FILL THE EMPTY SPACES

KARENNA COLCROFT

Vegan Wolf Productions

This book is a work of fiction. Names, characters, places, and incidents either are products of the author's imagination or are used fictitiously. Any resemblance to actual events or locales or persons, living or dead, is entirely coincidental.

©2023 Karenna Colcroft

ISBN 978-1-958346-09-9

Published by
Vegan Wolf Productions
7 Oak Avenue
Belmont, MA 02478

Cover Art by Kim Ramsey-Winkler
Special thanks to Uri Harel of Kitty Cat Café and Adoption Center for allowing the use of the photo of Charlie (the cat)

AUTHOR'S NOTE

WARNING: *Fill the Empty Spaces* discusses loss of a partner and depicts a grieving process. The story includes discussions of child abuse and child death, suicide, and homophobia and transphobia. But it also includes an adorable cat who wears sweaters.

This is not a romance. There are romantic elements and a hopeful ending, but the story is about a man healing from the loss of his life partner and realizing love after loss is possible. It depicts the progression of Del's journey rather than being a plot-driven, action-packed jam.

This author's note includes discussion of dementia and loss of a parent and an animal. And it's kinda long.

In the fall of 2022, I got a phone call from my dad. This was unusual. My dad despises talking on the phone. If one of my parents called me, it was almost always my mother; most of the time, I called them instead of the other way around, and my father sat in the background and listened while my mother talked to me. And because of a complex relationship between my parents and me, quite often several weeks would pass with no contact. Which wasn't necessarily a bad thing.

So when my dad called, I knew something was wrong. And it was very wrong.

My mother's health had deteriorated drastically. She was suffering from dementia, which my parents had hidden from me during phone calls by having my dad listen to the call and give my mother written notes and visual cues to help her act like she remembered who I and my kids were and understood what I was talking about. But now, she was hospitalized again and about to be moved to a care facility, and my dad was at the breaking point. He needed help, and as their only child, I was the one he turned to.

I did what I could to help him navigate the processes. He wanted to bring my mother home, but her care professionals and I were able to convince him that she had slipped too far for him to safely be able to care for her.

For a couple of months, she bounced between hospital and care facilities. She made it to her 79th birthday at the end of November, but that day passed with her in the hospital on a ventilator and unaware of what day it was. And on December 2, 2022, after a long and painful discussion with a doctor who said there was no longer any possibility of quality of life for my mother, my dad and I made the decision to disconnect the vent and let my mother go.

Part of me felt guilty for walking out of the hospital that day. The doctor had said my mother might linger for a few days or even longer, so there really wasn't a point in sitting with her. More importantly, my dad wasn't in a headspace to stay in the hospital once we told the doctor to disconnect the machines, and I was Dad's transportation, so if he needed to leave, I needed to leave. I paused in the doorway of my mother's ICU room and said, "It's okay, Mom. You can go now. Dad will be all right." And my dad and I left.

First thing the next morning, I got another call from my dad. "There was a message on the answering machine when I got up this morning. Your mother passed at about two a.m."

As I said, I had a complicated relationship with my parents, especially my mother. I wasn't sure whether to grieve her or not. I didn't know if I was grieving her as she was, or grieving the loss of opportunity to reconcile with her and get acknowledgement from her of her share of responsibility for the complicated nature of our relationship.

I didn't know how to feel, and meanwhile I had to support my kids (who are both adults and don't live with me) through the loss of their third grandparent in less than two years, and support and assist my dad through the loss of the woman he'd been with since 1966. My husband, who had lost his father less than a year and a half earlier, tried to be supportive but wasn't sure how; my partner, who before I met him had experienced multiple losses of loved ones, including his wife, and had recently lost his sister, stepped up to try to support me and help me and my dad with the aftermath.

When I was growing up, and through my toxic/abusive marriage to my kids' father, writing was how I survived. I wrote to process things that were happening to and around me. I wrote to escape from those things. I created worlds where characters I identified with had lives I wanted, and worlds in which those characters kept going through trauma and pain I'd experienced in real life. So as I tried to figure out how to feel about and deal with my mother's death, I turned to writing. And *Fill the Empty Spaces*, titled partially after the first line in "The Show Must Go On" by Queen, was born.

Fill the Empty Spaces was originally intended to just be a short story about how Del gets through the immediate aftermath of losing his long-term partner Austin. But as I kept writing, the story took on a life of its own. And then Lochlan showed up...and so did the cats.

Shortly before the day we lost my mother, I saw something online about a new cat café that had recently opened about 10 miles from where I live. I thought a trip to that café would make a great Christmas gift for my younger kid, who at the time was in their third year of veterinary school, so I went ahead and booked a visit for them and me. I honestly can't remember now—things got a bit blurred—whether I did that before or after my mother passed, but after her passing, the pending trip to the cat café became something to hold onto. Cats are healing.

We visited the café a few days after Christmas. The cats were furry and warm and adorable, and the humans were kind. Just what my kid and I needed. When I discovered that the café has volunteer workers,

I applied to become one. And, as *Fill the Empty Spaces* continued to grow, the cats found their way into the fictional world.

Especially Charlie, who adopted my kid's lap for nearly the entire duration of our visit and who quickly became my companion (or maybe I became his) during my volunteer shifts. Charlie was a stray who'd been found a couple of towns over from the café. He had fur so matted that he had to be shaved. When the café workers discovered that Charlie loved to be covered with blankets, one of the volunteers started knitting sweaters to cover him. Charlie loved the sweaters to the point of considering them part of himself.

I can't count the number of days that I went into my volunteer shifts struggling with my emotions and life stresses and was soothed by sitting with Charlie the Sweater Cat, petting his head, having him curl up on my lap, even having him purr for one of the first times since his arrival at the café. Charlie tended toward the "grumpy old man" personality—catality?—but he was a lovable grump, and he made an impression on everyone who visited the café. Sadly, due to multiple untreatable health issues that were causing him pain, on July 3, 2023, Charlie crossed the Rainbow Bridge.

I'm not ashamed to admit I cried as much about Charlie's loss as I did about my mother's.

In *Fill the Empty Spaces*, Charlie has a happier ending. As I wrote the book, I incorporated the real-time information I received about Charlie's health. By the time I finished the first draft of the story, it appeared that Charlie's conditions were treatable and that he might be adoptable at some point. So I went with that as I wrote, and in the story, Charlie is successfully treated and finds a fur-ever home with Del. Although I was informed when things changed with the real-life Charlie, and as I worked on editing the book I knew he wouldn't be finding a home outside the café, I chose to keep the book version's survival and adoption as written.

All of the other cats named in *Fill the Empty Spaces* also resided at the real-life café during the time I was writing the first draft, and other than one whose real name was a trademarked brand name, I used the real cats' names in the story. Some of them (Ice, Lord Purrington, Piper, and Choco Chip—the one whose name I had to change) have since been adopted, and new cats have come to live at the café in their place. Other cats named in the story (Clooney, Moonbeam, and the "chonk" brothers Bailey and Remy) are still there as of the writing of this note on September 4, 2023.

Kitty Cat Café and Adoption Center in Peabody, Massachusetts partners with two local cat rescue organizations, PAWS Wakefield and PALS Animal Lifesavers Salem. These two organizations take in cats who are found as strays or surrendered by their owners. Some of the cats have spent time in pet store "adopt me" cages. The cats are given temporary—or, as in Charlie's case, permanent—homes at the café. At the café, these cats experience socialization with each other and with humans, receive medical care and monitoring as needed, and are given food, treats, and tons of love.

I spoke with Uri Harel, one of the owners of the real-life café, about my use of Charlie and the other cats in the story. Uri approved and gave me permission to use one of my photos of Charlie as part of the cover art for the book. Yes, that is the real-life Charlie the Sweater Cat sitting beside "Del" on the cover, and I am very thankful to Uri for granting me permission to mention the cats and use Charlie's picture, and for accepting me as a volunteer. I'm also thankful to the other volunteers I've spoken with about this book for cheering me on. And especially thankful to the cats for...well, for everything.

Kitty Cat Café and Adoption Center is a nonprofit and operates partially on donations. PAWS and PALS are also nonprofits. If you'd like to donate to any (or, heck, all!) of these wonderful cat-supporting organizations, please visit their websites at the links below. And if you're going to be in the Peabody, MA, area, you might want to schedule a cat café visit!

Kitty Cat Café:
https://www.kittycatcafema.com/
PAWS Wakefield:
https://pawswakefield.rescuegroups.org/
PALS Salem:
https://palscats.org/

CHAPTER ONE

Everything was empty.

Not literally. My apartment was still filled with the remnants of my life with Austin. That was the problem.

The things were there. Austin wasn't, and he never would be again.

For just over a month, I'd pretended that Austin's clothes in the closet, his papers strewn across the dining room table, his shoes in the middle of the floor instead of the shoe holder beside the front door all meant that he would come bouncing through the door with stories about the audience at the club or the obnoxious Karens at the bookstore, depending on which job he was returning from. He would show off the new lipstick he'd bought for his drag persona, Toppa DaWorld, and ask me to "grill a cheese" for him.

And then we would go to bed. Make love. Spoon together. *Be* together.

Except none of that would ever happen again, because some drunk asswipe had run a red light and taken my husband away. The last time I'd seen him...

I didn't want to think about that. Couldn't let myself remember his battered body on the stretcher in the hospital or the pity on the face of the doctor who said, a few hours later, "We're sorry, Mister

Nethercott. His brain was severely injured. He might never function on his own again. It might be better to let him go. You're his medical proxy. It's your decision."

The last time I'd seen my colorful, sparkly Austin was the moment I told the doctor to shut off the machines that maintained the appearance of Austin being alive. I'd kissed Austin goodbye and walked away before his life faded. I was too much of a coward to stay in the room. I hated myself for telling them to turn everything off. To turn *Austin* off. But even I could see the doctor was right. Austin's body was too broken, and Austin was no longer there. I'd made the right decision.

But I still hated myself for it.

I didn't want to remember him that way, but that was the memory that came in the darkest hours of the night, as I lay on my side of our queen-sized bed even though I could have moved into the middle. I'd barely slept the past several weeks; or, rather, I'd dozed off and on and awakened from nightmares about the man of my dreams.

My bereavement leave from work had become an indefinite leave of absence. The three days the school district offered hadn't been nearly enough to process losing Austin, especially right before Christmas. At first, I told them I was staying home until after winter break, then, a few days later, I applied for a longer sabbatical. I wouldn't go back until March at the earliest now, and I'd alerted my principal that I might wind up taking the rest of the year off. I missed my students, missed having a regular schedule, but I was in no shape to counsel a bunch of high-schoolers. I couldn't get my own shit together, let alone advise them on theirs.

In the immediate aftermath of Austin's death, other people had filled the apartment, friends and chosen family who mourned Austin alongside me. His best friend-slash-honorary sibling Remy Doucette, a/k/a Remington Real at the club. Her mother, brother, and sisters, who had driven down from Maine to say their goodbyes. Remy's family had taken in Austin at sixteen, after he came out and his parents booted him onto the street. Since I'd cut ties with my parents halfway through college and had no siblings, Remy's family had become mine too.

I wouldn't have gotten through the days after Austin's death without Remy's mom cooking for me and his youngest sister, Mya, handing me glass after glass of water. Remy, even in her own depths of mourning the man she considered a brother, had run interference with the other queens from the club who nearly smothered me in their attempts to honor Austin's memory. The Doucettes hadn't kept me from falling apart. Nothing could have done that. But they'd at least made sure my pieces stuck around to be gathered up at some point in the future.

Some point when I healed. If I ever did.

We'd held a funeral for Austin at the nondenominational church where Remy led the choir on Sundays. Neither Austin nor I had much use for organized religion, but we'd attended a few services to hear Remy's solos, and he'd told both of us if anything ever happened, he wanted a church funeral. Mainly as a "fuck you" to everyone who'd ever said God hated him for being a gay drag queen. The service was three days after his death, followed by a memorial at the club so the queens who weren't comfortable entering a church could say their farewells. I always felt out of place in the club, but Austin's fellow performers had done their best to make sure I was included. It wasn't their fault I felt awkward. Over the years, I'd attended a few of Austin's shows, but mostly the club had been his space the way the high school was mine.

Christmas had come and gone, and I'd ignored it completely. I hadn't even decorated the apartment. That had always been Austin's thing. Neither of us retained happy holiday memories from our families of origin, but he'd had the Doucettes, and thanks to them, he loved Christmas. All the sparkles and lights and colors. Some years, he went so overboard I swore I'd moved into a Christmas shop. But even though I grumbled, I loved it because Austin did, and I loved Austin.

Without Austin, I saw no point in pulling out the decorations or wrapping the presents I'd bought him, which were still half-hidden on the floor of my closet. Without Austin, there was nothing to celebrate.

After a couple weeks of trying to cajole me out of my self-imposed exile, most of our friends had drifted away. Not entirely by their own choice. I'd shut people out. I didn't want to put on a false face and pretend to be social when grief and pain pulled me down like quicksand. I'd isolated myself to the point that other than Remy, nearly everyone had given up on me.

Remy was too damn stubborn for that, and even though she pushed a little too hard sometimes, I was thankful that she hadn't gone away yet. Today, though, I wished she had.

Today, she was coming over to start packing Austin's belongings. All the bland, boring clothes he'd worn to his bookstore "day job" and all the sparkly, colorful, fantastic outfits he'd worn as Toppa. The bland clothes would land in a donation bin somewhere. His drag clothes, makeup, and so forth would go to the club to be split among his fellow queens, with anything they didn't want going to an organization that provided clothing to trans and nonbinary teens who couldn't afford clothes that fit their true gender. Austin and I had never gotten around to end-of-life planning, but Remy and I agreed on what he would have wanted.

Giving away his clothes, though, wasn't what *I* wanted. I didn't want to give away anything of Austin's. Some of it still smelled like him. But maybe emptying out his closets and bureau would help me process and move on.

Remy texted me at eight a.m. on the dot. *I'll be there in half an hour. Bringing coffee and donuts. Be up and dressed.*

I was already awake. Had been for a few hours. The nightmares didn't let me sleep for more than an hour or two at a stretch anymore, and sometimes I couldn't bring myself to try falling asleep again after waking up. But I hadn't gotten around to dragging myself out of bed, and I didn't want to now. I could get away with staying put until Remy actually arrived. She had a key. She didn't need me to let her in.

Stop being so lazy and move your ass, Austin's voice said in my mind. Or, rather, my mental recording of his voice, saying what he'd said to me so many times when he'd planned "excursions" for us on weekends and school breaks. The day trips had run the gamut from visiting the top of the Prudential Center in downtown Boston to collecting shells and sea glass from the beach near Gloucester after a storm. And every time, he'd had to tell me to move my ass, because I hadn't wanted to give up a day off from work to go out.

Actually, I hadn't minded. Spending a day with him was worth it. But he'd enjoyed having to motivate me, and I'd played along.

This time, I wasn't playing. I didn't want to leave the bed. But Remy would be here soon, and she would worry if she walked in and saw me still lying there. Plus I hadn't showered since her last visit three days earlier, and I probably smelled a little funky. A shower and a clean T-shirt and sweats wouldn't hurt me.

Reluctantly, I pushed back the comforter—bright blue and purple flowers, Austin's choice—and forced myself vertical. I grabbed some clothes that looked relatively clean out of the basket of laundry I hadn't bothered putting away for the past few weeks and stumbled into the bathroom. Into the double shower Austin had had installed so we could clean up together.

I pretended not to remember all the times we'd showered together, or how hard it had been at first for Austin to convince me it was a good idea. I'd grown up in a conservative family. Being gay was the height of my rebellion and the furthest I'd gone toward doing anything my family considered outside the "norm." Austin had pushed me, gently but firmly, into broadening my comfort zones and my experiences of the world. I'd gone along with his ideas, like the double shower and the excursions, because they made him happy, and his happiness was more important to me than giving into my discomfort.

Who would drag me out into the world now? Who would encourage me to do things like installing a double shower or painting a wall of the kitchen as a poor imitation of Van Gogh's *Starry Night*?

Who would hold me when the grief and pain grew so intense my knees buckled and the wall wasn't strong enough to keep me upright?

I managed, barely, to finish doing something approximating cleaning myself, then pulled on the shirt and sweatpants I'd grabbed. A shirt that, as it turned out, had belonged to Austin. My Chemical Romance, a band I'd only vaguely heard of before Austin started listening to them on repeat. I'd managed, after haunting the ticket sales site, to score seats for us during their most recent tour stop in Boston, which had coincided with Austin's birthday that year, and I'd bought him the shirt as an additional gift.

He was so excited about the show and the shirt. He'd worn that thing constantly for weeks afterward, while he wandered around the apartment singing—or at least trying to sing—the band's songs. Singing wasn't Austin's strong suit. He claimed that was one of the reasons he'd become a drag queen, so he could lip synch instead. But hearing his happily off-key warbling had brought me joy too.

Now the shirt was only another reminder of how empty everything had become. But a knock on the apartment door meant I didn't have time to change it. Barefoot, I made my way to the door and opened it to reveal Remy, in a glittery orange sweater and torn blue jeans, holding a cardboard tray that contained two coffee cups and a paper bag.

"Step one. You're out of bed." She came in and sniffed the air in the general vicinity of my head. "And you showered! Step two. Well done." She planted a kiss on the air next to my cheek. "Let's caffeinate and calorie-ate, and then we can decide how we're handling this."

Without waiting for an answer from me, she breezed past me to the kitchenette, as graceful in her battered sneakers as she would have been in the four-inch heels she wore onstage, and set the tray on the counter. I followed, deciding it was better to just let her do her thing. She took one of the cups out of the tray, gave it a sniff, and took a dubious sip. "Ugh. That's yours." She wiped the rim with the edge of her sleeve and set the cup on the counter, then took the other one and drank. "Ah. Much better. Have some coffee, Del."

"Thanks." I picked up the cup she'd set down. It was warm. Warm was good. But I didn't drink any of it, and it had nothing to do with Remy having taken a sip. I wanted the caffeine, but drinking the coffee just felt like too much work. Just like eating whatever was in the bag.

"Drink." Remy opened the bag and took out a blueberry muffin, which she set on the counter in front of me. "Eat. We won't be merry, but we'll at least be sustained."

"Yeah." She'd brought my favorite, and I couldn't bring myself to touch it. "How are we doing this?"

"Breakfast?" She took another muffin, this one chocolate chip, out of the bag and took a bite off the top without removing the paper. "We're eating it. Coffee, we're drinking."

"You know what I mean." To get her to stop giving me the stink-eye, I nibbled at the sugar on top of my muffin. "Packing. Donating."

"I will answer your question after you drink some coffee." She set down her cup and muffin and folded her arms. "Del, please. I'm not going to say I know how you feel, but I know how losing Austin feels for me. Grief takes time, so I'm certainly not telling you to get over it, but Austin would hate seeing you like this." She grimaced. "Shit. I promised myself I wouldn't get all cliché on you."

"You're probably right, though." I took a sip of coffee to make her happy. Black with caramel swirl, my usual order ever since Austin had talked me into trying it one day. I hadn't had it since the accident, and the taste brought back too many memories.

I set down the cup and turned away. "I drank some. Answer my question."

She rolled her eyes. "We're going to pack up Austin's day clothes. Garbage bags will do. I'll drop them off at a donation bin on my way home." Remy owned a car, a rarity around here. I'd never bothered to buy one myself. Every place I needed to go was either walking distance or an easy trip on the T, Boston's public transportation system. "I have boxes and bins for his drag."

"That's going to the club, right?"

She nodded. "The fancy stuff, anyway. And the girls would love to see you if you want to come with me when I bring the things there."

"Let me think about it." There was no way in hell I would go to the club again. Not without Austin. The club was his place. It was *Austin*. And I wouldn't be able to go there without remembering that he would never be there again.

The club might be filled with drag queens and other performers, and their adoring public, but without Austin it would be just another empty space.

"Sure." She gave me a skeptical look. "Anyway, his drag that's more costumey will be going to the club. The more day-wear kinds of things, skirts and blouses and some of the blander dresses, I'll bring to Casilla's Closet for the kids. You're still okay with that, right?"

I nodded. "Yeah. Austin would want those kids to have clothes that suit their gender." I'd sent a few of my trans and gender-noncon-forming students to the Closet for support and resources over the years, and Austin and I'd put in a few volunteer shifts when our schedules allowed.

"Right." She hesitated. "I got some of my stuff there when Austin and I first moved to the city. Still feel guilty about it, since I actually had my family's support."

"You came here with almost nothing, though." Austin had told me the story. Even though Remy came out as trans before they moved, she hadn't yet been able to replace her guy wardrobe with clothes that fit her gender, and the cost of moving had taken what little money the two of them had managed to save. Her family had emotionally supported her transition, but they hadn't had the money to help with financial support.

"Yeah."

"They can probably use some of his regular clothes too," I said. "They work with trans boys and nonbinary kids who might want 'guy' clothes." I made air quotes.

"Good point," she said. "I'll pack some of his day clothes up to bring to them. You can...Do you want to help me sort out what goes where?"

I didn't. I didn't want anything to do with getting rid of what was left of Austin. But it wouldn't be fair to make Remy do it all herself.

"Sure." I said. "As soon as we finish our coffee."

CHAPTER TWO

The apartment had three closets. Two of them belonged to Austin. The walk-in contained his drag. The second held what he called his "normie bore-me" clothes.

The third closet, the smallest, was mine. I didn't own enough clothes to fill it, let alone occupy the space in Austin's closets once his clothes were gone. Those closets would just be more emptiness.

But I couldn't justify keeping Austin's things. They would only collect dust and remind me he wasn't coming back. And if some after-life existed from which he was watching me, he would be pissed if I didn't find new homes for his belongings. He would want people to wear his clothes and wigs. To use the makeup. He would want to make other people happy. I couldn't bring him back, but I could at least go through with what I knew he would want me to do. No matter how much it hurt.

And it hurt like hell. Saying goodbye to each piece of Austin was like saying goodbye to him all over again. We only managed to get through about two-thirds of the drag before Remy and I both started crying too hard to continue. But at least we'd managed to pack up some things, both for the other queens at the club and for Remy to bring to the trans youth organization.

"Let's go out for lunch," Remy suggested after we decided to stop packing for the day. "You need to be out of this apartment for a little while."

"Sure." I didn't want to go out, but maybe Remy was right. Getting out of here, even for an hour or so, might be good for me. It certainly wasn't something I'd done much of lately.

"There's that buffet around the corner," Remy said. "We can go there."

"Okay." That was one of Austin's favorite restaurants. It looked like just a tiny hole-in-the-wall Chinese place, but the restaurant stretched back through the entire building, and they provided an array of freshly cooked foods every day for lunch and dinner. Austin had always said he loved it because he didn't have to make decisions.

Every day for a week after Austin passed, the owner of the place had packed up food and brought it to me. Free of charge and delivered by him personally. I'd barely eaten any of it. I hadn't been able to eat much of anything that week. And I couldn't recall whether I'd thanked him or not. Although going out in public wasn't my preference today, going to the buffet with Remy would show support for the place. It was the least I could do.

We left the boxes by the door, planning to load them into Remy's car when we got back, and headed around the corner. The buffet was just opening for the day, and the owner greeted us with a warm smile and, "Welcome. Anything you like. Eat free today. For Austin."

"That's very kind," Remy said as I blinked back tears I wasn't willing to display in public. "Are you sure?"

The owner nodded. "We miss Austin. Happy to share today."

"Thank you," I managed through what felt like a Boston-sized lump in my throat. "We'll make sure to recommend this place to our friends."

The owner's smile widened. "Yes, yes. Thank you. Help yourselves. You want drinks?"

"Just water, please," Remy said. I nodded my agreement with the choice.

We chose our food from the buffet tables and returned to find the owner setting a table beside the window. "If you want to bring anything home, we have boxes," he said, gesturing toward the kitchen. "Enjoy."

"Thank you," Remy and I said in unison.

To my relief, the owner left us alone when we sat down with our plates. He was kind, but right now I couldn't deal with kindness. I was so choked up I wasn't sure I'd be able to swallow the food. Or if I even dared to try.

"Austin always loved coming here," Remy said quietly. She took a forkful of shrimp fried rice and nibbled at it. "He made friends everywhere. When we moved to the city, I thought we'd be completely on our own, but he built a community for us within the first couple of months."

"He could walk into a room and have a dozen new best friends before I even made it through the door." That was one of the things about Austin that had both annoyed and attracted me. I'd always been an introvert. I could be friendly enough when a situation called for it, but I preferred being on my own. Austin was my polar opposite, the social butterfly who adopted caterpillar me and showed me what flying was like.

Remy sniffed. "Yeah, that was Austin. Always. Even when his parents kicked him out and he didn't know where the hell he would end up, he was light, you know? Something about him just lit everything up even when he was struggling."

"Yeah." My eyes watered, and I closed them tightly for a moment. I couldn't cry here. Not where total strangers would see. "Can we talk about something else?"

"Of course." The sympathy in Remy's tone pushed me even closer to letting go of the tears. "What do you think of cats?"

"Huh?" I opened my eyes and stared at her. "The show or the animal?"

She chuckled. "The animal. The show was a phenomenon. We won't mention the movie."

I snorted. "Okay. I like the animal. I wanted to get a cat before I met Austin. He's—he was allergic."

"I know. Mya was furious when he moved in with us because Mom and Dad promised her a kitten, and then they backtracked because of Austin." She shook her head. "Mya loved Austin, but she was glad when we moved down here and she could finally have her kitten."

"Okay." I didn't know what to say to any of that.

"Sidetrack," she said. "Anyway, so you like cats."

"Yeah." She wasn't about to suggest I get one, was she? I was definitely not up for a pet.

"That's good, because I scheduled an afternoon for us at a cat café."

I blinked. "Um... you what now?"

"I scheduled an afternoon for us at a cat café."

"Yeah. That's what I thought you said." I ran my hand over my face. "Why would you do that, Remy?"

"To get your ass out of the house for a few hours." She ate a little more of her fried rice.

I took a bite of the spring roll I'd picked up, which was almost cold now. I decided it didn't matter. Food was food, and eating gave me the opportunity to avoid asking Remy why the hell she'd done something so completely ridiculous.

So completely Austin-like.

"What do you think?" she asked.

Apparently avoiding was not going to happen. "I think I have no idea why you decided a cat café, of all things, was a good way to get me out of the house."

"Because it's there?" She batted her lashes. Her version of trying to look innocent. "The place just opened a couple months ago. It's worth checking out. And cats."

"You actually want to go, don't you." I could have said no. I *wanted* to say no. Coming to Austin's favorite restaurant was enough. I didn't want to go hang out someplace where people petted cats while drinking coffee, or whatever one did at a cat café. But Remy looked hopeful, and I realized I hadn't seen that expression on her face since before Austin died.

I was mourning, but I wasn't the only one. If going to the stupid cat café would make Remy happy, I could manage it for an afternoon.

"Yes, I do," she said. "But if you don't, that's okay. It was just an idea. I booked two spots, but I can find someone else to go. Mitch, maybe. He's been begging Solara to let him have a cat." She was talking far too fast by the time she stopped.

She thought I was mad at her. Which, to be honest, I was. A little. But her heart was in the right place. "I'll go," I said.

"You will?" Her face lit. "Excellent. Tomorrow afternoon. I'll pick you up at twelve-thirty."

"Sounds good," I said automatically. It didn't sound good. It sounded like the worst idea I'd heard in a long while. But Remy was trying to help. She wasn't as extroverted and flamboyant as Austin, but she thrived on being around other humans. She couldn't understand why that was the last thing I wanted.

Neither did I, really. I liked my alone time, but even before Austin, when depression would kick my ass for a few days at a stretch, I hadn't isolated this much. I'd kept to myself, but I'd also made forays into the world. Of course, I'd still been in college and grad school. In those days before online classes were widely available, I hadn't had much choice about leaving the house, but I hadn't minded. No matter how much I'd wanted to be alone, I'd also wanted to be out in the world, breathing what passed as fresh air in Boston and seeing other humans even if I didn't talk to them.

During the two decades Austin and I were together, staying shut in the apartment alone was never a thing for me. Even in 2020, we'd made a point of taking walks around our neighborhood and had even taken a couple of trips to local beaches to get outside and see—from a distance—other people. Austin had brought me out of the cocoon I'd constructed around myself. I'd made friends, though in my mind I'd never fully adjusted to thinking of them as *my* friends. They were Austin's, and I was part of the package.

With Austin gone, I didn't know how to exist in the world. With Austin gone, the world was too empty.

"You're being way too quiet," Remy said. "You don't actually want to do this cat café thing, do you." It wasn't a question.

I pulled my thoughts back to the present, where Remy was looking at me with pity and concern and even the restaurant owner was lingering nearby with a worried expression.

"Sorry," I said, pitching my voice so the owner would hopefully hear and walk away. "My mind was just wandering. I'm fine. And honestly, Rem..." I hesitated. She thought she was doing something nice. I didn't want to shut her down completely. "No, I don't actually want to, but I think I need to. I don't actually *want* to do much of anything lately, and that isn't good for me. I appreciate you coming up with something I can do to break out of hiding in my apartment all the time."

She nodded. "I know how you feel, Del. Maybe not exactly, but I grok the grief and depression. Austin loved you. He would be so sad to see you pulling away from everyone. I'm not doing this to pressure you or anything."

"It's for Austin. I get it." I gave her a smile. A fake one, plastered on to reassure her, but hopefully it looked at least somewhat authentic. "We should finish eating before everything gets cold."

"I can warm up for you," the owner said, hurrying over.

"Thank you, but maybe we should take the rest of this to go," Remy said. "Boxes, please?"

"Sure, sure. One minute." He hurried away again.

Within a couple of minutes, we had several takeout containers filled with not only what we'd put on our plates but additional portions of our choices and a few things from the buffet that we hadn't chosen. Evidently the owner wanted to make sure we were well fed for the next week or so. He put the containers in bags to make them slightly easier to carry, and Remy and I left.

In silence, we walked back to the apartment. When we got there, she arranged all of the food in my refrigerator, which was otherwise mostly empty. "Some of that's yours," I said.

"All of it's yours. I have too many half-eaten takeout meals in my fridge." She closed the door and turned around. "Del, you have friends. I'm one of them. Mitch and Solara. Donnie and Marco. Other people who loved Austin. A couple of them are a little pissy that you haven't been in touch, but that's their problem, not yours. Most of us know you're mourning. They aren't reaching out to you because they don't know where you're at, but they're waiting for you when you're ready. Try being ready."

"I don't know what to say to most of them." Not knowing what to say had never been a problem with Austin around. He could fill the empty spaces in a conversation as easily as he could fill the club with those who came to see his shows. It didn't matter if I knew what to say. Half the time, I couldn't get a word in anyway, and that hadn't mattered either, because Austin wasn't overbearing about it. He just enjoyed talking and including those around him in whatever he said.

I couldn't fill a conversation, especially with people I only knew because of Austin. In my work, not being much of a talker was a bonus. As a counselor, I was supposed to listen more than I spoke. But in other parts of my life, without Austin to fill the gaps, conversations seemed doomed to being a few words broken by uncomfortable silences.

"Start by saying 'how are you,'" Remy advised. "And maybe tell them how you are. We're your friends, Del. We don't expect you to be Chatty Cathy." She sighed. "Like I said, when you're ready, we're here for you. Meanwhile, how about you help me get those boxes down to my car? I need to drop things off and get to the club."

"Sure."

We managed to fit all of the boxes into her little two-door hatch-back. She had to put all her weight into slamming the hatch shut, but she managed it. Then she hugged me. "It's okay to cry, you know."

"Been doing too much of that." I sniffled. Clearly she hadn't missed the way my eyes were watering. "Thanks for helping with all the stuff."

"Thanks for letting me bring it to those who can use it. I'll see you tomorrow. Twelve-thirty." She got into the car.

I stayed on the sidewalk until she drove away, then went back into the apartment. I expected it to feel even emptier now that most of Austin's drag was gone, but it didn't. The place was still unquestionably empty. Austin wasn't there. But after spending some time with Remy, the emptiness felt a little more comfortable. Like hope was waiting in the wings, ready to start filling the space.

CHAPTER THREE

The following morning, I woke to a silent apartment, the same as I had for the past few weeks. Empty and still. No one here except me and the echoes of Austin.

I didn't want to get out of bed. Especially since that would mean seeing the empty racks and hangers in the walk-in closet. More of Austin was gone than the day before. The items had gone to good homes, but the selfish part of me wanted the clothes back. As long as they'd hung in the closet, I could pretend Austin was still around.

I knew damn well how unhealthy that was. He *wasn't* here. That was reality. No matter how much I pretended or wanted to deny it, I'd seen his body in the hospital. I'd chosen the urn for his ashes, and I'd chosen to send it home with Remy's mother because the thought of having an urn of Austin was worse than not having him at all. Maybe I should have kept the damn thing to prove to myself that he really was never coming back.

I dragged my ass out of bed and went over to the closet. Remy had closed the door. It was the first time that door had been closed since Austin and I moved in. He liked keeping the closet open so he could see all the sparkles and bright colors. I was pretty sure there was some deeper symbolism for him as well, though we never talked about that. I put my hand on the doorknob. Austin would have wanted it open.

But some of the colors and sparkles were gone. There was no point in opening the door. Some of his things remained, but I would only see the emptiness.

I trudged into the bathroom for a quick shower, then pulled on a pair of old jeans and a sweater Austin had given me for our first Christmas together. The sweater's forest green color had faded. The jeans had the beginning of a hole in one knee and were so worn they felt like pajama pants instead of denim. They were clothes I wouldn't mind getting cat hair on, which was something I assumed would happen at a cat café.

I was going to a cat café. That was not something I'd foreseen. I liked cats. I'd had a few as a kid, and my biggest regret about leaving home was leaving the cats behind. I'd wanted a cat or two as an adult, but the apartments I lived in before meeting Austin hadn't allowed pets, and with Austin's allergies, having a cat together wasn't possible. I liked the idea of hanging around with felines for a little while.

But I didn't know what to expect at a cat café. Would we just sit and drink coffee while cats stared at us from cages? Did the cats wander freely? Questions I probably should have asked Remy when I accepted the invitation.

I spent most of the morning mindlessly scrolling social media and trying to build the motivation to do some cleaning. During Remy's visit the day before, I'd mentally registered the dirt and dust and clutter I'd been ignoring for the past month. Not wanting to notice it was one of the reasons I'd resisted having anyone visit, but now I couldn't pretend it wasn't there. The house wasn't exactly filthy, with me being the only one there, but it needed some work.

Somehow, by noon, I managed to sweep the floors and even drag a mop over the kitchen linoleum. It wasn't spotless, but the improvement was noticeable. And accomplishing the task boosted my mood. I'd actually done something besides wandering the internet and binge-watching shows I couldn't remember afterward.

At exactly twelve o'clock, my phone chimed. I picked it up from the counter and read, *Downstairs. You have two minutes before I come up there to drag you out.*

On the way, I typed. I quickly slipped on my shoes and headed down to meet Remy.

She was out of her car, leaning against the curb, looking resplendent in an iridescent purple coat and over-the-knee purple boots. She'd picked up the coat at a thrift shop during a shopping trip with Austin and me a couple of years earlier. I had no clue where she'd gotten the boots, but they were a nearly perfect match for the coat.

"I was wondering if you'd actually go through with this." She hugged me. "I'm glad you are. This will be fun. Two hours of cats, coffee, and conversation."

"Great." I tried to sound enthusiastic, but to my own ears it came off more sarcastic than anything. "Two hours?"

"Or less if you really feel like you need to get out of there, but I booked us for two hours." She opened the passenger door and gestured at it. "Get in and I'll explain more on the way."

We settled ourselves in the car, and she drove away from the curb, barely missing a bicyclist who either didn't see us or decided racing to get past a moving car was smarter than stopping to let us out of the parking space. "I was going to tell you to bring a book or something," Remy said as she navigated through traffic to a left turn lane. "But then I realized you would probably just sit in a corner and read the entire time."

"Yes, that's often what one does with books," I said.

She snorted. "Yes, it is. But it isn't what I intended when I scheduled this. I'm not expecting you to be Mister Extrovert, but I'm hoping you'll interact with the cats and me, at the very least. I've missed hanging out with you and Austin. He was my family, but you are too, and I'd like to keep our connection going."

A lump rose in my throat, and my eyes watered as I nodded. "Yeah. Same. Austin called you his sister, which I guess makes you my sister-in-law. We are family."

"Then maybe do a little less shutting me out?" She glanced at me as she steered around a delivery truck blocking our lane. "I know grief fucks mightily with people. I'm going through it myself. There's nothing wrong with us handling things differently from each other, but it feels like you just want nothing at all to do with me or Austin's other friends." Her voice choked. "And that hurts."

The last word ended on a sob that struck my heart like an ice pick. She stared at the windshield, a tear trickling down her cheek.

Lost in my own fog, I'd been aware that Remy and the others mourned Austin. I hadn't stopped to consider how they felt about me pulling away from them.

"I don't..." I stopped. Apologies didn't start with excuses. "I'm sorry, Rem. Really. I'm sorry for hurting you and the others. I want you around. I just don't know how to be around you."

"You can start by just *being* around us." She sniffed. "You aren't like Austin. No one expects you to be. But there's a huge range between super-mega-extrovert and hiding in your apartment not talking to anyone who doesn't put themself right in your face."

"You're right." I paused. Overapologizing wasn't much better than making excuses, but I didn't know what else to say besides, "I'm sorry."

"No, no." Another sniffle, then she took a deep breath. "I'm the one who's sorry, Del. We all lost Austin, but he was more to you than to the rest of us. He was my brother, as far as I'm concerned. He was the others' friend. But he was your..."

"He was my everything," I said quietly.

She nodded. "Yeah. And I don't know what losing everything feels like. It isn't up to you to make the rest of us feel better. I shouldn't have said anything."

"I'm glad you did." I leaned back and closed my eyes, both to try to keep the gathering tears from falling and to give myself a moment to mentally compose what I wanted to say. "It's true that Austin was a massive part of my life. Hell, other than my job, he *was* my life. Maybe that wasn't healthy, but that's how it was. But you had him in your life longer than I did. You and the others knew part of him I was barely acquainted with. I was only thinking about how losing him affected me. I didn't put much thought into how it affects you all."

"Grief fucks with people," she said again. "We don't want to grieve at you, Del. We want to grieve *with* you. We're your family as much as we were Austin's, if you want us to be. You aren't alone."

Those words did it. Or maybe the love and compassion in her voice. Either way, I couldn't hold back the goddamn tears anymore. They fell, I sobbed, and I felt like an idiot.

"Let it out," Remy said softly, and that made it worse.

By the time she pulled off Route One into the parking lot of a small strip mall, I was a freaking mess. Tears streaked my face, my nose ran like a faucet, and I couldn't stop the loud sobs that were more like wailing. All the grief I'd tried to ignore poured out, and as it did, Remy just sat in the driver's seat, not speaking but still so obviously present, so emphatically there, that for the first time since Austin's accident, I felt like I wasn't on my own trying to find a way through the grief.

"There are tissues in the glove compartment." Remy pulled into a parking space and turned off the car. "We have five minutes until we're scheduled to be in there, so take your time."

Not trusting myself to speak, I nodded and opened the glove compartment. Getting myself to a point where I didn't look like I'd spent the entire drive crying took almost an entire pocket pack of tissues. Fortunately, Remy didn't seem to mind.

The tissues and several deep breaths calmed me. "Sorry," I managed to mumble after a couple of minutes.

"For?" Remy turned in her seat to face me. "Del, what would you say to one of your students at a time like this?"

"Grief is normal and healthy, and crying is nothing to be ashamed of." I recited the words in a monotone. Over the past couple of decades, I'd dealt with too many grieving teenagers to count, and the reassuring words came automatically.

"Maybe listen to yourself, then." Her tone was gentle. "I know you've spent a lot of time crying, Del. Believe me, I have too. And it is nothing to be sorry about."

"Yeah." I inhaled slowly and wiped my nose yet again with yet another tissue. "I don't want to snot all over the cats."

She chuckled, a sound that was more tolerant than amused. "Don't worry, they have hand sanitizer at the door. Are you ready to go in? We can sit another few minutes if you need to."

I looked toward the building. Sandwiched between an auto parts place and another business I couldn't immediately identify was a small storefront with a sign identifying it as the café. In the front window, a black and white cat lay on a shelf, while a gray and black striped cat sat on the floor casually licking its paw.

I wanted to pet them. I wanted to feel something alive and soft beneath my hand. The cats my family and I'd had when I was growing up had always comforted me, even the ones who wanted little to do with humans in general. Maybe these furry little beasts would help ease my grief, at least for a little while.

"Let's go in," I said.

CHAPTER FOUR

We got out of the car and walked over to the building. The café's door led into a narrow entryway with a cooler of drinks, a basket of individually wrapped brownies, and a coffee machine on a shelf at one side and window taking up most of the wall beside the door that led into the café proper.

A short man with slightly straggly light brown hair and a matching mustache waved through the window and came to open the door. "Hi, I'm Liam Patrick," he said brightly. "Are you signed up for a slot?"

"We are." Remy beamed almost as brightly as Aaron. "I'm Remy Doucette, and this is Del Nethercott. We signed up for two hours?"

"Absolutely." Liam's smile grew. "Sanitize your hands, please, and then come on in and I'll show you around. Oh, if you want any drinks or snacks, go ahead and take them. Drinks are free. For snacks, we'll settle up when you leave."

Despite her talk about coffee, Remy took a couple of bottles of water out of the cooler. We each used the hand sanitizer beside the door, then followed Liam into the café.

The space stretched back farther than it had appeared to from outside. A few couches occupied some of the area, along with various cardboard boxes, cat toys, and of course food and water dishes. A large white cat with piercing yellow eyes came over to sniff my foot.

"Taking your duties seriously, huh, Ice?" Liam bent to pet the cat. "Ice here thinks he's in charge of the place. He's only two, one of our younger cats, but he's good at helping."

"I'm sure he is. And he's beautiful." Remy dropped to one knee to scratch between Ice's ears. "So the cats all live here?"

Liam nodded. "They're all up for adoption, and until they find their permanent homes, they're here with us. Some of them lived in cages in pet stores before this, so we have them here to get more used to socializing with humans and other cats. Others were found on the streets and picked up by our cat rescue partners and brought here to be cared for. There's a QR code on the wall in a few spots; if you scan it, you can find bios of all the kitties."

Remy took out her phone and headed to the nearest QR code. Arms folded, I stayed near the door, resisting the temptation to kneel down and start petting the heck out of Ice. "So how does this work? Us being here, I mean."

"Just play with the cats." Liam smiled. "There's a table and stools over there where people usually sit if they're working on a laptop or something. Couches. Some of the cats love laps. Please don't pick them up, though. It's fine if you're sitting down and one of them settles on your lap, but don't hold them. Just pet. Or give scritches, as the case may be."

A gray and black tabby, not the one we'd seen in the window, came over and sniffed tentatively at Ice, who immediately lay down. Liam crouched and petted her. "Hi, Piper." He looked up at me. "Piper's one of our youngest. She's only a year old and she's already had two litters of kittens. And she has FIV. But she gets medication, and we want to show that cats with FIV, as long as they receive treatment, can live long lives and be safe around other cats."

Piper looked at me and meowed, and my heart melted. I gave in to the impulse to sit on the floor. I held out my hand so she could sniff it, and after a second she head-butted it.

"She likes you." Liam sounded approving. "There are toys around.

She loves to play. Just have fun. Our shy cat room is in there." He pointed to a doorway through which I saw a closed door and another open room. "We have a couple of cats who are just getting the hang of being here and need to be separated from the rest for a little while." He glanced toward the front door. "We have more guests coming in. Ah, and one of our volunteers. I have to go let them in. Just let me know if you need anything."

"Thanks."

He walked away, and I yanked my hand back as Piper decided it was a cat toy that looked fun to chomp. Remy came back and sat on the nearby couch. "There are eight cats here." She looked around, her mouth moving as she counted. "I only see six."

"Liam said some of the cats are shy and stay in another room." I moved up onto the couch, my knees reminding me that sitting on the floor wasn't as good an idea as when I was younger. A fluffy black cat in a cardboard box nearby stretched and came over to sniff me.

"Oh, that must be Lord Purrington!" Beaming, Remy scrolled through her phone, then leaned over me to pet the cat. "Hello, beautiful. Oh, I wish I could bring all of them home. How about you, Del? Are you considering adopting any of them?"

"Probably not." For the past few weeks, I'd barely been responsible for myself. I definitely wasn't in the headspace to be responsible for another living creature, especially one that would be totally dependent on me. "I might come back here, though."

"Yay!" Despite the interjection, she kept her voice low. Probably so she wouldn't startle the cats. "Let me know. I don't mind coming with you if I'm off from my day job."

"Okay." I leaned back. "You know, you could switch places with me so you can pet him more easily."

"Yeah." She studied me for a moment. "Sorry."

I got up, and Remy moved closer to Lord Purrington. By the door, Liam was talking to a woman about my age and a girl who appeared to be in her teens, while a guy with blond-streaked black hair knelt to pet Ice. The space was small enough for me to hear most of what Liam was saying, but I didn't absorb it.

A low black sofa sat along the back wall beside the doorway Liam had indicated. A cat lay by itself there, idly licking one paw. His face, legs, and paws were black and white, and a blue and green striped sweater covered his torso. As he half-heartedly groomed himself, he surveyed the room with what I could only describe as disgruntled judgment.

He looked like my kind of cat.

Remy seemed pretty occupied with Lord Purrington. I walked over and sat beside Sweater Cat. "Hi, pal," I said, holding out my hand for him to sniff.

He sniffed and gave me a "what's your problem" look that dissipated when I gently petted his head. For a few seconds, he submitted to that, then stood and stretched. I expected him to walk away, as cats tended to do when they'd had their fill of humans, but instead he walked onto my lap and looked up at me.

I gave him a couple more light pets and stopped. He hissed.

"Ah, I see, I'm now your petting servant." I started stroking his head again. He purred and settled down.

"You're doomed now." The guy who'd been petting Ice walked over. "Charlie loves being in someone's lap. Last time I was here, one poor woman sat there for three hours with Charlie monopolizing her until Liam managed to distract him."

"I'm only here for two hours." I stopped petting Charlie when I spoke, and once again he made his displeasure known.

The man chuckled. "He'll give you what-for if he thinks you're ignoring him. I'm Lochlan, one of the volunteers here."

"Del." I thought about shaking hands with him, but I wasn't sure Charlie would be happy about it. "This guy has a nice sweater."

"Charlie loves his sweaters." Lochlan sat beside me. "They found him on the street. His fur was so matted they had to shave most of it off. One of the other volunteers makes the sweaters for him. The only problem is he thinks they're part of him and keeps grooming them, so we have to keep replacing them."

I looked down at Charlie, who was glaring at Lochlan as if unimpressed by the interruption, even though I hadn't stopped petting him this time. "He's up for adoption too?"

Lochlan nodded. "Well, he probably will be in the future,

depending on his medical needs. He's twelve and being treated for some kidney issues, and we're keeping him here until he's more stabilized. Between that and the fur thing, not many people are interested in him. Which is too bad. As you can see, he loves people."

"Yeah."

He stood. "I need to go check in on the shy cats, but let me know if you have any other questions. Or, of course, ask Liam."

"What do volunteers do here?" I blurted the question without thinking about it and instantly realized how ridiculous it sounded.

I wanted to know, though. I wasn't ready to go back to work yet, and socializing had never been one of my favorite things. At the same time, especially now with so much of Austin's stuff out of the apartment, staying home to stare at the walls all day every day was losing its appeal. Being alone with my grief wasn't doing me any favors.

Volunteering at a cat café might not do me any favors either, but at least it would give me someplace to go. Without work and Austin to keep me on a schedule, I'd begun to lose track of the days. Maybe it was time to do something. At least the cats wouldn't expect much from me besides a hand to pet them and a lap to sit on. Adopting might not be a good idea, but I could get my cat fix occasionally.

"Various things," Lochlan said. "I'm pretty good with the shyer ones, so I spend time just sitting with them and encouraging them to explore a little. Volunteering is mostly about socializing the cats so they're more adoptable. The other volunteers and I play with them, encourage them, and give them plenty of attention." He tilted his head. "Is that something you're interested in? I can ask Liam to come talk with you about it."

"Um." I looked down at Charlie. "Maybe later. Thanks."

"Okay." He smiled, a kind smile that for just a second reminded me of Austin, until I shoved that thought away. "Just let me know. Nice meeting you."

"You too."

He went into the shy cat room. I glanced toward Remy, who was grinning at me with a look I couldn't mistake even from halfway across the room. I ignored it. I'd had a conversation with someone. It wasn't as big a deal as Remy seemed to think.

For the rest of the afternoon, I sat with Charlie on my lap and watched Remy wander around petting and playing with the other cats. Liam checked in with me a few times about whether I wanted him to try to remove Charlie, but I was perfectly happy to sit with the Sweater Cat. He seemed pretty content as well. He even let me stop petting him a few times, though if I tried to move him or shift my position at all, he hissed.

I lost track of time. For the past month, that had only happened when grief and thoughts of Austin took over. Today, though, I barely thought of anything at all. Petting Charlie and watching the other cats running around and deigning to interact with the other humans was better than any meditation I'd tried.

Eventually, Liam came over to me. "I have to start closing up. Do you want to help feed them? Your friend already is."

"I don't think Charlie will let me." I started to try to ease out from under Charlie, who swiped at my arm. "Yeah, he isn't in favor of that plan."

Liam laughed. "Charlie does get possessive of his laps. I think when he realizes it's feeding time, he'll move on his own. If not, I'll help you escape."

He went into the other room. I tuned out his voice and the voices of the others who were apparently helping with feeding. Charlie, however, perked up, staring toward the room, until the sound of a food can lid opening motivated him to meander off my lap and into the room where the food was, stopping on the way to hiss at another cat who made the mistake of getting in his path.

I stood and stretched. My legs were a little stiff, but I didn't mind. I wouldn't have said I felt positive, but the deep black cloud that had surrounded me for weeks wasn't as dark.

"I see Charlie finally left you." Lochlan walked through the doorway. "Did you have a chance to talk to Liam about volunteering?"

"Not yet." I hadn't fully decided whether I wanted to. But the way I felt right now, the healing I'd received from Charlie the Sweater Cat's presence, convinced me. I needed something besides the empty space of my apartment.

"I heard my name." Liam came out of the other room. "Did you need something?"

"Lochlan was telling me a little about volunteering here." Without thinking, I stood straighter. "I was wondering if you could use another volunteer."

His face lit up. "Absolutely. You were wonderful with Charlie." He started toward his desk by the front door and motioned for me to follow. "Tell you what. Give me your email and I'll send you some information and the volunteer application." We reached the desk, and he typed something on his laptop. "Email?"

I gave him my email address, which he typed in. "And sent," he said. "Thursday is the day that works best. You saw we get quite a few people in on Thursdays. Is that a day you're usually available?"

"Yes. I have a pretty flexible schedule right now." That would change when I went back to work, but since I didn't yet know when that would be, I opted not to bring it up.

"Why don't you come back next Thursday, then?" He closed the laptop. "I mean, of course, I have to see the application and all that formal stuff, but like I said, I watched you with Charlie. I think you'll be fine. So next Thursday at one?"

"I'll be here. Thank you."

He smiled. "No. Thank *you*."

As Remy and I left, my heart did something it hadn't done in quite a while. I wouldn't say it exactly soared, but it definitely felt lighter.

"You look, dare I say it, happy," Remy said as we got into the car.

"I'm volunteering here starting next week." I fastened my seat belt.

"You're *what*?" She stared at me. "That's amazing, Del!"

"It's not that big a deal."

"It is, because it means you're getting back into the world." She backed out of the parking spot. "I'm glad to see it. Let me know if you need a ride next week."

"I will." I paused. "Thanks for bringing me here, Remy."

"You're welcome. Don't get sappy on me, now." She grinned. "Let's stop someplace and I'll buy you dinner to celebrate."

A couple hours later, after an early dinner and a battle with rush hour traffic, Remy dropped me off at my building. Bracing myself against the inevitable weight of emptiness, I walked into my apartment.

The place was still empty. Austin was still gone. But it didn't feel as desolate. Maybe there was a chance I could fill the empty spaces after all.

CHAPTER FIVE

Weekends were the times I struggled most. Before the accident, Austin spent hours at the club from Thursday through Sunday, but he always made time for me. Breakfast, which usually wound up being closer to lunch since Austin tended to sleep late, in bed. Binge-watching some random show curled up together on the couch until he had to leave again. Our excursions.

Showering together. Making love. Staying connected even when Austin's schedule made seeing each other almost impossible. Sometimes on weekends, I'd felt a little lonely, but I'd always known I wasn't alone. Austin would come home and be with me again.

Now, Austin would never come home. I was truly alone.

Between Thursday night and Monday morning, I didn't even reach out to Remy, who was busy at the club. I only left the apartment once to take a trip around the corner to the buffet. Not that I was particularly keen on another round of pity food, but it was preferable to navigating the grocery store. The restaurant owner wasn't there, but one of his employees recognized me and loaded me up with several takeout containers for which she refused any payment. I felt guilty about accepting, but posting a five-star review on social media assuaged the guilt a little. At least I had enough food to last until I decided I could cope with shopping.

Aside from that, I sat in my living room and pretended to watch TV. Pretended because my mind was barely on the old 1980s detective series I found on one of the streaming services, though I did manage to amuse myself a few times by identifying the 1980s version of parts of Boston I'd become familiar with over the years. The city had changed a lot in the intervening decades.

Monday morning, I woke up actually looking forward to getting out of bed. For the first time since Austin's death, despite the literal emptiness of the place, it didn't *feel* empty. Quiet and unoccupied, but not the deep, pressing emptiness to which I'd become all too accustomed. I had no idea what had changed, but I was thankful for it. Maybe today, I could function.

I got up and pushed myself through my first shower since Saturday, when I'd only showered because I didn't want to offend anyone at the buffet. This time, I cleaned up because I wanted to. I actually wanted to soap up and rinse off, to shampoo my hair, to put on clean clothes that I wouldn't mind wearing in public. Not that I was planning to go out anywhere, but putting on clothes in which I *could* go out opened possibilities.

Right up until I walked into the kitchen, I felt hopeful for the first time in weeks. And then, as I stepped from carpet onto linoleum, the grief hit me again. Not for any reason I could identify. It was as if grief had simply waited for the right time to strike, and it had decided now was the time. Maybe because I'd finally run out of Austin's favorite cookie-flavored creamer. Or because I had to measure the coffee grounds and water more carefully since I would be the only one drinking it. I'd been making coffee the same way for the past several weeks, but this time, it hit me.

Austin was gone. For the rest of my life, I would only need to make enough coffee for myself. I would never again fill a cup halfway with coffee, top it off with far too much creamer, and bring it to him in bed. I would never hear him laughing at me as I scrambled to get ready for work while he lounged around since his shifts at the bookstore didn't start until early afternoon.

I leaned on the counter as a wave of grief nearly knocked me off my feet. The tears began to fall, and a sob tore from my throat.

Austin was gone, and I was still here, and I wished to fuck it was the other way around.

I didn't bother trying to stop myself. Crying was going to happen. Grief would sneak up on me when I least expected it, and there was no point in forcing it away. Especially when the dark depths of it had become so familiar. Despair was my new partner, because the partner I'd loved more than life itself would never be with me again.

In the bedroom, my phone rang. I was afraid to go retrieve it; that would mean letting go of the counter, and I didn't know if my legs would hold me up. Nor did I trust my voice not to betray my anguish. Whoever was calling would probably leave a message if I didn't answer, but somewhere in the back of my mind, I felt like I should answer anyway. Maybe the voice of another human being would help pull me back out of the grief pit, or at least bring me closer to its surface.

By the time I managed to get myself into the other room, I'd missed the call. I sat on the edge of the bed and checked the call log. Remy. Of course. She probably wanted to make sure I'd made it through the weekend.

Before I could call her back, she called again. I jumped as the phone started ringing again and then answered. "Hi, Remy."

"Hi." She paused. "Are you all right?"

"Dandy." She knew I wasn't all right. There was no need to admit it. "What's up?"

"It's been a few days. I'm just checking in." Another pause. "Well, okay, that isn't a hundred percent true. Some of the girls asked about you over the weekend. They'd like to see you if you're up for it."

"I don't want to go to the club, Rem."

"I don't mean at the club," she said. "I was thinking more of food and drinks at my place. Tomorrow night, maybe? Or Wednesday? You, me, of course Marco and Donnie since they live here, and probably Mitch and Solara. It's okay to say no, but we talked a little about this last week, right?"

"Yeah. Let me think for a minute." Part of me wanted to concoct a good excuse for turning her down, though honestly, I didn't need an excuse. "No" was a complete sentence.

Except she was right. We had talked about how she and Austin's other friends felt like I'd shut them out since his death. They mourned him too. Seeing them in full drag at the club would have been more than I could deal with, something Remy acknowledged implicitly through referring to her roommates by their "real" names instead of as Georgia and Robin. Going to Remy's place might be something I could handle.

To her credit, Remy didn't say a word while I considered. Finally, I said, "Yes, okay. Which night?"

"Let's do Wednesday," she said. "That gives me time to let them all know and figure out food and such. They really do want to see you, Del."

"I know." I couldn't quite bring myself to say I wanted to see them. I liked all of them, though Mitch was sometimes a little grating. But in my mind, they'd always been Austin's friends who accepted me for his sake, not *my* friends. I wasn't sure I'd be able to shift my thinking.

I could try, though. Austin would have wanted me to stay in contact with the people who'd become his family. He would have given me a lecture or two about assuming they merely tolerated me.

"Will you need a ride?" Remy asked. "Speaking of rides, by the way, how about the cat café? You're volunteering there this week, yeah?"

"Oh." I hadn't even gotten around to checking my email since Thursday, let alone opening the application Liam had sent. Something I probably needed to do if I still wanted to volunteer.

Which I wasn't sure about anymore. Going to the cat café once a week, or however often Liam wanted me there, had seemed like a good idea while I was there surrounded by the cats. Now, though, I questioned whether I wanted to commit to anything.

"Del." Remy sighed. "You were happy there the other day. Okay, maybe happy isn't the right word, but you were different. In a good way."

"I know what you mean." I did, and she was right about this too. Happiness probably wasn't the right word, but sitting on the couch with Charlie the Sweater Cat, I'd been content. Talking to Lochlan, I'd felt like I was back in the world instead of viewing it from a distance through a grief-tinged lens.

Committing to something—anything—would be better than the constant days running into more days of emptiness. That was why I'd asked Liam about it in the first place. I needed to follow through.

"I should check my email," I said.

"Yes, you should," Remy agreed. "Why don't you go do that? I'll give you a call later to let you know for sure about Wednesday."

"You mean you'll call to nag me about checking my email."

She laughed. "I won't rule that out. Talk to you later, Del. Take care."

"You too."

She hung up.

The call left me calmer. Not as hopeful as when I woke up, but heading in that direction. I could breathe, and grief no longer threatened to pull me under. I could function, at least.

I returned to the kitchen and got my coffee, then sat down with my laptop to check my emails. I didn't remember the last time I'd opened the account. I wasn't sure if I'd checked it at all since Austin's accident. Judging from the number of messages, I probably hadn't. There were a couple hundred, many of them spam or things I'd subscribed to and forgotten about. I was thankful that my work emails went to a different account or there likely would have been several hundred more.

Fortunately, the email from Liam was near the top of the list: a short note thanking me for my interest in volunteering and asking for my schedule. The application was attached. It was a brief, easy form, which I had no way of printing out since I didn't own a printer. I usually printed things at work. For some reason I'd assumed the volunteer application would be a digital document.

That didn't have to be an obstacle, though. I wouldn't let it be. Reading the email and the application form brought back the memories of sitting on the low black couch with Charlie the Sweater Cat on my lap. Watching the other cats play. Talking to Lochlan.

I wanted to be there again. Not only because it was better than staring at the walls of my apartment, but because it was a place I actually liked being.

I typed a quick email to Emmet. *Hi, Liam. I'm available any day of the week, but we had talked about me volunteering on Thursdays. That works well for me. I'm looking forward to being there this Thursday. I'm having a little trouble printing the application. Can I just send you the information?*

I added my name and phone number and sent the message. Within a few minutes, Liam replied confirming Thursday afternoon at one as the time he was expecting me and promising to have a printed application form for me when I arrived because he needed the information on file. I thanked him and debated whether to spend my mental energy on reading the rest of the messages, knowing I probably should. They were piling up, and I couldn't avoid them forever. Most of them could be deleted anyway, and maybe clearing out the inbox would let me feel as if I'd accomplished something.

I sipped my coffee as I got rid of all of the unnecessary emails. That took a little while. Most of them were unnecessary. I probably should have unsubscribed from the mailing lists and such, but I didn't have the emotional bandwidth to deal with opening every single email from those lists so I could click the "unsubscribe" link that didn't work half the time anyway.

When I returned to work, I would have to do this all over again. I could access my work email from home if I wanted, but I refused to. From the day I took my first job, as a teacher's assistant while I attended school to get my master's degree, I'd sworn to Austin that I wouldn't let the boundary between work and home get blurry. Now I was keeping that promise for my own sake.

There was no point in thinking about the work emails now. My principal and the counselor who was filling in for me both had access to the account and were hopefully checking it regularly to address anything that required immediate attention. I wouldn't be returning to the job for a while. Possibly not until fall. If I went back at all, which was something else I couldn't think about right now. I was still too deep in grief to make any life-impacting decision.

Once I got rid of the junk emails, I moved on to the others. Most were from friends and colleagues offering their condolences about

Austin. I didn't read them, but I didn't delete them either. Eventually, responding to them would be the polite thing to do. It just wasn't something I could handle today. Maybe I would ask Remy if I could forward some to her to deal with, though she'd probably received messages from some of the same people.

I found it near the end of the list. An unread email from Austin.

The sight of his name stabbed me through the heart and brought tears to my eyes, and breathing became painful. The weight of his loss, a weight that I'd been stupid enough to think had begun to lift, slammed down full force, and I shoved the laptop away so I could put my head down on the table and cry. Wave after wave of dark pain broke over me, breaking *me*, and all I could do was sit there and wonder who was crying out Austin's name, because it couldn't have been me.

Except it was. Sobs and Austin's name tore out of my throat, and I couldn't move from the heaviness pressing down on me so forcefully I couldn't believe it would ever go away. After all, I'd thought I was doing better, but the mere sight of Austin's name in my inbox was more than I could take.

Grief was a spiral. I'd told students and colleagues that more times than I could count, but I'd never fully understood until now how true that was. Grief wasn't a straight path through the forest of loss. It was curves and turns and switchbacks. It was getting lost amongst the trees and undergrowth. It was finding yourself stuck in the darkness, with the only way out blocked by obstacles you couldn't begin to move.

Gradually, the tears ran dry, as they always did. I managed to sit up and reach for the box of tissues on the other side of the table. Tears still flowed, but more slowly, and I felt a little more in control.

I couldn't avoid the email forever. I needed to see what Austin had said. Since it was unread, he must have sent it the day...

I didn't want to think about that day.

Staring at the screen, I finished my coffee and tried to summon the courage to open the email. It probably wasn't anything important. A reminder of his schedule at the club, maybe, or a request that I pick up lasagna ingredients on the way home from work.

Except if it had been something like that, he would have texted, not emailed. Just as I didn't check my work email at home, I didn't check my personal email at work, and he knew that.

My cup was empty. I could make another, keep prolonging the wait until I saw what was in that email. Hell, I could ignore the email entirely. It wasn't as if Austin was waiting for a reply.

I wouldn't be able to answer the email. No matter what it said, no matter what it was about, I could never answer it. If Austin was letting me know about a problem, the problem would never be resolved. Because Austin was gone, which meant there was zero point in opening that email.

Except I wanted to know what it said. It was the last thing Austin had sent me other than his usual Heading home now, love you text at the end of his night at the club. The night he hadn't made it home. I'd deleted that and all of his other texts in the thick of the first, harshest round of grieving because seeing his name on my phone infuriated me. How dare he go away and not come back?

Now I wished I'd saved the texts. They might be backed up somewhere. I would have to find out. That was something else I could do today, maybe, since I seemed to be in a mood for doing things.

Right now, though, that last email from him was staring me in the face, waiting for me to decide what to do with it. And as hard as seeing his name was, as difficult as it might be to read that email, I needed to know what it said. I clicked on it.

Hey, babe. Merry almost Christmas! Okay, you'll say I rushed the season again, but at least it's after Thanksgiving this time. And I couldn't wait to tell you about the present I chose for you. Mostly because I didn't want to buy it without talking to you. What do you say to a trip to Prince Edward Island this spring? April break, maybe? I got some info from a travel agent. It's attached. Love you, babe, until the sun turns blue.

I didn't know what sent me into another fit of sobbing. The fact that Austin had actually listened all the times I'd said how much I wanted to visit Prince Edward Island to see where my favorite fictional character of all time, Anne of Green Gables, originated, maybe. Seeing his humor and stream-of-consciousness personality in text. The phrase he'd used to end the email, something he'd first said to me on a drunken night not long after we met, when I was still convincing myself it was too soon to be in love.

Or, most likely, all of it.

"You didn't love me until the sun turned blue, you fucking bastard!" I shouted at the laptop, tears streaming down my face. "You didn't stick around that long. Why didn't you stay? Why didn't you..."

The tears took over again, drowning the words, and I let them. There was no point in saying anything. Nothing I could say would bring Austin back.

CHAPTER SIX

Austin had planned to book us a trip to Prince Edward Island. That stunned me. Every time I'd talked to him about the place, he'd said Canada was too cold to visit. He'd also teased me, lovingly, about my reasons for wanting to go. No surprise. The Anne of Green Gables books weren't exactly aimed at grown-ass men.

But as strange as it might have seemed—as it certainly *had* seemed to my family and classmates when I was young—I'd always loved those books. Something about the story of an unwanted, atypical orphan who not only found a home but earned love and respect from everyone around her had appealed to the unwanted, "abnormal" preteen me. Those stories had kept me going during the times I'd wondered if living to see adulthood would even be worthwhile. In my heart, I wanted to see the land Anne and her author had called home.

Something else that goddamned drunk driver had taken from me. Sure, I could still go to Prince Edward Island someday, but I would always know Austin had intended to bring me. He wouldn't be there, and it wouldn't be the same.

After reading his email, I couldn't bring myself to check the rest of the messages in the inbox. The grief-fog engulfed me so heavily I couldn't do anything except pray it would lift. I spent the day avoiding my computer and ignoring most of Remy's messages, other than to tell her that something had come up and I wasn't in any shape to chat. She sent a couple more messages after that but finally gave up.

Tuesday morning, I forced myself out of bed and into clothes. I made my coffee and some toast, which was the only food that even remotely appealed to me. And then I sat down at the table with my laptop. I needed to get through the rest of those emails.

Austin's was still there, of course. I hadn't deleted it. I *wouldn't* delete it. That email was one of the last things I'd received from Austin. I would save it for as long as email existed.

Until the sun turns blue.

A lump rose in my throat, and I swallowed hard. I refused to spend today dissolved in a puddle the way I had yesterday. Everything still hurt. The grief still shrouded me. But today, I needed to get some things done. Tomorrow, I was supposed to go to Remy's. Thursday, I would go back to the cat café and become Charlie the Sweater Cat's throne again. I had things to do. Grief could—and definitely would—accompany me in those tasks, but I had to stop letting it take over and leave me nonfunctional for days on end.

Grief was a spiral. Sometimes, I knew, it would hit when I didn't expect it. And at those times, for a little while, even an hour or two, I could let it rule. But not for a solid day anymore, and definitely not for weeks. Austin was gone. He would always be gone. But I believed in some sort of afterlife, and I believed if Austin was there, he wouldn't be too happy to see that his loss of life had caused me to stop living. There was a balance between allowing myself to grieve and barely allowing myself to exist.

When I was sure I had myself under control, I drank more coffee and went through more emails. I moved the condolence messages into a folder to answer some other time, though by now, most of the senders had probably given up on receiving replies. A few emails were from my principal and the superintendent. Those, I saved. I couldn't deal with them today, but I would need to read and respond soon.

As I drained the last dregs from my coffee cup, my phone rang. Remy, of course.

"Hello?" Balancing my phone between my ear and shoulder, I got up to rinse my cup.

"I'm getting ready to go to some shopping for tomorrow's soiree," she said. The whooshing in the background suggested she was already outside. "Should I pick you up?"

"Why on earth would I want to go soiree shopping, Remy?" I set the cup on the sideboard and returned to the table. "Grocery stores are the fifteenth circle of hell."

"On a Tuesday morning, grocery stores are pretty quiet." Something thudded, and the whooshing stopped. She must have gotten into her car. That was confirmed when the call cut out for a second then returned echoing as if Remy had fallen down a well. "Did you leave your place at all the past few days?"

"No," I admitted. "Not since Saturday."

"Then I suspect your cupboards are running bare and a trip to the grocery store might be in order."

She did have a point. I still had a reasonable amount of canned goods and other nonperishables on hand, but I'd run out of some things, and the perishables I'd bought the last time I'd bothered to shop had probably already perished. "Fine. Can you give me half an hour to get ready?"

"It'll take me almost that long to get to your place. Traffic's a bitch this morning."

"All right. See you then." I hung up.

Exactly half an hour later, Remy texted to say she was out front. The text, rather than her coming to the door, meant she was probably double-parked, so I grabbed my jacket, made sure I had my wallet, and headed out to meet her.

Sure enough, she'd pulled up beside one of my neighbors' cars, barely leaving room for me to open the passenger door wide enough to squeeze through. I didn't blame Remy, though. Almost everyone in this part of East Boston had to park on the street. Buildings with off-street parking were extremely rare. With cars parked along both sides, the streets were narrow as hell. Remy had pulled over as far as she could to leave room for other drivers to pass.

"I was a little surprised you only asked for half an hour," she said as

I fumbled for the seat belt. "I need to drive. There's a very large pickup coming who won't be able to get by."

"Go ahead." I fastened my seat belt, and Remy started driving—at maybe ten miles an hour—down the street.

"You were already out of bed, I take it," Remy said as we approached the nearest intersection.

"Up, dressed, and caffeinated." I leaned back. "I know how much you just love driving around here, but do you mind going to the store in Revere instead of the one by Central Square? It's usually quieter."

"I was already planning on it. The Revere one's cheaper, too." She glanced at me. "What motivated you to get up and ready? I'm not complaining, mind you. It's great. Just unexpected."

"I had things to do today. I didn't finish what I was working on yesterday." I hesitated, debating whether to share with her about the trip. Then again, Austin told Remy everything; she probably already knew. "I started going through my emails yesterday. Personal ones, I mean. I found one from Austin about my Christmas present."

"Ah." She tensed, staring fixedly at the windshield. "I didn't want to bring that up with you. I wasn't sure how you would feel about it."

"So you knew."

She nodded. "I helped him find an LGBTQ-friendly travel agent. He wanted to make this the perfect trip for you. For the two of you, I mean. He had...plans for the trip."

"Plans?" I repeated.

"Del, I don't want to make this harder on you." She took a long breath, and a split second before she spoke, I realized what she was going to say. I almost stopped her, but I needed to hear it. "He was going to propose. He loved you and loved being with you, and he wanted to make it legal. You and he called each other 'husband,' and he wanted the paperwork to back it up. He said you might say no, that the two of you had only talked about it a couple of times and you'd made it sound like legal marriage wasn't something you would want, but he was going to ask anyway. In Prince Edward Island. He thought you would like that even if you did turn him down." She spoke rapidly, as if the faster she dumped out the words, the less likely I would fall apart.

I didn't fall apart, which probably surprised me more than her. Austin had planned to propose. It was another "never" in the long list of things Austin would never do now that he was gone, and I couldn't understand why it wasn't shoving me into another grief tar pit. But I felt nothing. Maybe because Austin had been right. Legal marriage, even though it would have made things much easier for both of us in terms of things like health insurance and other benefits, was something I'd never wanted. He and I'd had a spiritual ceremony shortly after we moved in together, and that was enough for me.

He'd said it was enough for him, too. Apparently it wasn't.

"Del?" Remy said cautiously. "You good?"

"Yeah." Closing my eyes, I took a deep breath, just in case tears were lurking and waiting to attack when I was off guard. "He never even hinted about any of that."

"Keeping secrets wasn't Austin's strong point, but once in a while, he pulled it off." She held up a finger. "Quiet for a moment, please. I almost hit a couple of kamikaze pedestrians on the way to get you, and Maverick Square looks worse than it was just a few minutes ago. I need to focus until we're on One-A."

I mimed zipping my lips, which got a chuckle from her.

When we were safely away from Maverick Square and the streets around the nearby health center, Remy said, "Austin didn't want to give anything away until he was completely sure he would go through with the proposal. He really wanted to, but he was worried about how you would react. And I think he was a little worried about whether the trip would actually happen. He wasn't sure you'd want to spend the money."

"I would have been okay with it. It was a wonderful thought." My voice choked up. For a few seconds, I just sat there, until I was sure I could trust myself to keep talking. "I'm glad he didn't book it. I wouldn't be able to go alone. And no offense, but I wouldn't want to go with anyone else either."

"No offense taken," she said gently. "It was supposed to be something for you and Austin. Going with anyone else wouldn't make sense."

"No." I pressed my lips together. There was nothing else I could say. Without Austin, nothing made sense.

We made it through the grocery store without too much stress. I hadn't thought to make a list, so I just picked up whatever seemed reasonable and tried to remember I only needed enough for myself. Of course things like meat came prepackaged, but I could portion it out and freeze the individual portions. Things I hadn't had to think about before losing Austin. Not only had we obviously eaten more together than I would on my own, but he'd usually handled the grocery shopping. He claimed to actually enjoy it.

When we returned to my place, Remy helped me carry in the three bags, even though I could probably have managed on my own. Then again, they were the store's flimsy paper bags. I'd forgotten all about Austin's reusable shopping bags, which were sturdier and had handles.

"Next time, I'll help you make a list," Remy said, putting down the bag she'd brought in on the counter. She stepped back and regarded me, hands on her hips. "You look better."

"Thanks?" Not sure I wanted to know what she meant, I put down my bags and started unpacking things.

"You're standing up straighter." Apparently she intended to explain even if I didn't ask. "You even smiled a couple of times. And you chatted with the cashier. I've never seen you chat with anyone."

I snorted. "I'm not completely incompetent in the real world, Remy."

"You know what I mean. Small talk isn't your preferred language." She leaned against the counter. "I'm not putting you down, Del. It's all good things."

"I know." I did know what she meant. That didn't stop a pang in my heart at the thought that maybe it seemed like I was forgetting Austin. "Yesterday was hard. Today was easier."

"Grieving is like that." She turned and started taking things out of the bag she'd brought in. "You're coming over tomorrow night like we planned." It wasn't a question.

"Yes." I stared at the can of spaghetti rings in my hand and tried to remember why I'd bought it. Or even the act of buying it; I didn't recall putting it in my cart. Hopefully I hadn't wound up with some preschooler's lunch or something. "I'll take a rideshare."

"So you can make a faster escape?" She chuckled. "Fine. Be there around five if you want to arrive before the others. Donnie and Marco have to work, so they won't be home until five-thirty or so, and I told Solara and Mitch to show up at six."

"Thank you." Even with a small gathering, I preferred being one of the first to arrive. It was easier to deal with other guests one or a couple at a time than walking into a roomful. Remy's acknowledgement of that warmed me. "I'll aim for between five and quarter past."

"Sounds like a plan." She looked around. "Do you need anything from me? I can hang out. Help with cleaning if you want. Or I can head home and give you space. Your choice."

For whatever reason, Remy's kindness brought another lump to my throat, and before I was able to swallow it, tears started trickling down my cheeks. A gray film clouded my vision, and my chest ached. Remy would have said she wasn't doing much of anything, but she was. Austin had always given me choices like that. He'd understood that sometimes I just didn't want to "people," as he put it, and he never took it personally when I said I wanted space. Or at least, if he did take it personally, he never said so.

"Um, space, please." I didn't trust myself to be able to say anything else.

"You got it." She hesitated. "Are you all right?"

All I could do was shake my head. She stepped toward me, arms outstretched, and I held up a hand to stop her. Right now, I couldn't tolerate even a hug meant to comfort.

Her face fell, but all she said was, "Call if you need me. I'll text you tomorrow to make sure you're still coming over."

"Thanks," I croaked.

"You got it." Still looking unsure, she left.

The moment the door closed behind her, the trickle of tears became a tidal wave. I sagged to the floor and let it flow.

CHAPTER SEVEN

By the next afternoon, I'd almost talked myself out of going to Remy's "soiree." The grief-fog had settled in again, and it showed no sign of burning off. The last thing I wanted to do was spend the evening surrounded by humans, even those I considered friends.

But I'd promised Remy, and when she texted me shortly after I finished the peanut butter toast I'd forced myself to eat for lunch, I told her I would be there. And then spent the next couple of hours cursing myself for the decision.

At quarter to five, wearing a Toppa DaWorld T-shirt Austin had given me for my birthday a few years ago and a pair of jeans that reminded me I hadn't done laundry in a while, I got into my rideshare and headed off to the Dorchester apartment Remy shared with Marco, a/k/a Robin Goodlady, and Donnie, who performed as Georgia Marietta.

Remy had lived in that apartment for decades. She and Austin had rented it along with two others they'd met at the club shortly after arriving in Boston. Since Austin moved in with me nearly twenty years earlier, Remy had had a revolving door of roommates. Whenever someone showed up at the club needing a home, she gave them one, or at least gave them an air mattress and sleeping bag on her floor for a few nights. No matter how long they stayed, to Remy, they became chosen family.

The apartment was on a quiet street, which Donnie alleged was the same street on which the Wahlberg brothers had grown up. I suspected that was wishful thinking on his part, especially given that he'd named himself—his guy self—after Donnie Wahlberg. The rideshare dropped me off right out front, and I took a moment to breathe in the cold, snow-scented air. Despite the implication of a storm and the many streetlights, when I looked up, a star shone directly above me.

Maybe that was a good omen.

I went upstairs and knocked on Remy's door. She opened it within seconds. "Were you lurking?" I asked as I walked past her.

"We agreed five, and you're usually on time or early." She closed the door. "You look...decent."

I couldn't help laughing. "Yeah. Not all of us are blessed with in-unit laundry. I need to make a laundromat run tomorrow, I guess."

"You could have brought some things over to wash." She surveyed me head to toe. "How are you doing? You don't look like you regret being here."

"I'm here for dinner, not to run up your electric bill. And I wanted to see the others." To my surprise, the words were true. I did want to see them. Even Mitch, who talked at warp speed and didn't always comprehend personal space.

"Solara promised to keep an eye on Mitch," Remy said as if she'd read my mind. "He's been clean since we lost Austin, and she's trying to make sure he stays that way. I know he gets on your nerves. Hell, he gets on everyone's sometimes. But only when he's high."

"Okay."

She tilted her head. "Are you actually something resembling happy?"

"I don't know." I honestly didn't. The only thing I could have said for certain was that I wasn't wallowing in the grief tar pit. Not that I particularly wanted to talk about my feelings. "So what are we having for food, and what can I do to help?"

"You're here for dinner, not to do my dirty work." She grinned and led me into the kitchen. "Vegetarian lasagna. Garlic bread. Homemade lemon pie. It was supposed to be lemon meringue, but the meringue didn't want to meringue, so we'll have to make do with whipped cream. And whatever Solara and Mitch bring, if they bring anything. I told them not to, but you know Solara."

"Yeah." Loud, opinionated, and Austin's best friend aside from Remy, Solara nurtured everyone she met. She'd tried to take care of me after the accident, but I hadn't been in a place where I could let her. She was the first one I pushed away, and I felt like shit for it. "Think she's still pissed at me?"

"Huh?" Remy glanced at me over her shoulder. "Solara? She was never pissed at you. Why would she be?"

"I was kind of a dick the last time she saw me." I pulled out one of the heavy oak chairs at the kitchen table, as always cringing at the sound of the legs scraping across the linoleum, and sat down.

"You were a dick to me a few times too, and I stuck around." She opened the oven and waved her hand in front of it. "Smell that? That is the scent of incredible Italian cooking. Solara understood why you were acting that way, Del. She's had losses too. She didn't back off because she was pissed. She just didn't want to piss *you* off by being in your face."

"I wasn't pissed at her." Now I felt worse. Solara should have been angry with me after I yelled at her and told her to leave me alone. I'd treated a friend like crap, and that was worthy of anger. If she wasn't angry, I wasn't getting what I deserved.

"She knows that too," Remy said soothingly. She closed the oven. "That isn't quite ready yet, but by the time the girls get here, it will be. Del, listen to me. You told people to leave you alone, so they left you alone. Some of us were a little hurt, yes, but we all understood. Grief fucks mightily with people, and we were all grieving. You wanted to grieve alone, and even though we wanted to be there for you, we knew we had to let you grieve your way. If you want to apologize, I won't stop you, but I'd bet this lasagna that every one of them will say there's no apology necessary."

"If you bet the lasagna and I win, does that mean I get to take it home?"

I meant it as a joke. Fortunately, Remy laughed. "Hell no. I worked way too hard on this." Three rapid thuds sounded against the front door. "That'll be Solara and Mitch. I told them six, but..."

"But I know Solara." I took a breath and pasted a smile on my face. It wasn't as difficult or inauthentic as usual. "Go ahead and let them in."

I stayed in my seat and listened as Remy opened the door and Mitch bounded in, at least judging from the sound of his footsteps, followed by Solara's more placid entrance. They chattered as Remy brought them into the kitchen, then fell silent.

I stood and faced them. Solara was taller than me and just as imposing in dark jeans and a striped button-down shirt as in the evening gowns and multi-inch platform heels she wore on stage. The shirt's periwinkle and lavender checked pattern made a striking contrast against her dark skin. Mitch, even thinner than the last time I'd seen him, barely reached Solara's shoulder. He'd chopped off most of his brown hair sometime in the past month, and he regarded me with a solemn expression, though the typical mischievous glint showed in his eyes.

Neither of them spoke. It was up to me to say something.

"I'm sorry." My voice caught on the last word. I cleared my throat. "I appreciated everything. I just couldn't..." Not sure how to finish the sentence, I shook my head.

"Couldn't accept it." Solara fluidly moved forward and enfolded me in her arms. I wasn't a big fan of hugging, but it was Solara's native language, so we'd agreed long ago that she had permanent hug privileges with me. "It's okay, boo. We understand." She stepped back, keeping her hands on my shoulders. "How are you doing?"

I shrugged. "It depends on the day. Today, pretty much okay."

"Good." She flashed a smile and stepped back. "Mitch?"

"I'm sorry too." Mitch chewed his lower lip. "For last time. I was... Shit, I was high. I shouldn't have been, but I was. And I acted like an ass. I'm really sorry, Del. Austin was so amazing, and I didn't want to think about him not being here." His eyes widened. "And neither do you. I'm doing it again."

"Hey, boo, you're fine." Solara gave me a look that said I had better agree with her.

I didn't need the look. Seeing the fear in Mitch's expression was more than enough. "It's okay, Mitch. I appreciate the apology."

He relaxed. "Okay. Thanks. God, Sol, why didn't you let me come here as Starry? I'm so much better at humaning when I'm her."

"You *are* her, boo," Solara said sternly. "So be her without the drag."

"Yeah." Mitch took a deep breath and straightened his shoulders. "Sorry, Del. We're supposed to be here to support you, and I'm being..." He waved his hand at himself. "This."

"You're being you." Mitch did get on my nerves sometimes, but I knew enough about his past to understand. I'd dealt with teens like him, using substances to numb the pain of the abuse they lived with. Even if the abuse ended, it lived on in their minds. Knowing that, I fell back into counselor mode without thinking about it. "Let's not get stuck in endless apologies, okay? I'm glad to see both of you. Remy claims she's making an amazing dinner, so let's enjoy ourselves." I blinked back tears, unsure whether they were due to my own grief or Mitch's pain. Possibly both.

"Yeah." Mitch took another long breath and smiled. "Yeah, let's have fun tonight. Missed ya, Del."

"Same." And I meant it. I'd missed both of them. All of them.

Donnie and Marco got home not long after, and the six of us settled in to tackle Remy's lasagna. During the meal, I listened to the others sharing the club gossip. New queens who wanted to perform there, new ideas for the shows, the frustration of dealing with the club's manager. I didn't say much, but none of them seemed to notice. And there wasn't much for me to say. I wasn't part of their world. Austin was the bridge between them and me, and with him gone, even though they tried to include me, I felt like I didn't belong.

During dessert, Donnie asked the question I'd been dreading. "Del, how have you been doing? You know you're welcome at the club, right?"

"Oh." I looked at the forkful of lemon pie I was holding and put it down. My appetite had just vanished. "I've been managing, I guess. Remy has helped a lot."

"That's good." The pity in Donnie's expression hit me like a blow to the gut. "We've been hoping to see you around."

"I just needed time." I paused, trying to find words that wouldn't hurt their feelings. "The club isn't really my thing. Especially without Austin."

"It definitely isn't the same without him." Donnie narrowed his eyes. "But we're all still there."

"Donnie, drop it." Solara's voice boomed across the table.

"I'm just asking."

Yeah, the pie was definitely no longer appealing. I shoved back my chair and stood. "Remy, thanks for having me over. It was good to see all of you. I think it's time for me to head home." Even though home was the last place I wanted to go.

"Del, wait." Remy shot a death glare at Donnie as she got up. "Please stay."

"I'm sorry." Donnie sounded anything but. "Like I said, I was just asking."

"This was a nice evening. Best to leave it that way." I walked away, ignoring the multiple voices calling me back to the table.

Remy followed me to the door. "Donnie's a mouthy bitch. Please don't let him push you out like this."

"I pushed all of you out, so I guess it's payback." I put on my jacket. "I'll wait downstairs for my ride."

"Solara can probably drive you if you stick around."

The desperation in Remy's tone struck me in the heart, but it didn't change my mind. I wasn't even all that angry with Donnie. He was being a dick, but he had reason to be. I just wasn't in the mood to deal with it civilly, and I respected Remy and the others too much to let conflict wreck their night. "I'll be fine, Remy. I'll let you know when I get home."

Looking defeated, she held out her arms, and I let her hug me. "Do you need a ride tomorrow?"

The idea of having to deal with a rideshare again the next day didn't thrill me, but I felt wrong about asking Remy to drive me to the café after the way tonight was ending. "I'll figure something out, but thanks. Talk to you later." I looked past her toward the kitchen. "Have a good night, all."

"Keep in touch, boo." Solara sounded uncharacteristically subdued.

"You too." A lump rose in my throat, and I walked out before it could bloom into full emotion.

So much for a pleasant dinner with friends.

CHAPTER EIGHT

Thursday morning, I woke up feeling smothered by the weight of guilt on top of grief. I'd messaged Remy the night before, as promised, but ignored her response. Someone else had texted me as well, and I hadn't even bothered checking my phone to see who it was.

Remy had put together an evening to bring me back into our circle of friends, and I'd bailed. Regardless of my reason, I shouldn't have just walked out. I could have stayed and sorted things out with Donnie. I just didn't have the emotional bandwidth. Yet again, I'd pushed away the people who wanted to be there for me.

At the same time, though, Donnie was out of line. He knew damn well I rarely went to the club even when Austin was alive. It obviously wasn't anything personal against him or the others. He could have dropped the subject, but he'd chosen to keep pushing. Maybe out of his own grief. He wasn't one of Austin's close friends, but he'd taken Austin's death hard.

I wasn't the only one grieving. I knew that. But my grief had blinded me to how others were feeling, even Remy and her family. I'd taken advantage of their kindness despite knowing they'd suffered just as much of a loss as I had. More of one in some ways, given how much longer they'd known Austin. I hadn't taken advantage of Donnie, and

I'd known Austin longer than he had, but that didn't mean he wasn't mourning just as much.

"Shit." I pushed back the covers but didn't get up. Getting out of bed would mean making decisions. Should I apologize to Donnie? To Remy and the others?

I decided I should have coffee. Maybe it would help me make the rest of the decisions. I started the coffee maker, then took a quick shower and dressed in old, worn jeans and a light-colored sweater that seemed appropriate for hanging out with Charlie and the rest of the cats.

I would be spending the afternoon with cats. Maybe hanging out with Charlie the Sweater Cat again. The prospect brightened my mood a bit. With the cats, I wouldn't have to worry about how I acted or what they might say. I could just be there, the way I'd been the previous week.

Of course, I wasn't going there just to play with the cats. The information Liam had sent didn't really indicate much about what volunteers did, but surely it involved actual work. I would find out when I showed up.

Cup of coffee finally in hand, I got my phone and sat at the table to schedule a ride to the café. I'd found in the past that prescheduling a ride, especially outside the city limits, made having a driver actually show up on time to get me where I was going more likely. Before I opened the ride app, though, a pair of texts distracted me.

One was Remy's reply from the night before. Thanks for letting me know. Glad you made it home okay.

From the words, I couldn't tell whether she was annoyed with me for taking off the way I had. I would have to call and find out. And apologize. That much was a fairly easy decision. Remy had gone above and beyond to try to keep me going and help me fill the empty spaces left by Austin. She didn't deserve to have me act the way I had last night.

The other message, from Donnie, surprised me. I was out of line. Hurts not seeing Austin around, kinda thought seeing you would help. Not your job to help me. Sorry for pushing.

Guilt pushed in on me again. As I'd speculated, Donnie had acted the way he had because of grief. And I'd pretty much shit on him for it, even though God knew I'd done my share of acting like a dick. I owed Donnie an apology too. And while I was at it, I might as well apologize to Solara, Mitch, and Marco for the way I'd walked out of the get-together.

I scheduled the ride to the café and then started in on the apology texts, Remy's first. By the time I finished the others, all variations of *sorry I ruined the mood last night, I appreciate you being there*, Remy had replied: All good. Wish you'd stayed, but I get it. Need a ride this afternoon?

I debated. Taking a ride from Remy would save me a fair amount of money, even if she only drove me there and I took a rideshare home. At the same time, after getting pissed at myself for taking advantage of her and her family, accepting a ride from her seemed wrong. Thanks, all set this time.

LMK if you change your mind. Not doing much today.

Will do. I set down the phone, then picked it up again. Words on a screen didn't tell me enough. I called Remy.

"Del?" She sounded surprised when she answered the phone.

"Yeah, sorry if I'm interrupting you." I paused, searching for the right words. "You did something awesome for me last night. I'm really sorry for bailing on you."

"No need." Her tone warmed. "I get it. Donnie was getting on your case, and that was not what you needed right then. I wasn't upset. None of us were. Well, except maybe Donnie, but that was his own damn fault."

"He sent me an apology text."

"Did he?" Her voice rose. "Good for him. And you accepted it?"

"I sent him an apology back." I sipped some coffee. "I apologized to everyone."

"You didn't have to, but I'm sure they appreciate it." She was silent for a moment. "I'm glad you came over, Del, even if it didn't go the way I'd hoped. You were here among friends, and that was the most important thing as far as I was concerned. I wish it had ended differently, but like I said, I get it."

"Thanks." I let out a long breath. At least Remy was still in my corner. I didn't know how I rated her continued friendship, but I was thankful for it. "So you aren't working today?"

"I'm working tonight at the club. It's Thursday." She chuckled. "No, I'm not doing the day job today. That's the brilliant thing about working for myself. I can give myself days off. Just like I've been doing for the past month-plus, or hadn't you noticed?"

"I..." I trailed off. For the past month-plus, as Remy put it, I'd barely been aware of my own daily routine, let alone anyone else's. I was also used to Remy working odd hours. In her offstage life, she was a certified life coach who focused on supporting other transgender people through their social and emotional transitions. She'd been doing that work for over a decade now and had not only a full client roster but a waiting list, since the internet allowed her to work with people internationally. Having clients in various other corners of the globe meant accommodating other time zones, so she didn't have a typical nine-to-five schedule. "I hadn't noticed."

"I wouldn't have expected you to," she said gently. "I took a couple of weeks off, and some of my clients had already arranged to take a break over the holidays. I'm not back to my full client load yet, so I've had extra time on my hands."

"Which you've been spending with me."

"Some of it. Some of it I've been spending with me." She paused again. "Del, I don't have any problem supporting you in any way you need. You're my brother as much as Austin was. I've told you that. Guilt is part of grief, but try not to let it eat you alive the way the grief has been, okay?"

"Thanks." I didn't feel guilty for her spending her free time supporting me. Did I? When I honestly thought about it, I wasn't sure. "And thanks again for offering me a ride today, but like I said, I'm set."

"Rideshare?" She muttered the word as if it tasted disgusting.

"Well, yeah, but I don't mind. It doesn't make sense for you to go out of your way to pick me up here and drop me off there. Unless you signed up to volunteer when I wasn't paying attention." I wasn't about to say that I didn't want to impose on her, at least not in those words. That would only get me another lecture.

"No, today I'm volunteering at the Closet," she said. "So I guess it is good that you don't need a ride from me. I have to be in Cambridge by two."

"Yeah, Peabody to Cambridge in an hour isn't impossible, but why rush?" I relaxed. Now I didn't have to come up with an excuse for turning down her offer. "I'll be fine, Rem. Rideshare isn't the worst fate in the world."

"And then you get to play with cats."

"Exactly." I ran my finger around the rim of my mug. The coffee was getting cold. "I'm going to let you go, Remy. I just wanted to make sure we're good."

"We're always good, Del." Warmth filled her tone. "I'll give you a shout tomorrow and you can tell me all about your fuzzy little friends."

"Sounds good. Have a good day, Remy."

"You too."

I hung up and drank the rest of the coffee, which wasn't quite cold enough to be unpleasant. It was only eight-thirty. My ride to the café wouldn't arrive for nearly another four hours. Four hours of time to fill. I'd grown accustomed to time just kind of passing, without anything to occupy it, because grief had occupied everything. But today, I felt like doing things. I just didn't know what.

I decided to start with my emails again. I could make sure I'd replied to all of the ones that needed replies, including any that had shown up since Monday. Maybe I would even have the mental bandwidth to read the information Austin had attached to his email.

Probably not. But anything was possible. Right now, I almost believed that cliché.

CHAPTER NINE

I ate a light lunch just before my rideshare was due to arrive and was waiting outside when the car pulled up. The driver, to my relief, didn't speak beyond asking me how my day was going, and we completed the half-hour trip to the accompaniment of a decent variety of classic rock and show tunes. The music and lack of conversation put me in a state of calm relaxation that seemed optimal for spending the afternoon with cats.

Liam met me in the entryway of the café. "Welcome, welcome! Glad you could make it. Sanitize your hands, please, and then come on in."

I did so, then took off my coat and hung it up while Liam chatted with Ice. "So what do you need me to do?" I asked when I was ready.

"Mostly the volunteers are here to help socialize the cats." Liam gestured around the space. "Obviously some of the cats are already pretty good with humans, but some need more attention. I saw Charlie kind of took you over last week. He can definitely use more human interaction, so if you want to sit down and let him have your lap, that's fine. We have our shy cat room, too, and you're welcome to spend time sitting in there with the cats who are a little more reluctant to be out."

I raised my eyebrows. "That's it?"

He smiled. "That's it. There are some things we can't ask the volunteers to do because of regulations. And honestly, giving these cats love and attention is an important job in and of itself. We have a few people scheduled for visits this afternoon, so I'll be talking with them, but feel free to chime in. And ask me anything you want to know."

I nodded and scanned the room. Charlie the Sweater Cat was lying alone on the black couch, blinking at me in what appeared to be a disgruntled manner, though I wasn't sure if cats actually got disgruntled. I thanked Liam and headed over to sit beside Charlie, who immediately made his way onto my lap.

"He's not even going to give you a chance to protect yourself." Lochlan came out of the other room and nodded to the blanket beside me. "Charlie sheds. Sometimes it isn't fur."

"Great." I stroked Charlie's head, and he started purring loudly. "Good thing I wore my oldest jeans."

"That was a wise choice." He grinned. "Del, right? I'm Lochlan."

"I remember." I smiled back. "Good to see you again."

"Likewise." He glanced around. "So you signed up to volunteer, I take it. That's good. These cats can always use more people to care for them. Do you want a water or anything? I'm happy to get you something. I don't think Charlie will let you move."

"I suspect you're right." I stopped petting Charlie, who glared up at me balefully. As soon as I touched his head again, his eyes slipped closed and the purring resumed. "Yes, apparently the possibility of me getting up offends his sensibilities. I don't need anything right now, but thank you."

"Sure, no problem." He looked toward the entryway, where Liam was greeting a trio of young women. "Drinks are free while you're volunteering here, so if you want anything, just flag down Liam or me. Or try to get up if Charlie gives you permission. I'll be in the shy cat room, but I can hear from in there. Those cats are pretty quiet." He bent and peeked behind the couch. "So is that one."

I did a double take. "There's a cat back there?"

He nodded. "Clooney. One of our new ones. He's claimed that space for now, but he comes out at night when the humans are gone.

Hopefully he'll get bolder over time. He's only been here since Friday, so he's still getting acclimated."

The young women, chattering excitedly, followed Liam into the space. Lochlan straightened. "I'm going back into the other room. Nice talking to you."

"You too."

He returned to the shy cat room, and I returned to petting Charlie. His sweater was a little more ragged than last week, but that didn't seem to matter to him. He curled up on my lap and, still purring, fell asleep.

There wasn't much I could do besides continuing to pet the slumbering cat on my lap. Having Charlie lying there, a soft, warm pile of fur under my touch, was incredibly soothing. My mind wandered, not to anything in particular but more to a lack of thought. I was simply here, being a cat cushion, watching some of the other cats play with the other humans while still other cats slept or perched and surveyed their domain.

Volunteering here was a good idea. I hadn't been sure, but now I was glad I'd done it. If I could spend one afternoon a week petting cats and not thinking about Austin, maybe healing would happen sooner.

Liam walked by and smiled a couple of times as he showed the visitors around. I smiled back but otherwise barely noticed the other humans in the room. Ice wandered over and sat on the floor in front of me, not quite within range for me to pet him without disturbing Charlie, who did not appear to want to be disturbed. Piper jumped up on the other end of the couch and lay like a loaf, blinking at me, also out of my reach.

Finally, Charlie decided he'd had sufficient lap time. He stood and yawned at me, then clumsily hopped down and wandered off in search of food or a litterbox. Or both.

I checked my watch. I'd been sitting there for over an hour without even noticing and without moving even the slightest bit. No wonder my legs were starting to ache. I leaned over to let Piper sniff my hand, hoping I would be able to pet her, but after one sniff she leapt off the couch and ran to the cat tree along the nearby wall.

"She's persnickety." At Lochlan's voice behind me, I jumped. He chuckled. "Sorry. Didn't mean to sneak up on you."

"No worries." I stood and turned to face him. "Charlie decided it was break time."

"I see." He gave me a warm smile that lit his entire face, including his hazel-green eyes. It tugged at me in a way I wasn't willing to acknowledge. "Do you want to meet the shy cats while you're up?"

"Sure." I went to the end of the couch and crouched. Eerily glowing eyes looked back at me from the shadows. "Looks like one is still here."

"Clooney." Lochlan knelt beside me, close enough I could feel his body heat. Suddenly uncomfortable, I moved back. He didn't seem to notice. "Hello, Clooney. It's okay. Someday you'll come out and see all of us." Turning to me, he rose to his feet. "Come meet the brothers."

"Brothers?" I stood, ignoring my legs' complaints.

"Bailey and Remy."

I couldn't help laughing. "Remy? That's my friend's name. The one who was with me last week." She would probably find it hilarious to know she shared a cat's name. "I'll have to call him Remy-the-Cat to keep them straight."

"Sounds like a plan." Lochlan grinned. "She wouldn't have met him when you were here before. He and Bailey came in a day or so after Clooney." A large black and white cat sauntered out of the shy cat room and blinked up at Lochlan, who knelt again to scratch the cat's head. "Speak of the devil. Hi, Bailey, you incredible chonker."

"He is a bit large," I said. It was an understatement. I'd known full-grown dogs—not counting Chihuahuas—who were smaller than this cat.

Lochlan snorted and stood again. "Yeah, you could say. Twenty-three pounds. Remy's a little smaller, but not much. He's also considerably shyer. Come meet him."

I followed him into the shy cat room. Two small plastic carriers sat side by side on the floor. One was empty. In the other, when I bent to look, I spotted a furry face, black around the eyes and mostly white on the nose and mouth, other than one black smudge beside the nose. "You must be Remy-the-Cat. Nice to meet you."

"He sometimes comes out of the carrier, but he hasn't been out of this room with humans present yet." Lochlan sat on the floor and leaned against the door frame. "He's lovable, just scared. He and Bailey were with their humans for quite a while, but they're both diabetic and need some extra care their humans couldn't provide."

"Ah." I sat cross-legged near the carrier. The second I was settled, Remy emerged and nudged my leg. I petted him, and he rubbed against me. "You are a lovable kitty, aren't you?"

"And you're a cat whisperer." Lochlan sounded pleased. "This is the first time I've seen him go right up to someone like this."

"He's soft." I continued running my hand over the silken fur. "You're a soft old sweetheart, aren't you, Remy-the-Cat?"

Ordinarily, I might have felt awkward talking to a cat that way in front of another person. I loved cats, but I'd never been one of those who acted as if a cat could hold an entire conversation. But I didn't feel weird in front of Lochlan. I felt as calm and at peace with him as I did with the cats themselves.

"He and Bailey will have to be adopted together," Lochlan said. "They've been together since they were kittens, so we need to make sure they aren't separated now. They won't be adopted out for a little while yet, though. We need to get their diabetes and weight a little more under control first."

"That makes sense." Maybe I would adopt them. I had no experience with diabetic cats, of course, but I could learn.

Or maybe I would adopt Charlie. Once I returned to work, having a cat to curl up in my lap after a long, stressful day would be wonderful. Though Charlie might object to being alone all day five days a week.

Shaking my head, I scoffed. "Here I sit plotting to adopt the lot of them."

Lochlan laughed. "Yeah, that happens. I've considered it myself, except my landlord doesn't allow pets. Which is why I'm here. Do you have pets?"

"No. My partner is—was allergic." And just like that, a bucket of icy pain poured over my mood. My voice caught in my throat. "Um, I lost him a little after Thanksgiving."

"Oh." Lochlan's eyes widened. "I'm so sorry."

"Thanks." I took a couple of breaths to steady myself. The last thing I wanted to do was burst into tears in front of Lochlan and Remy-the-Cat, who was now lying against my leg blinking up at me in an oddly reassuring manner. "It was sudden. A drunk driver. I'm still adjusting."

"Of course you are." The sympathy that shone in his eyes almost killed my resolve not to cry. "I'm really sorry, Del. I'm glad you're here, though. These furry little guys help a lot." He reached behind him as Bailey wandered back in, and Bailey butted against Lochlan's hand.

"Yeah." I looked down at Remy-the-Cat. "They do."

Lochlan leaned back against the doorframe, legs outstretched. Bailey tentatively moved onto Lochlan's lap. "Oof. You're heavy." Lochlan scratched between Bailey's ears.

Remy-the-Cat stayed where he was, eyes closed to slits as I continued stroking his incredibly soft fur. As with Charlie, petting Remy-the-Cat became almost a meditative action. My mind shut itself off, though the pain of talking about Austin remained.

Lochlan, too, stayed where he was, petting Bailey and not saying a word. I was grateful for that. Nothing he might have said would have helped, and I definitely wasn't in the right headspace to talk anymore. But Lochlan's presence, like that of the cats, was soothing.

After several minutes, Lochlan leaned through the doorway to look out at the other room. "Uh oh. Charlie is disgruntled. He doesn't have a lap."

I managed a sound that was somewhere along the lines of laughter and gave Remy-the-Cat one last pet. He sniffed, an almost human sound, and meandered back into his carrier. I stood. "I guess I'd better return to Charlie, then."

"I'm sure he'll appreciate it." Lochlan smiled. "I'll be in here hanging with Bailey and Remy."

Feeling annoyingly awkward about walking away from him and with no idea why I felt that way, I went back to Charlie's couch and put the blanket over my lap. Charlie almost instantly curled up on it. And there we stayed until Liam started getting cans of food out of a cupboard along the back wall of the space. At that point, Charlie decided food was far more interesting and stalked away without even a backward glance.

I stood and stretched. The three young women who'd come in just after I arrived had left at some point, probably while I was in the shy cat room. A man and a young girl who looked around ten were helping Liam open cat food cans and place them on the floor, while most of the cats surrounded them. Charlie hung back until the girl, at Liam's direction, put a can directly in front of him, at which point Charlie, as one of my students would have said, "chowed down."

"Will you be back next week?" Lochlan asked from the doorway of the shy cat room.

I hadn't realized he was standing there, but this time I at least managed not to jump. "That's up to Liam, but I hope so."

"You're welcome to." Liam, kneeling beside Piper as she ate, looked at me over his shoulder. "Same time as today?"

"Yes." My heart rose. "Thank you."

"Thank you. I know Charlie appreciated the attention." He turned back to Piper. "Good girl, Piper. Del, we'll see you next week."

"Absolutely."

I stood watching the cats for a little longer. Liam might have intended his "see you next week" as a dismissal, but I wasn't yet ready to leave the serenity of being surrounded by so many furry creatures. The man and girl who had helped feed the cats left, and two other cats, both black and white, one with short fur and one very fluffy, came out from under the couch closest to the feeding area. "Moonbeam and Choco Chip!" Liam said. "Welcome. Come have food."

The cats joined the others at the collection of cans. I started feeling awkward about standing there, which told me it was time to go whether I was ready or not. I walked over to the coat rack. Lochlan followed. "I'll see you next Thursday."

"Yeah." I paused, trying to come up with something else to say. "Thanks for talking with me."

"You're welcome." He touched his tongue to his upper lip. "Um, look, can I give you my number? If you ever want to talk. I kind of know what you're going through. You barely know me, but I could still be someone you can reach out to if you want. I make my own schedule, so I'm usually available."

I started putting on my jacket slowly, so I would have time to consider Lochlan's question. I had friends' numbers in my phone. Until this morning's round of apology texts, I hadn't contacted anyone besides Remy in weeks, so if I took Lochlan's number, I probably wouldn't contact him either. Then again, taking his number didn't obligate me to anything, and I liked talking to him. Maybe a little more than I should have.

"Yeah, I'd appreciate that," I said finally. The way he'd just stood there, not even looking slightly impatient, while I debated didn't escape my notice. I took out my phone and realized I hadn't ordered my rideshare yet. "Just a sec. I have to arrange my ride."

"You don't drive?"

I opened the rideshare app and clicked what I needed to click. To my annoyance, it informed me that the nearest driver was thirteen minutes away. At least the sun was shining and the temperature outside wasn't ridiculously cold. I could wait in the parking lot. "No, I don't," I said, answering Lochlan's question. "I live in East Boston with no off-street parking, so owning a car didn't make sense. I might have to sign up for one of those rent-by-the-hour services or something." Austin had an account with one of those services for our excursions, since sometimes we went too far from home for rideshare to be feasible. Maybe I could find his information and get the service to transfer his account to me. "I *can* drive, I just don't own a car."

"Got it." He opened his mouth as if to say something else, then closed it.

I opened my contacts list. "You were going to give me your number?"

"Yes, and then please text me so I have yours." He quirked the corners of his mouth. "Assuming you want me to have it."

"I think I can trust you with it."

He chuckled. "I promise to guard it carefully and use it well."

He recited his number. I typed it into my phone, then texted him Hi. His text tone, like Lochlan himself, was soothing: a faint, deep chime.

"Well, I'm sticking around a while longer." He stuck his hands in his pockets. "I usually stay for an hour or two after Liam and everyone else leaves to spend time with the shyer cats. It's easier on them when it's only me here. I'll talk to you soon."

"Yeah. Thanks."

He turned and headed back to the shy cat room. I put my phone in my jacket pocket and went outside to wait for my ride. The sunshine felt warmer than when I walked into the café two hours earlier. The winter chill still lingered in the air, but I barely felt it.

Lochlan shouldn't have had so much of an impact on me, but there was something about him. Something I looked forward to learning more about.

Austin hadn't even been gone two months. It was far too soon to be this interested in someone else. I could try to convince myself I wasn't really interested in Lochlan, that he was just being kind and I needed kindness. But that wasn't completely honest. There was something about him, and I wanted more of that something in my life. And I hated myself for wanting it.

CHAPTER TEN

Remy—the human, that was—sat cross-legged on my couch, leafing through a fashion magazine she'd brought with her. The scent of vanilla and cinnamon filled the air, emanating from the oven full of sugar cookies Remy had decided we needed to bake. She'd done most of the work. My contribution to the cookies had mainly consisted of standing back so I wouldn't cry in the dough.

I sat at the other end of the couch using the smell of the cookies to try to keep myself together. After spending all day Friday and Saturday actually functioning, I'd awakened this morning in full-on collapse mode. I didn't know why the grief pit had decided to drown me today, and I hadn't been able to combat it on my own.

"I'm glad you called." It was the fourth time Remy had said so. "I needed an excuse to try this cookie recipe."

I couldn't pull myself out of my pain enough to even chuckle at that. "Thanks for coming over." It was the third time I'd said that. The first time Remy had told me she was glad I'd called, I'd been crying too hard to say anything. Being able to talk was an improvement.

"Anytime." She closed the magazine, keeping a finger in the page she'd been reading. "I mean it, Del. I know you didn't want to wake me this morning, but I'm here for you even after a night at the club."

"I know." I sighed. I really wished she hadn't reminded me that she'd been at the club until two or three this morning. I felt guilty enough as it was for disrupting her Sunday. At least I'd managed to wait until ten to call her.

"Hey." She reached over and rested her hand on my knee. "Del, it's okay, really."

I wanted to believe her. The depression that went hand in hand with my grief wouldn't let me. I didn't say so, though. Remy was here to support me, and I didn't want to shit on that.

"This place feels different," she said after a brief uncomfortable silence during which I managed to pull myself somewhat together. "I can't put my finger on it."

"Must be the cookies."

She laughed. "Sure, that's it. I'm serious, Del."

"It still feels empty to me." I leaned back, one arm over my eyes. "I've been doing things. Cleaning. Even walked to the store and bought something resembling food the other day." That had been Friday's chore, spurred both by my need to eat and by bright sunshine and warmer than normal weather that had meant I didn't even need a jacket.

The sunshine had helped my mood on Friday. Too bad neither had lasted; my mood had gone down the sewer, and the sky outside my window today was a steel gray that foretold either rain or snow. Possibly both.

"Maybe that's it," Remy said. "You're putting yourself out in the world again instead of spending all your time sitting here."

"But it still feels empty."

"Yeah." She sniffled and put the magazine on the coffee table. "It does."

"I don't think that's going to change." I uncovered my eyes and looked around. At times, the place had felt too crowded when Austin and I were both home. It wasn't exactly a huge space, barely eight hundred square feet, and sometimes it had felt like he and I were tripping over each other. But without him here, with all the empty spaces, the place felt too big. "Maybe I should move."

"You could." Remy uncrossed her legs and turned to face me.

"Where would you move to? You're going back to work, right? So you'd probably want to stay near the school."

"You aren't going to try to talk me out of it?" I wouldn't move. The apartment was one of the few pieces of Austin I had left, and as long as I could afford it, I intended to stay. But now that I'd mentioned the possibility, my brain didn't want to let it go.

"I'm not going to talk you out of something you actually want to do." The stove timer started dinging, and Remy stood and headed for the kitchen. "Cookies are done. I should have brought stuff to make frosting. I love frosted sugar cookies."

"The convenience store on the corner might have frosting." I followed her to the kitchen and watched her remove the cookie sheet from the oven.

She shook her head. "Store-bought frosting is not the same. Making the frosting is part of making the cookies. But we'll have to do without." She set the sheet on top of the stove. "Those need to cool a bit."

"We could go to the grocery store to get what you need to make the frosting." From crying to moving to frosting. My brain refused to stick to anything today. Then again, that was probably a good thing. And I did like frosting, even though I usually didn't allow myself to eat it.

"We could," Remy said slowly. "Though I'm not sure you need the sugar. You're all over the place right now."

"Yeah." I shrugged. "I don't know what's going on today, Rem. I just need to ride it out." I'd had days like this early on, when I was still in the thick of pain and anger and disbelief. The first couple of times, I'd tried to force myself out of it. Bad idea. The harder I'd tried to focus, the more the grief had taken over. Letting my mind do its random thing had kept it from getting sucked into the knowledge that Austin was gone.

Remy nodded. "I get it. Okay, so let's go get stuff to make frosting."

We drove to the nearby grocery store and got what Remy needed. When we returned to the apartment, she informed me in no uncertain terms that I was only allowed to assist with putting the frosting on the cookies, not with actually making it. She mixed up a large bowl of plain frosting, then portioned it into smaller bowls she found at the back of one of the cupboards. I'd forgotten we—I—owned them. Into each of the smaller frosting portions, she added a drop or two of food coloring, yielding brightly colored stuff that looked like it belonged in small plastic cylinders in a playroom.

"We used to do this sometimes on weekends at home." She handed me a small spoon from the silverware drawer and took out one for herself. "We'd bake cookies and Mom would make the frosting, and then us kids would have a contest to see who ended up with the wildest looking cookies."

"We aren't kids anymore, Remy." I stared dubiously at the spoon.

"No shit. My back reminds me of that every morning." With her spoon, she scooped up a bit of monster-blue frosting and splorted it onto one of the cookies. "Sometimes acting like a kid helps, Del. Playing. Having fun. Hell, that's part of what drag's about, for me at least. I get to play dress-up four nights a week and sometimes during the day so I can go read stories to kids. Who, contrary to the pearl-clutchers' deepest fears, just think I'm a 'pretty princess,' as a few of the kids have put it."

"That was one of the reasons Austin did it too." My throat felt like it was closing up as I spoke Austin's name. *No.* I couldn't deal with another tidal wave of tears, and I doubted Remy wanted to put up with it again.

"I know. We agreed on that when we started. As long as it was fun and we got to play with it, we would keep doing it." She smooshed the frosting blob with the back of her spoon and started spreading it on the cookie. "Come on. I'm getting ahead of you here."

"I didn't realize we were racing." Reluctantly, I took a blob of neon yellow frosting and smooshed it onto a cookie.

"We aren't. Unless we are." Grinning, she reached past me for some green frosting.

We didn't exactly race, just kept reaching past each other for frosting and putting it on the cookies, sometimes multiple colors on each, until we had a dozen ridiculously brightly colored cookies on the sheet. Eyes sparkling, Remy licked some frosting off her spoon. "Done. I declare it a tie."

"And what happens in case of a tie?" Unable to resist, I licked at the last of the frosting on my spoon. It tasted far too sweet, which was part of the appeal.

"We eat the cookies. Duh." She dropped her spoon in the sink and picked up what might have been a cookie but looked more like a monstrosity of red, blue, and purple where the other two colors had gotten mixed. "Probably not all of them, though. That was what my sibs and I always did. Frosted the cookies and then ate every last one of them." She laughed. "Always pissed Dad off, because there were never any left for him."

"I can see where that might have been annoying."

She took a bite of the cookie and grimaced. "Damn, that's sweet. Oh well." She took another bite and chewed. "Good. Just way sweeter than I meant it to be. Try one."

I wasn't sure that was such a good idea, but I picked up the yellow cookie I'd done first and took a bite. It was so sweet my mouth felt like it was turning inside-out. But it was delicious, none-theless.

We finished our cookies, then Remy started cleaning up. "Is your dishwasher working? Have you even been using it?"

"It was working in November." When Austin and I had hosted "Friendsgiving." I pushed the memory away. "No, I haven't been using it. I don't dirty that many dishes. It makes more sense to wash them by hand."

She rolled her eyes and glared at the pile of bowls she'd put in the sink. "Then I guess by hand it is. I'll wash, you dry."

"Why dry?" I took the dish rack out of the cupboard under the sink. "We put them on this. They dry. Then I put them away."

"Oh, good grief. Fine, then I'll wash half and you wash the other half." She turned on the water. "I'm not solely responsible for this mess, so I'm not doing all the work to clean up."

"That's fair." I leaned against the counter as she started washing the frosting bowls. "This was kind of fun."

"Yeah, it was." She flashed a smile. "This apartment needed some laughter. How are you feeling now, Del? Honestly?"

I'd been feeling pretty good until she asked. But her question brought back the pain from earlier, and a new sorrow cloud drifted over me.

"Better," I said, hoping she wouldn't spot the lie. It wasn't entirely a lie anyway; I wasn't dissolved in a lake of tears, which was better than a few hours earlier when Remy first showed up. "You're taking the cookies home, right?"

"Half." She looked at the cookie sheet. "Maybe two-thirds, because Donnie's a freaking piglet sometimes. Though he's trying to fit into this vintage evening gown he found at the thrift shop, so maybe he won't eat every single one of these." She rinsed the bowl she was holding, studied it, then washed it again. "The problem with this frosting is it's impossible. Del, have you thought about getting help?"

"With the dishes?" I knew damn well what she meant, but I wanted her to say it.

"With the grieving." She glanced at me, pity heavy in her gaze. "You're a counselor, Del. You know good and well that sometimes people need help. I haven't wanted to bring it up because I didn't want you to get upset with me, but I'm worried about you."

I pressed my lips together. Part of me was pissed off that she'd brought this up, but the more rational part of me knew she was right. I'd recommended grief counseling to students and their families who had lost people, but it hadn't occurred to me to seek it for myself. Or if it had occurred to me, I'd pushed the idea away. Who was I to get help?

Human, that was who. I was human, and Remy was right. I'd been trying to get through losing Austin alone, with only Remy to help hold me together most of the time, and that wasn't working. I was doing better, but not well enough to say I couldn't use more support.

"I'm worried about me too," I admitted. "Every time I think I'm getting through this, it comes back. Grief is a cycle, not a straight line, and I'm not handling it on my own the way I would like to. I'll make some calls tomorrow." Thanks to my job, I had a list of resources I could contact to try to arrange counseling for myself.

She nodded, looking relieved. "Thank you. I'm here for you, you know that. I'm not going anywhere. But..." Biting her lip, she trailed off. "Del, I love you, but sometimes trying to get you through your grieving keeps me from dealing with my own. It isn't healthy for either of us. I'm not going anywhere, like I said, but I need to take care of me, too."

The pain in her voice stabbed me through the heart. I really had been taking advantage of her. And I felt like shit for it. She and Austin had been friends—more like family—for longer than I'd known either of them, and I'd been so engulfed in my own grief that I'd just kept taking from her.

"You need to take care of you *first*," I said quietly. "I'm so sorry, Remy."

"Don't be sorry!" Some water splashed up from the bowl she was washing onto her shirt. "Shit!" Her voice broke, and she dropped the bowl back into the sink. When she turned to face me, tears were rolling down her cheeks. "Don't be sorry, Del," she said, her voice cracking. "I love you as much as I loved Austin, and I wanted to be here for you."

"But I asked you to be here too much." I put my arms around her. "I love you too, Rem. I'll get help. I promise. And I'm here for you, too."

"I know." She burrowed her face against my shoulder.

The moisture of her tears set off my own. And we held each other and cried.

CHAPTER ELEVEN

I kept my promise to Remy. The prospect of seeking grief counseling didn't exactly appeal to me, but I couldn't deny that I could use more support in recovering from losing Austin. And seeing exactly how much my pain impacted Remy pushed me to do something about it. It wasn't fair for her to put aside her own mourning to coddle me through mine.

I placed a few calls first thing Monday morning. By lunchtime, I'd scheduled an intake appointment for the following week with a counselor named Tammy, whose office was within walking distance of my apartment. It turned out we'd met at a conference a couple of years earlier, which gave me a bit more confidence. At least I wouldn't be spilling everything to a total stranger.

Even without having a session, arranging counseling helped clear some of the grief fog from my mind. I would have someone to talk to for an hour a week—well, forty-five minutes, at least—who wasn't directly involved. Someone who got paid to listen, which meant I wouldn't feel like I was burdening or taking advantage of them. Someone who might be able to tell me how to begin filling the empty spaces left by Austin's death.

Although I wouldn't officially be on Tammy's client roster until after our first appointment, she gave me an assignment to accomplish in the meantime. I'd admitted to her that I'd barely left my apartment for the past month and a half, so she wanted me to at least take a walk up the street and back each day. Weather permitting, of course.

I wasn't excited about the idea, but I did it, starting right after the phone call with Tammy. Piers Park, right beside Boston Harbor, was only a few blocks away. At this time of year, the park wouldn't be crowded, and I would be able to stand near the ocean for at least a few minutes. It was as good a plan as any, so I put on my jacket and went.

It was a walk Austin and I had taken numerous times since moving into our apartment. He loved the park at any time of year, and he could stand for hours watching boats moving back and forth in the harbor. He would have been thrilled by the oil tanker that plodded by on the water as I reached the railing along the edge of the harbor.

But he wasn't here. I was alone, stuck in the memories of his child-like excitement when tankers and boats passed by and all the times he'd talked about renting a sailboat so we could be out there with them. We'd never done it.

Maybe this summer, I would. In his memory. If I could ever have memories of him without tears streaming down my face the way they were suddenly doing now. It was a good thing no other humans were around.

Except for the one who spoke from behind me. "Excuse me, are you all right?"

Shit. Quickly swiping my gloved hands over my face, I turned, forcing something that I hoped resembled a smile. "Just reminiscing about someone," I said, even though all I'd intended to say was "yeah."

The woman was shorter than me, with black hair and wide-set eyes in a light brown face. She smiled, and a sense of peace, not as strong as with Lochlan and the cats but similar, spread through me. "Reminiscing sucks sometimes. I'm Suzannah."

"Del." Out of habit, I extended a hand. Suzannah shook it. "Nice to meet you."

"Likewise. I'm sorry I interrupted you." She put her hands in her jacket pockets. "I just wanted to make sure you were all right."

"I will be." I managed to curve my mouth into something that felt like a smile. "Thanks for checking."

"You're welcome." She glanced over her shoulder. "I'll leave you alone. Take care."

"Thanks. You too."

She walked away. Despite my embarrassment at a total stranger catching me crying, I gave myself credit: I'd actually had a conversation with someone. Something more than banal small talk. I would have to tell Tammy about that during our session. I'd interacted with another human being.

Turning back to face the harbor, where the tanker was still slowly floating by, I pulled my phone out of my pocket. Being here, in the spot where Austin and I had so often stood, hurt. The brief conversation with Suzannah had helped a bit, but now that I was alone again, the pain pressed in on me.

I stared at the phone. Usually at a time like this, I would call Remy. But after our discussion the day before, I didn't want to dump my grief on her again. She needed a break from me. She never would have said so, but she didn't need to verbalize it. I'd depended on her too much since Austin's death, and now she needed a break.

I wasn't close enough friends with the other performers to consider calling any of them. Given how much I'd pushed them all away, I suspected they wouldn't want to hear from me now.

A gust of wind off the harbor knifed through my jacket. It was still warmer than a typical January day, but the wind was picking up, and it was getting a little too chilly to stay there. Reluctant but relieved, I turned away from the water and headed back toward the street, still holding my phone.

There was one person in my contacts list I could reach out to. I hadn't planned on using his number, but it was there. I barely knew Lochlan, but maybe that was a good thing. I hadn't worn out my welcome in his life or pushed him away. And I was much less likely to start emotionally dumping on him. I didn't know where Lochlan lived, or if he was even available right now, but maybe we could meet for coffee.

That wasn't something I'd anticipated doing. Asking someone out for coffee. Even before I lost Austin, I hadn't been the type to ask people to hang out. That was Austin's thing. My thing was hanging around the apartment when I wasn't working unless Austin convinced me to go out somewhere.

Austin. Would asking Lochlan to meet for coffee be disloyal to Austin?

Of course my brain couldn't let me have nice things. With the question came a wave of guilt so strong I stopped in my tracks. What the hell was I thinking? Lochlan was a nice guy, and I couldn't deny finding him attractive. Which only served to increase the guilt. I shouldn't be finding anyone else attractive. Not when Austin hadn't even been gone for two months yet.

I wasn't contemplating dating Lochlan, though. He'd given me his number in case I ever wanted to talk. I wanted to talk. Talking in person while drinking coffee felt like less pressure than trying to have a phone call. Or maybe that was just an excuse.

I couldn't call him or even send a text. I wanted to reach out to him —wanting to reach out to anyone other than Remy wasn't like me at all, but there we were—and I couldn't bring myself to do it.

I managed to get home before I started crying again. One step forward, a hundred fucking steps back. I'd left the apartment without Remy pushing me. I hadn't even called Remy for moral support. I'd had a conversation with a total stranger. More than one step, maybe.

And then I'd fallen apart at the possibility of asking a guy I barely knew if he wanted to grab a coffee. Now I stood here, leaning against the kitchen counter, barely balancing on the edge of the grief chasm. I didn't want to reach out to Lochlan. Or anyone. I just wanted to be alone, because that's all I was.

Alone. The empty spaces weren't only in the apartment. They were inside me, and with Austin gone, I didn't know if anything could fill them.

Grief wasn't a straight line. "Just getting over" losing someone you loved wasn't possible. It was okay to make progress and then fall back. I would have said all of those things to one of my students. But trying to say them to myself, all I heard was bullshit. I should have been doing better than this.

I should have been able to pick up the phone and ask a guy if he wanted coffee without feeling like the biggest traitor on the planet.

My phone chimed, yanking me out of the self-pity wallow I was heading for. I fumbled it off the counter where I'd dropped it and blinked at the screen through a blur of tears.

Hey, it's Lochlan. From the café. Just wanted to see how you're doing.

How had he known I was thinking about him? I wiped my eyes with my free hand and read the message again. Lochlan had texted me out of the blue right when I was thinking about texting him.

Right when I was deciding texting him was a bad idea. That texting him would be equivalent to betraying Austin.

"I shouldn't answer, should I?" I said it aloud as if someone would answer. As if maybe Austin's ghost was standing there waiting to give me advice on how to be friends with someone.

Friendship was all I was aiming for with Lochlan. Maybe not even that. Just a friendly acquaintanceship. Talking to Lochlan would be no different from talking to Remy or any of the others. It wasn't a betrayal of Austin if I wanted to have people in my life whom I could talk to.

I grabbed a piece of paper towel to wipe my nose and eyes while I figured out how to respond to the text. As I tossed the paper towel into the trash, I decided simple was best. Hey. Doing okay, I guess. How are you?

Out of it. I was thinking coffee might help. Want to join?

Lochlan texting when I was thinking about him might have been coincidence. His asking if I wanted to get coffee when that was exactly what I'd been considering? I wasn't sure my belief in coincidence stretched quite that far.

Or maybe my mind was just trying to find something else to ponder besides how wrong it would be to go get coffee with Lochlan.

Where were you thinking? I'm in Eastie. Had I already told him that? I must have, when we were talking about why I'd taken a rideshare to the café. But if I didn't remember whether I'd said it, he might not remember either.

I can pick you up if you want.

Being stuck in a car with the guy I felt like I shouldn't even be talking to outside the cat café didn't sound like the best choice, but there weren't many other options unless he picked something in walking distance. While I struggled to make that decision, another message showed up. Public transit or rideshare also options, right? Or walking. I'm really bad at this. I don't even know where to suggest.

Me neither. Maybe the fact that we couldn't come up with a place to meet was a sign that we shouldn't meet. At the very least, it made a good excuse.

But before I could suggest that we put coffee on hold until some other time, Lochlan said, Looks like there's a place near Maverick Square. Corner of Orleans and Marginal. Is that near enough to you?

It was. The walk would be a bit long but still within reason, if it was reasonable for me to even go. I knew the place he meant, though I'd never visited it because it had always looked too crowded. Then again, I'd generally seen it during the morning rush while I was walking to work. At this time of day, it might not be too bad.

I couldn't seriously be considering meeting up with Lochlan, though. Even though I'd been thinking about exactly that only a little while ago, that was before my meltdown.

But I'd told Tammy I would try to spend less time at home. And knowing I'd gotten out of the house to see someone else might ease Remy's mind.

I can be there in about half an hour, I told Lochlan.

Give me an hour. I don't know how traffic is between here and there.

Got it. See you then.

He didn't respond. I set down the phone and leaned against the counter again. "Am I doing the right thing?" I asked the empty room.

The echo of Austin's voice, which had to be my imagination, replied, *Yes.*

CHAPTER TWELVE

An hour later, I stood in front of the tiny coffee shop that occupied a corner of one of the condo complexes along the waterfront. Despite my winter jacket, I shivered; the wind that had risen during my earlier walk had grown even stronger, carrying the scent of snow. The buildings around me blocked some of the wind, but not enough.

Lochlan hadn't arrived yet. I didn't know where he was driving from, but it was quite likely he'd run into heavier traffic than he'd anticipated. That was what the logical part of my mind told me. The much less rational part tried to convince me that Lochlan had no intention of showing up. After all, he knew I'd recently lost my partner. Maybe he figured I was too broken to bother with.

That was grief and depression talking. Lochlan had issued the invitation. He wouldn't have done so if he hadn't intended me to take him up on it.

Just as I was about to let the irrational brain-part win and head home, I spotted Lochlan hurrying up the street toward me. His hair was messy from the wind, and the long gray coat he wore didn't look warm enough for the weather. His face was flushed, which I thought was from the cold until he said, "I'm sorry. I couldn't find parking, and you've just been standing here. I texted you, but you didn't answer."

"I didn't hear my phone." I took it out of my pocket.

Sure enough, there was one text. *On my way. I didn't realize parking sucked so much around here. I understand if you don't want to wait.*

I put away my phone and smiled at Lochlan. "I waited."

"I see." He grinned, and the redness of his face faded. "I'm glad you did. Should we go in?" He looked dubiously at the small storefront we stood beside. "*Can* we go in? Place looks pretty small."

"It is. But there's a table open, it looks like." I opened the door and motioned him through. "After you."

Inside, we ordered our drinks and sat at one of the three small round tables to wait. I took a breath to check in with myself. Now that I was actually sitting here with Lochlan, I didn't feel as if I'd betrayed Austin in any way. No more than I would have if I'd met Remy or one of the others for coffee. Lochlan was just being friendly, and there was nothing wrong with me having friends. The serenity I'd felt around him at the cat café was even stronger here, sitting close to him across the tiny table.

In a small corner of my heart, though, the doubt lingered. Not because I was wrong to grab a coffee with someone who wanted to be friends, but because of possibilities. Lochlan was attractive. That little blush of his, whatever the reason for it had been, was downright cute. His snub nose and wide hazel-green eyes were adorable. Even the splotches of blond in his black hair appealed to me. I shouldn't have been noticing any of this, not so soon after losing Austin. Maybe not ever, since I couldn't see myself with anyone other than Austin. He'd been my life for nearly my entire adulthood, and I couldn't just put him aside for someone else.

"It's weird," I said, mostly to break the silence.

"What is?" Lochlan glanced toward the counter. "Oh, looks like our drinks are ready. Hold tight. I'll get them."

He launched himself out of his chair and hurried the few steps to the counter as if running away from something. From *me*. Which put my guard back up. I'd barely said anything, and maybe I should keep it that way.

He returned with two ceramic mugs containing our coffees. Mine was a basic coffee with cream and sugar; his had foam on top. With a foamish rendering of a cat face.

"Pretty appropriate." I nodded toward his mug. "You didn't say anything to them about cats, though."

Looking uncomfortable, he shrugged. "Coincidence, I guess. Maybe that's all they know how to draw with the foam." He touched the corner of one eye with a fingertip. "Maybe it's the eyes. Some people say they're cat eyes."

"Maybe you're a cat shifter."

He snorted. "Nope. Those don't exist."

"'There are more things in Heaven and Earth,'" I quoted.

"Not cat shifters." He sounded pretty definite about that. "You said something was weird."

"Yeah." I studied him for a few seconds, covering it by taking a sip of coffee. If I said what I'd intended to say, he might take off again. "Just before you texted, I was thinking about asking if you were available to get coffee. I was feeling low and wanted to talk to someone. I talked myself out of contacting you, and then your text showed up."

"Huh." He didn't meet my gaze as he drank some of his foamy thing. "Interesting."

He seemed even more uncomfortable. I tried to joke him out of it. "I'd almost say you read my mind, except mindreading doesn't exist either."

"No. That does." Looking completely serious, he set down his mug and took a long breath. "There are more things, Del. You wouldn't believe half of them."

"I can believe—"

"Yeah, yeah, six impossible things before breakfast." He drummed the fingers of one hand on the table, still holding the handle of his mug with the other hand. "It's after lunch. And I didn't ask you for coffee to spill deep, dark secrets that might make you think I've lost my mind."

"Have you?" I had no idea what he was talking about, but I had more than a passing familiarity with feeling like I'd gone off the deep end. Especially over the past several weeks.

"No." He quirked the corners of his mouth. That was good.

Amusement was preferable to discomfort. "Most people would think so, though."

From the context, it was pretty easy to guess what he was refusing to say. I decided to take the plunge and speak my guess aloud. "So you did read my mind?"

"In a way." He sighed. "I'm going to sit here and brace myself for you getting up and running away from the madman."

"I'm not running away." Maybe he was full of shit. Or had actually lost his mind. But I didn't think either was the case. Whatever he was about to tell me was real, at least to him.

"We'll see about that." Mouth set in a grim line, he picked up his mug but didn't drink. "I didn't read your mind exactly. It was more a connection. Like picking up someone else's random call on a cell phone or something. It's hard to describe. I was wondering how you were doing and sort of felt you wanting to talk to me. And then not wanting to."

"I wasn't sure if you were busy." I hoped he wouldn't catch on that I was lying about why I'd decided not to reach out to him.

He might realize it. If he'd detected from wherever he'd been that I was considering contacting him, how easy would it be for him to detect a lie sitting face to face with me?

With that question, I realized I believed him. I didn't even have to think about it. Mindreading couldn't exist, but I believed what Lochlan was saying. Somehow, from some other part of the metro area, he'd heard me thinking about him. A miniscule niggle of doubt tugged at my mind, but for whatever reason, I believed Lochlan.

If he had picked up on the lie, he didn't mention it. "I was working, but I work for myself. Flexible schedule and all. Hence being able to sit here with you."

"Okay."

He drank more of his coffee. That reminded me that I had a cup in front of me, which I sipped from slowly. It was getting cold, but I didn't really want coffee. I'd wanted to talk to someone. And now that Lochlan was right here, I had nothing to say until he finished what he was trying to tell me. If he finished.

"Anyway." He put down his mug and took a breath. "You haven't taken off yet."

"I said I wasn't going to."

He looked surprised. "I knew what you were thinking. That doesn't freak you out?"

I shrugged. I didn't understand it myself. In my experience, psychic abilities didn't exist any more than cat shifters did, but there were certainly plenty of people in the world who believed in them. Clearly Lochlan was one of them. And given the evidence, who was I to say he was wrong? The possibility that he'd known what was going through my mind did feel intrusive, but I didn't believe he'd intended to intrude. He'd just overheard it, as if I was having a conversation too close to him.

That was what I told myself, anyway, because it was the only way to comprehend what he was telling me. "I mean, it isn't exactly typical, but it certainly explains you texting me right at that moment. You believe it. I believe you."

"You're open-minded." He sounded relieved.

"I work at a high school. I have to be open-minded." I gave him a smile that I hoped appeared reassuring. "I've heard less believable things from my students, and they were telling the complete truth. I don't have any reason to think you aren't."

Visibly relaxing, he nodded. "Okay. I'm glad to hear that. I didn't ask you to meet up so I could spill this to you, though. You needed to talk."

"We are talking." My grief and pity-party wallowing seemed far less important now. His little bomb about psychic abilities had distracted me. Maybe that was better than trying to talk things through. "I had a good morning and then hit a rough patch. My friend Remy's been letting me lean on her more than is healthy, and I remembered you'd said to call if I wanted someone to talk to."

"Except you didn't call." Head tilted, he studied me. "I'm not sure if you're really okay with what I told you or if you haven't processed it yet. You're being oddly unreactive."

"I guess I am still processing." I drank more of the cooling coffee. "My mind is all over the place right now. You telling me you magically knew I wanted to hang out is only one of the things bouncing around up here." I tapped my temple with a finger.

"Not magic." He smiled slightly. "Psychic, maybe. It's just a thing I do, or, rather, a thing that happens. I don't intentionally hear what people are thinking."

"It's like overhearing other people in a coffee shop," I said, verbalizing the analogy I'd come up with.

"Kind of like that, yeah." He glanced toward the window. "Looks like it might snow."

"It does that sometimes in January." Now I felt suddenly awkward. Was he changing the subject to avoid talking about himself anymore? Should I be dumping out my issues instead of continuing this conversation?

I could have just thanked him for meeting up and called it a day, but I didn't want to do that. He was the first person other than Remy with whom I'd had more than a few minutes of conversation since losing Austin, and I didn't want to end it just yet.

"I took a walk earlier," I said so I would have something to say. "My partner and I used to go to Piers Park so he could watch the boats. I didn't mean to wind up there, but I did."

"And it reminded you of him." Sympathy filled Lochlan's eyes. "Was that why you thought about reaching out to me? To talk about how that felt?"

When he put it that way, it sounded like I was using him. Which was a pretty shitty thing for me to do. But I couldn't deny it. "Yeah. I'm sorry. I was a jerk for that."

"Not at all." He reached across the table and rested his hand near mine. "That's exactly the kind of thing I gave you my number for. You're grieving, Del. I understand grief, believe me. Sometimes you just need to talk to someone who isn't involved in it and have them tell you it's okay to feel how you feel."

"Yeah." As he spoke, the sense of peace emanating from him grew stronger. He wasn't just mouthing words. He was making me feel like everything was okay.

I wanted to ask if this was part of the psychic stuff too, but I didn't quite dare.

"Were there boats on the harbor?" he asked.

"A tanker." I leaned back and moved my hand just a wee bit closer to his. I couldn't bring myself to touch him, but I convinced myself I could feel the warmth of his skin against mine. It was incredibly comforting. "Austin would have been so excited. I don't know why he was so into boats. He never told me. But he loved watching the big tankers come in guided by the little tugboats. All I could think while I was standing there today was how happy he would have been to see it." I swallowed hard. "And how he'll never see it again."

"I don't know if that's true." Lochlan looked thoughtful. "I don't want to tell you what to believe. Personally, I believe there's an after-life, and that people who are there can still see what's going on in our world. So Austin might be watching the boats from wherever he is."

"Maybe." I wasn't sure what I believed happened after death. I'd never really given it much thought.

Then again, until Austin, death hadn't really affected me. All four of my grandparents had passed away when I was too young to under-stand what was going on. During my years working at the school, a few students and staff members had passed away, and I'd mourned them alongside everyone else, but I hadn't truly *grieved* them the way I was grieving Austin. And I hadn't wondered what happened to them after their souls left their body.

I hadn't even really pondered whether people had souls. The reli-gion in which I'd grown up taught that we did, and that after death God judged our souls and decided whether we went up or down. Since that religion had also taught that I deserved to burn in hell for liking other guys instead of girls, I didn't put much stock in anything it preached.

I liked the idea of Austin eternally standing by a sunlit railing in Piers Park, warm and happy and watching the boats. If any kind of afterlife existed, I hoped that was the one he'd wound up in.

"You're smiling," Lochlan said. "It's hard to think about people we love being gone. Sometimes there's comfort in thinking they're in a positive place."

"Yeah." I finished my coffee. "Yeah, it does help."

"So does coffee." He picked up his cup and took a drink. "I should get back to work soon. I can hang out for a little longer if you want, though."

"I'm good. Thanks." I was good. Approaching it, anyway. If nothing else, I no longer felt like I was about to break down crying, so that was progress.

We brought our mugs to the counter and headed outside. "Do you want a ride home?" Lochlan asked. "My car's up the street a bit." He looked up. "It's starting to snow."

"I think I'll walk, but thanks. I don't mind the snow." I hesitated. "If you don't mind my asking, why do you believe in an afterlife?"

"That's kind of an odd question." He looked amused but guarded. "Why don't you?"

"I don't know if I do or not." Sensing that I'd struck a nerve, I chuckled. "You're right, it's an odd question. Forget I asked."

"No, it's okay." He looked thoughtful. "It's a complex question. Maybe something to talk about another time, because I really do need to get going. See you Thursday?"

"Thursday? Oh. Yes." The cat café. Of course I would see him there. "Yeah, see you then."

"Okay." He placed his hand on my arm. Just a very brief touch, but the warmth and connection it held struck me. "Take care of yourself, Del. And don't worry about whether I'm busy. If you want to talk, please reach out."

"Do I even need to?" I said, trying to make a joke even though it hadn't worked out so well the previous time.

Fortunately, this time he seemed to take it as I meant it. "Phones are easier than random bits of thought floating about in the ether."

"Fair point." I felt like I should say something else, but I couldn't come up with anything. "Thanks for taking time to meet up with me."

"Anytime." He sounded as if he meant it. "See you."

He walked away just as the awkwardness reached a peak. Unsure whether I was relieved or regretful, I headed home.

This time, as I walked home, I didn't dread entering the apartment. The empty spaces didn't scare or anger me. Home was where Austin had been, and if Lochlan was right that some kind of afterlife existed, maybe Austin was still there. Hadn't I heard his voice telling me meeting up with Lochlan was the right thing to do? Of course, that was probably a combination of my imagination and wishful thinking. Austin definitely wasn't haunting the apartment. Even so, maybe he wasn't entirely gone.

I could almost make myself believe that.

CHAPTER THIRTEEN

On Tuesday and Wednesday, I took walks around the block. I wasn't quite able to work up the nerve to go back to Piers Park. Even though the grief pit didn't seem quite as deep and dark, I was afraid I would have another breakdown if I returned to someplace I associated so strongly with Austin. Watching the boats from the park was more his thing than mine, and it reminded me of him in a way the apartment, which belonged to both of us, didn't.

Simply going outside in the cold, crisp air and nodding at passing neighbors as I went around the block was more than I'd done the past few weeks. I interacted. I put myself out in the world. I even stopped at the nearest convenience store and bought a chocolate bar, not because I wanted candy but because buying it gave me a reason to speak to another human.

Both days, I texted Remy. I didn't try to lean on her. I'd pretty much made up my mind to cut way back on doing that. I just wanted to let her know I was okay and to find out how she was doing. She responded with pictures of a few of the kids at the Closet wearing Austin's clothes. Seeing the pictures didn't bother me as much as I'd feared it would. Austin would have loved knowing his stuff was helping these kids present their true selves to the world, so I loved it on his behalf.

I didn't contact Lochlan. I wanted to. Sitting with him in the coffee shop, I'd felt more comfortable and at ease than I had in a long time. Even more than with Remy, which was saying something. I wanted more of that comfort.

The wanting was exactly why I didn't reach out to him. I couldn't let myself impose on someone else the way I'd done to Remy. With Remy, I could at least justify it. She was the closest I had to family other than Austin. But even though I'd gotten to know a little more about Lochlan during our conversation, I still didn't know *him* well enough to consider him more than an acquaintance. And even with the grief pit lurking just below my surface, I couldn't think of an acquaintance as someone to randomly reach out to.

Plus my desire to talk to him disturbed me. I thought I'd made peace with the idea of spending time with someone who wasn't Austin, but I clearly wasn't entirely okay with it yet. I'd met Lochlan for coffee because I needed someone to talk to, and because he'd been the one to reach out and suggest it. We could build a friendship based around the cat café, and maybe occasional coffee-fueled conversations, but I couldn't be the one to reach out. Even when a faint voice in my mind, which might have been mine or Austin's, urged me to do exactly that.

On Thursday, I took a rideshare to the cat café and walked in to find Liam and Lochlan wrestling with a large neon sign that said something about liking "chonky" cats. They were working on installing the sign on the wall near the merchandise shelves, but the sign didn't appear inclined to cooperate.

I walked over, torn between distracting them and leaving them alone, and decided speaking wouldn't be enough of a distraction to cause a problem. "Can I help?"

"Huh?" Liam jumped slightly as Lochlan flashed me a smile over his shoulder. "Oh, Del. Hi. No, thanks, we've got it. Would you mind spending some time with Charlie? I think he's feeling neglected because we've been working on this all day."

"Yeah, no problem." I nodded to Lochlan and went to hang up my coat.

Charlie the Sweater Cat was chilling on a blanket spread over the couch near the shy cat room. Another identical blanket was crumpled beside him. I sat down and spread the unoccupied blanket over my lap, then petted Charlie between the ears. "Hi, buddy."

He immediately started to purr, and after blinking at me a few times made his way onto my lap. I kept petting him as his purring grew louder and he moved around, trying to get comfortable.

Just like the previous week, the warm weight of cat on my lap soothed me. And when Charlie finally curled up and appeared to doze, I felt at peace.

Maybe I would ask about adopting Charlie. All the reasons I'd given myself the week before for not adopting a cat were still valid, but I was tired of going home to an empty apartment. Even though this was only my third visit to the café, I already felt a connection to Charlie. Going home after a day of work—when I eventually returned to work, that was—and having a warm, furry being there to curl up in my lap would be wonderful.

He wouldn't replace Austin, of course, though there had been times Austin had curled up with his head in my lap. But I wasn't considering adopting a pet as a replacement. Just a companion. Someone I could give love and attention to and receive it in return.

While Charlie snoozed, I zoned out. The café wasn't exactly quiet; from where I sat, I could hear, though not see, Liam and Lochlan trying to hang the sign. Visitors had arrived and roamed around talking to the cats and each other. One, a preteen girl, came over to pet Charlie, but as she reached for him, he abruptly raised his head and growled.

"He's not very nice." The girl looked offended.

"He's napping." I stroked Charlie's head until he lowered it again. "He's a very old cat and doesn't like having his naps interrupted, I guess."

"That's kind of like my grandpa," she said. "He gets really annoyed if we make too much noise when he's taking a nap. My grandpa's seventy-two." She crouched to look more closely at Charlie. "How old is he?"

"I'm not sure." I couldn't remember if Liam had told me. "Maybe not as old as your grandpa."

"Of course not. Cats don't live that long." She stood up. "I'm going to go play with one of the other cats."

"Okay." I wasn't sure why she was announcing it, but kids did that kind of thing.

She walked away, and I returned to my zoned-out nonthoughts. Even with other people around, sitting here with Charlie was restful. I wasn't used to just sitting and relaxing. Before I lost Austin, I was constantly doing something. Working, mostly. Cleaning. Cooking. Anything to be occupied, because I'd learned from an early age that I was only worth as much as the things I did.

Of course that wasn't the case anymore. It never really had been, other than in my parents' worldview, and I'd figured out when I was still fairly young that their worldview was more than a little problematic. But lessons learned in childhood, whether problematic or not, tended to linger, especially if those lessons were enforced by one's parents. Even though I'd learned new lessons as an adult, and Austin had done his best to show he loved and valued me whether I kept the apartment clean or not, a deeper part of me still felt like I wasn't earning my right to exist if I tried doing nothing.

Here, although the belief that I should be doing something worthwhile tugged at me, I could simply sit. I *was* doing something worthwhile. I was giving Charlie the Sweater Cat a safe lap to nap on and showing him that he could trust a human. Liam had said the main purpose of having volunteers at the café was to socialize the cats. That was what I was doing, even though the cat in question had gone back to sleep.

After a little while, Lochlan came in from the front room and stood, arms folded, smiling at Charlie and me. "Charlie likes you."

"He likes sleeping on me, anyway." I rubbed between Charlie's ears. He didn't even stir. "Did you guys get the sign up?"

"Finally, yes." He sat beside me. "It's meant to be a photo op for the visitors. Something they can take pictures with to put on their social media and help boost visibility for the place. Not a bad idea. People like taking pictures. But the sign was a pain in the backside." He snorted. "How have you been?"

"Okay, and you?" Feeling unexpectedly awkward, I petted Charlie again. This time, he lazily turned to look at me through a squinted eye. I hoped Lochlan wouldn't ask why I hadn't been in touch. I didn't have an answer I wanted to give.

"Not bad," Lochlan said. "Working and coming here. You might actually get to see Choco Chip today. He's been coming out and wandering a bit."

"That's good."

"It's progress." He leaned back. "I've spent a few evenings here over the past couple of weeks just sitting and letting the cats decide whether to come to me. When it's just me and them, they're a little more willing to show themselves."

"They don't like the noise when there are a lot of people here?" I said.

"Sometimes it's that. Sometimes we get cats who haven't had the best experience with humans, and it takes time for them to believe we can be trusted." He reached over and scratched Charlie's head. Charlie started purring again. "Just like some humans take time to believe they can trust each other."

"Learning to trust is a process." And the statement was a cliché, but I didn't know what else to say.

"Yes, it is." He stood. "I'm going to go hang with the shy cats. How late are you here?"

"Until Liam tells me to leave, I guess." I didn't even know what time it was. I'd lost track again. I checked my watch. "Another hour or so, probably."

"I have to leave earlier than usual today." He looked uncertain. "Around three, if you'd like a ride home. I'm cheaper than a rideshare."

All the reasons to turn down the offer rolled through my brain, and I ignored every one of them. "Sure, if it isn't too out of your way, that would be awesome."

His eyes widened slightly. "You aren't worried about being trapped in a car with me for half an hour or so?"

"Should I be?" I nodded toward the shy cat room. "If they can trust you, I think I can."

His face lit up. "It's a plan, then. I'll let you know when I'm ready to leave."

He went into the shy cat room, and I leaned back and closed my eyes for a moment. I did trust Lochlan. Being in a car with him for however long the drive from Peabody to Jeffries Point lasted wouldn't be a bad thing. The conversation might get a little odd, as it had at the coffee shop, but I didn't have a problem with odd.

I did have a problem with the way my heart gave a little leap at the idea of spending more time with him, though.

For the next hour, I stayed on the couch, acting as Charlie's cushion. Unlike the previous week, although he woke up a couple of times, he didn't seem inclined to wander away. Not that I minded. I didn't have anywhere else I needed to be.

When Liam announced the café was closing for the afternoon, Charlie finally decided it was time to get off my lap. Which probably had a lot to do with the cans of food Liam, the preteen girl, and her family started placing in the middle of the floor. Nearly all of the cats came hurrying over, even Choco Chip, who to my surprise made his way out from under the couch I'd been sitting on without even realizing he was there.

Lochlan followed Remy-the-Cat and Bailey out of the shy cat room and smiled at the collection of cats stuffing their faces. "Looks like everyone's happy. Liam, do you need anything else from me?"

"No, no." Kneeling and petting Piper, Liam looked up. "Thanks for coming in. Del, you too. See you next week?"

"Definitely." I stood and stretched, ignoring the tightness in my legs. "Thanks."

"Thank you." Liam looked down at Piper and murmured something I couldn't quite make out.

Lochlan and I got our coats and went out to his car, an older-model Toyota Corolla with a paint job that might have been bright blue once but had faded to a color resembling denim. He unlocked both doors with his key. "Old school," he said as we got in.

"As long as there's heat, it's all good." The weather had turned cold again, despite the brightly shining sun, and just walking from the café to the car left me shivering.

"The heat works quite well." Lochlan started the car and turned on the blower full force. "I just need to let the car run for a minute before I actually start driving. It isn't a fan of cold weather either."

"A kindred spirit. Or do cars have spirits?" I was teasing, but as soon as I said it, I felt like an ass. "I'm not making fun of anything."

"Um, I didn't think you were." Wrinkling his forehead, he put his phone on the dashboard mount. "Oh. The spirit thing. No, I can't read cars' minds, Del. You need to work on your material if you think you're a comedian."

"Yeah, I guess I'm out of practice." I fastened my seat belt and leaned forward toward the blower vent. The air coming through it was just beginning to resemble heat. "You don't have to drive me all the way to my place. If you drop me off at the coffee shop we went to the other day, I can walk from there."

"You sure? I don't mind."

I wasn't even sure why I'd said it, let alone whether I meant it. The coffee shop to my apartment wasn't a ridiculously long walk, but in this cold, I wanted to be outside for as little time as possible. There was no reason Lochlan couldn't know where I lived. It wasn't as if he was going to follow me home with an axe some night. At the same time, though, having him bring me home brought back the same sense of wrongness I'd had about meeting him for coffee. Home was Austin. Sure, Remy and the others had been there in the past few weeks, but they'd also been there while Austin was alive. Lochlan hadn't been.

Then again, I didn't have to invite Lochlan in. That probably wasn't even what he was planning on. He merely intended to drop me off.

"You can take time to think about it," he said. "As long as you tell me before we actually get there." He tapped his phone. "I'll GPS the coffee shop for now. You can give me directions from there if you decide you don't want to walk."

"Thanks." I watched as he set the GPS. "I'm sorry. You'd think that would be a simple decision."

"When someone's grieving, nothing's simple. It's okay, Del."

I sighed. It wasn't okay. Indecision had always been Austin's thing. I was the one who knew exactly what to do, when, and how. I should have been able to figure out whether I wanted to walk from the water-front to my apartment, but no decision felt right.

I really hoped Lochlan wasn't reading my mind right now.

"Charlie really likes you," Lochlan said. "Did he leave your lap at all today?"

"Not until the food appeared." Relieved at the change of subject, I sat up a little straighter. "He's such a sweet cat. I'm surprised no one's adopted him yet."

"Between the fur problem and some other health things, it won't be easy to find a home for him. And our cat rescue partner wants to keep him with us until we find out exactly what's going on for him health-wise and get him a little more stabilized." He held his hand over the vent. "Warm enough, I think. Let's hit the road."

I waited until he navigated out of the parking lot into Route 1 traffic before asking, "What health problems does Charlie have?"

"His fur isn't growing back the way it should, and we aren't sure why." Lochlan held up one finger. "He walks a little oddly. I'm not sure if you've noticed."

"He does kind of stagger," I said, thinking about it.

"Yeah, and Liam says when he's checked the camera at night a couple of times, it looked like Charlie was having a seizure. So there might be something neurological going on." He glanced at me, then swore as another driver cut us off. "Sorry, Del. I need to concentrate on the road until we're out of this mess."

"No worries." It was nearly three-thirty on a weekday afternoon. We quite likely wouldn't be out of the traffic mess at all. Certainly not until we got off Route One, which would take a while if we went to the exit my drivers usually took.

Which we didn't. Lochlan's GPS directed us off the highway in Lynn instead of Revere. "That's better," Lochlan said, visibly relaxing, as we turned onto the exit ramp. "Still traffic this way, but at least it's only one lane each direction instead of three. Anyway, Charlie. Maybe something neurological. There's the fur issue. And we think he has something going on with his kidneys. Liam's taking him to the vet next week for some bloodwork and other tests to find out what's actually going on."

"Poor old guy." I didn't like thinking about Charlie getting stuck with needles. Or about him having some incurable health condition. "But he's still up for adoption?"

"Yeah, for the moment. Depending on what the tests show, we might end up having to keep him at the café rather than sending him home with anyone. That way he'd be able to get immediate care if he needed it. We aren't at that point yet, though." He glanced at me. "You want to adopt him, don't you?"

"Reading my mind again?" I teased.

He snorted. "Nope. It's just pretty obvious from the questions you're asking. I think you'd be a good human for him. You could talk to Liam about it next week if you're honestly considering it."

"I might." A cat with health issues would need more attention than I'd be available to give once I went back to work, though. Charlie would be alone for seven or eight hours a day. If there was something seriously wrong with him, he would need more than that, assuming it wasn't serious enough that they decided to keep him instead of allowing an adoption.

Another decision I couldn't make. At least I didn't have to decide this right away.

We drove toward the city of Lynn in a line of cars that didn't give me much hope for the GPS's ability to get us out of traffic. Lochlan didn't seem fazed by it, though. "If it doesn't work out for you to adopt Charlie, maybe one of the others."

"Maybe." I hadn't bonded with any of the other cats yet, but that was mainly because Charlie had monopolized me each time I'd gone to the café. Maybe next week, I would have a chance to get to know some of them a little better.

I was actually planning to adopt a cat. Not something I'd antici-pated when Remy dragged me to the café that first time. But having someone waiting for me at home, even a furry, four-legged someone, would be better than all the time I'd been spending alone.

Alone, I barely existed. Having someone else in the apartment, some cute little creature who depended on me, might help me start living again.

CHAPTER FOURTEEN

As we drove through Lynn, I remembered the question Lochlan had brushed off at the coffee shop. The one he'd said he might answer when we had more time. Sitting in traffic seemed like it would give him enough time. "Why do you believe in an afterlife?" I blurted.

His eyes widened slightly, and he quickly glanced at me. "Right. You asked me that the other day."

"And you said you might tell me when you had more time." I didn't like seeing his discomfort at the question. "You don't have to answer. I just remembered we were talking about it. Damn, I really suck at having a normal conversation nowadays."

I'd hoped the last comment would get a laugh out of him, but he barely even chuckled. "I can relate. Sometimes I do far better talking to cats than to other humans. I don't mind answering. I just need a minute to figure out how to explain."

"All right." That sounded a little ominous, though I couldn't put my finger on why.

After we'd made it through a few intersections, he said, "I believe in an afterlife because I've seen it. Glimpses, anyway. The whole 'go into the light' thing? I've seen that light. Not what's on the other side, but the light itself."

He spilled the words so rapidly it took a few seconds for my brain to catch up both with what he was saying and the fact that he was nervous as hell about saying it. He was afraid I would judge him.

I couldn't deny that I felt some judgment. I'd never believed in the whole "go into the light" thing that prevailed among those who believed in life after death. Certainly I'd never anticipated talking to someone who claimed to have witnessed it.

But as with the discussion of how Lochlan had not quite read my mind, I could tell *he* believed what he was saying. And if he believed it, the least I could do was listen without judging.

"How have you seen it?" I asked. "I mean, did you have a near-death experience or something? Tell me if I ask anything too personal." I decided to try another joke. "Or just pull over and kick me out of the car."

"I'm not going to do that unless you ask to get out." He tapped the steering wheel. "No near-death experience. It's kind of a long story."

I leaned forward and looked at the GPS. "Apparently we have twenty-five minutes. Is that long enough?"

"Are you sure you actually want to hear this?" He glanced at me again. "You don't really believe in this kind of thing, do you?"

"I can see that you do." It was the most diplomatic answer I could come up with. "I don't believe in much of anything, but I'm open to other people's beliefs. Not necessarily embracing them, but at least hearing and accepting that not everyone thinks the way I do."

"Fair enough. I'm not trying to convert you." He flashed something that didn't quite reach "smile" territory. "I don't tell most people about any of this. Somehow I think you're someone who should hear it, but I'm a little leery about telling you. I'd like us to be friends, Del, and you wouldn't believe how many friends I've lost because of this."

"I'd like us to be friends too," I said quietly. "Listen, you don't have to tell me anything." Even though my curiosity grew stronger by the second, the last thing I wanted was to be the cause of his fear. And he was clearly afraid. "Friends don't have to know everything about each other. For example, you don't know I'm really shitty at juggling."

He let out a surprised laugh. "I do now. And that isn't quite the same thing, but thank you." Inhaling loudly, he stared out the windshield. "I've seen it," he said again. "Since I was a little kid. The first time, I was around five. My great-grandmother passed, and my parents thought bringing me to the funeral was a brilliant idea. I was the only kid there. Everyone was crying, and I couldn't understand why." He paused. "Gee-Grannie was standing there in front of all of them. Wagging her finger at the pastor, making a face at my grandfather when he got up to speak. She was right there, so I didn't get why everyone was so upset."

He didn't look at me as he stopped speaking. And I didn't say a word as I tried to digest what he'd just told me. Just as some people believed in an afterlife, some believed in ghosts, and who was I to say they didn't exist? I'd certainly felt Austin's presence since he'd been gone. An echo, maybe. Or the product of my imagination. There was no way to say for sure, and there was no way to know whether five-year-old Lochlan had really seen his great-grandmother at her funeral.

The silence stretched painfully. Since Lochlan didn't appear close to saying anything else, I needed to say something. I fell back on my counselor training. "That must have been confusing for you."

"To say the least." Looking relieved, he sighed. "It was even more confusing when I tried to talk to my mom about it after we went home. She yelled at me for making things up and then sent me to my room. Gee-Grannie was her grandmother, and they were really close. Gee-Grannie looked so sad when Mom yelled at me."

"So she was there, too? In your house?"

He looked at me out of the corner of his eye. "I'm not sure if you really believe this or if you're just humoring me. Either way, thank you for listening. Yes, she was in my house. I found out why after Mom sent me to my room. Gee-Grannie went with me. She said she didn't want to leave but knew she couldn't stay, and she wasn't sure where to go. She asked me to help her."

We'd reached the end of the street we were on. He turned a couple of corners, until ahead of us, the ocean stretched out, sparkling in the sunlight. It was deceptive; from the safety of the car, the bluish ocean water looked inviting, but in January, entering that water could be deadly.

Austin had always loved the beach, just as he'd loved standing by the waterfront in Piers Park. For a moment, the memories eclipsed the conversation with Lochlan. I should have spent more time at the beach with Austin. There were so many things I would have done if I'd known how soon he would be gone. So many things I wouldn't have said, and so many other things I would have.

I hadn't known. He was gone so suddenly I had no way to know. And for the rest of my life, I would hate the man who'd taken my lover away—and myself for all the things I hadn't said or done.

"Are you all right?" Lochlan asked.

I drew a shuddering breath, resenting him for breaking my train of thought even as I wanted to thank him for it. "I will be."

"Memories?"

Startled, I nodded. "Mindreading?"

He shook his head. "Just a guess. I don't read minds, remember?"

"Even though it's a real thing."

"Even though." He turned the corner onto the road that led along the shore. "Traffic through here won't be exactly light, but at least we can see the water for a bit. The ocean is beautiful. Even at this time of year."

"The people whose homes are destroyed by storms probably don't think so," I muttered.

My irritation didn't seem to bother him. "Probably not."

Another stretch of silence passed. I broke it because talking was preferable to feeling like an ass. "Your great-grandmother asked you to help her?"

"Yes." He caught his lower lip between his teeth. "How far does your mind open?"

"Tell me what you want to tell me." I couldn't judge whether I would believe him until I knew what he wanted me to believe.

He slowed to let an elderly couple cross the street. "I didn't really understand what she wanted me to do. She wasn't exactly talking to me. It was sort of like when I knew you wanted coffee the other day. Hearing a concept more than actual words, I guess. And I don't remember it very clearly anyway. I was only five. I just remember knowing she needed my help so she wouldn't be stuck the way she was. So she could go to wherever she was supposed to be. With my great-

grandfather and whoever else was waiting for her." We started moving
again.

"Pretty sophisticated thinking for a five-year-old." I did my best to
keep my tone neutral, but a little kid thinking something like that was
a bit hard to believe.

Yeah, out of everything he was saying, the part I was having trouble
accepting was that a five-year-old considered who might be waiting for
his dead great-grandmother.

"Like I said, I don't have an entirely clear memory of it." He
sounded a little annoyed. "Maybe my parents said something about
people waiting for Gee-Grannie on the other side or something. I
don't claim it as my own thought, but it was something on my mind."

"Sorry," I said.

"It's fine. I did say this might be hard to believe." He slowed again,
this time for a traffic light. "If you're having trouble with that, the next
part's really going to hurt your brain. I don't even really know how to
explain it. I lay down and closed my eyes, because that seemed like the
right thing to do. No one told me. I just did it. And then it was like I
was standing beside Gee-Grannie. We weren't in my room anymore.
We were in her yard. She had a cute little yard with a latticework gate
that had roses growing through it. She told me once that that gate was
the one thing she'd dreamed of having as a child that she'd actually
managed to get."

He was talking faster again, and when we took off from the traffic
light, the car jerked forward. His nerves were getting the better of
him, and my reaction to what he was saying probably hadn't helped.

"Do you think it was a dream?" I asked, trying even harder to
sound interested and nonjudgmental, though as soon as I spoke I realized the question itself came across as a judgment.

Lochlan didn't seem to mind, though. "I wondered that for quite a
while. Until the next time it happened. Not with Gee-Grannie. The
next time, it was a neighbor of ours, a boy a few years older than me.
He got hit by a car one night. My mother told me about it the next
morning when I got up, and when I went outside to go to school, the
boy was standing on my front porch. That was when I knew I hadn't
dreamed what happened with Gee-Grannie."

He hadn't actually told me yet what had happened with his great-grandmother. I wasn't sure I should ask. Before I made up my mind, he said, "When I was standing with Gee-Grannie, on the other side of the gate, there was a bright light. It was beautiful, and I felt calm looking at it. I could see a shape, a person, standing in the light, but I couldn't tell who it was."

He wet his lips with his tongue. "I pointed it out to Gee-Grannie. She had this big smile and said, 'Oh, it's Howard! He's there to bring me home!' Howard was my great-grandfather. I asked Gee-Grannie if she wanted to go through the gate, and she asked me to hold her hand and walk with her as far as I could. So I did. I had to stop when we reached the gate. It was like I ran into a wall. Gee-Grannie didn't have to stop, though. She thanked me and said goodbye, and she walked through the gate. And then I was back in my room, lying on my bed. Alone."

I wasn't sure what to say to that. The story was sad. The tone of Lochlan's voice when he said "alone" made my heart ache for the little boy who'd had to send his great-grandmother into the light.

I still didn't know if I actually believed in an afterlife, but I believed Lochlan. Whether he'd actually guided his great-grandmother to the other side or not, something had happened.

"That must have been hard," I said finally, as we headed onto the Lynnway, a stretch of multilane road lined on both sides with businesses.

"It was." Lochlan abruptly changed lanes to go around a box truck that had come to an inexplicable stop in front of us. "Asshole. Not you, Del."

"I didn't think you meant me."

He chuckled. "Good. Anyway, yes. The thing with Gee-Grannie was hard, especially how my parents reacted. I didn't know any better than to tell them. My dad told me to keep my mouth shut so I wouldn't get locked up. My mother said I was lying and that she hated me for making her think Gee-Grannie hadn't gone straight to Heaven." He shuddered, and a tear trickled down his cheek. "I might have only been five, but I've never forgotten my mother saying that."

"I'm so sorry." No child should hear words like that from their parent, though sadly, too many did. The thought of little Lochlan having to listen to such vitriol from his own mother made my eyes water.

"Thanks," he said quietly. "It was a long time ago, but it still hurts. After that, I didn't tell them when someone came to me for help. Which was really hard because there was no one I could talk to. No one human, anyway."

I wasn't sure I wanted to know, but I asked anyway. "No one human?"

"My parents called him my imaginary friend." He paused. "You haven't started begging me to let you out of the car yet. Either you're really good at pretending not to think someone's crazy or you actually don't think I am."

"I actually don't think you are." I was a little surprised to realize how much I meant it. "I'm going to go out on a limb and guess that your imaginary friend wasn't imaginary?"

"Jury's still out on that. I don't think he is. He knows too many things I don't have any way to know." He gripped the steering wheel more tightly. "Del, I really appreciate you listening to this. There are some things I'd rather not talk about right now."

"No problem." I pushed away my curiosity. He'd told me more than he told most people. I felt honored by that. I wasn't ready to completely change the subject, though. "You mentioned the boy who was your neighbor."

"Yeah. Leland. He was ten." He scoffed. "He was kind of a jerk to me, since I was younger, but the morning after he died, there he was, standing on my porch. Crying. He didn't know what had happened." He steered around a slower car. "Of course, I didn't know what had happened either. All Mom told me was that Leland died. I didn't know how to help him, but I couldn't just let him stand there crying, so I sat down and closed my eyes like I'd done with Gee-Grannie. And then Leland and I were on the school playground, and there was a light shining in the middle of the jungle gym."

"So you helped him go into the light?"

"He didn't want to go." He gave me a thin smile. "He wanted to go home. But then a man came to the edge of the light and called Leland's name, and Leland stopped crying and went to him, and they walked into the light together. And I was back on my porch."

"Wow." I tried to think of something else to say. "So you helped him the same way you helped your great-grandmother."

"Yeah. I wanted to tell my parents about it, but I was too afraid they would yell at me again. So I never told them." He took a long breath. "It feels really good to tell you all this. Over the years, I've had a very few people I trusted enough to share it with."

"I'm honored to be one of them." It sounded a lot sappier than I'd thought it would.

"I'd like to stop talking about it now, though." He steered onto a ramp that led off the Lynnway. "Let's drive along Revere Beach. More ocean. Probably more time and traffic, too, but I don't mind if you don't."

"I don't mind."

We didn't talk for a little while, but this time the silence was comfortable. It didn't matter if I believed Lochlan or not. He trusted me, and that felt good.

As we finally neared the coffee shop, I said, "Do you mind bringing me to my place?"

"Not at all." He smiled. "Can you direct me from here? Or reset the GPS. I can't really do it while I'm driving."

Directing him seemed easier, so I did. A few minutes later, he double-parked in front of my building. For just a second, I considered asking him if he wanted to come in for dinner, but there was no way I could do that. I couldn't bring him into the space Austin had occupied.

"Thanks for the ride," I said instead.

"I would say anytime, but I'm usually at the café later than this." He turned slightly to face me. "I enjoyed this, Del. God, that sounded better in my head."

I laughed. "It sounded fine to me. I did too."

"Give me a call or text if you want coffee sometime." He hesitated. "Or maybe I'll call or text you."

"That would be nice." *What the hell am I doing?* I took a breath. I was becoming friends with someone. That was all. "I'm going to be honest with you. I'm still a mess."

"We're all a mess in some way." He rested his hand on the back of my seat. "I know what grief is like, Del. Let it be what it is. I'd just kind of like to be here for you."

"Thank you." My voice croaked. I cleared my throat. "Um, thanks." I decided it would be best to get out of the car before I either said something stupid or my emotions got the better of me. I opened the door. "Talk to you soon."

He smiled. "Talk soon."

I got out of the car and went inside. When I entered my apartment, it felt a little less empty.

CHAPTER FIFTEEN

"So you have a new friend." Sprawled on my couch, Remy grinned. "I'm glad. You need more than an old drag queen to hang out with."

"You're not old," I said, giving the expected response. "And I like hanging out with you, but I don't want to monopolize you."

"You aren't." She sobered. "I like you, Del, but also...This sounds shitty, but you're what I have left of Austin. Being around you reminds me of him."

"It doesn't sound shitty." I understood completely. She and I got along well. We were family. But Austin had brought us together, and spending time with each other was a way of remembering him.

"Good." She sniffed. "Anyway. New friend. Cat guy. Tell me about him."

"Aren't we supposed to be packing?" After a weekend of walks outside and a couple of short text conversations with Lochlan, I'd finally decided I was ready to deal with what remained of Austin's stuff. I'd asked Remy to come over and help because I wasn't completely convinced I could do the job alone. So far, we'd packed two dresses, and then Remy had decided it was time to hang out and chat. About Lochlan, now that I'd told her about him giving me a ride home on Thursday.

"It's Monday. Georgia's going to come home in a shit mood. I'd rather hang out here." She stretched. "Which means I have all afternoon and evening to hear about cat guy. He's cute."

"We're friends." I spoke more harshly than I meant to, but I couldn't believe she would even hint at me being interested in someone. "It's too soon, Remy."

"I know," she said gently. "I wasn't trying to imply anything, Del."

"Sorry." I ran my hand over my face. "He is cute. I don't like that I've noticed."

"Del, honey, it is okay to notice that a cute guy is cute." She sat up. "It doesn't mean anything other than that you're observant."

"Yeah." I was done talking about Lochlan's cuteness. "He's a nice guy. We had coffee last week."

"Wait, what?" Eyes wide, she leaned forward. "Why didn't you tell me?"

"I just did." My heart raced. Her reaction was probably just because this was the first she was hearing about the coffee thing. At least I hoped she wasn't thinking I'd betrayed Austin.

"I mean when it happened." She sat back. "When was this?"

"Last week," I said again. My mind went blank. "Um…Monday? I think?"

"It obviously made an impression on you." She studied me. "Del, you don't think I'm pissed at you, do you? I'm not. There's nothing wrong with you having coffee with someone."

"I'll convince myself of that at some point." I took a breath. "I was having a hard time that day. I was watching the boats."

"Austin loved that," she said softly.

"Yeah. And it reminded me that he isn't here to see them anymore, and that hit hard. I didn't want to bother you, and then Lochlan texted and asked if I wanted to get coffee." I wasn't about to tell her he'd texted because he knew I'd thought about texting him. That would have been more than Remy could believe. Not to mention betraying Lochlan's trust.

"I'm glad he did." She hesitated. "You know I don't mind you texting me, right?"

"Yes, of course." I went over and sat on the edge of the couch. "*I* mind. We talked about this. You need time to take care of yourself. If Lochlan hadn't reached out, I probably would have texted you, but he did."

"I've been feeling guilty all week because of that conversation." She rested her hand on my leg. "I do need to take care of myself, but I'm here for you too."

"Don't feel guilty." I scoffed as I realized what I'd said. "I should take my own advice. I was feeling guilty for leaning on you so much."

"We need to talk more." She rolled her eyes. "Okay, so neither of us needs to feel guilty. Hey, completely random subject change, do you want to come to the club Friday night? I'll be debuting a new number in honor of Austin. 'The Show Must Go On.'"

"Freddy at his finest." Austin had loved that song. I'd lost count of how many times I'd caught him belting it—poorly—in the shower. My man definitely hadn't been a singer, let alone capable of matching Freddy Mercury's rendition. I started to turn down the invitation, but stopped myself. Remy knew I didn't like being at the club. She wouldn't have asked if it wasn't important to her. And it was in Austin's memory, which meant I needed to be there. "Sure, I'd love to see it."

Her face lit up. "Seriously? I'm so glad! I'll make sure Giorgio has your name so he doesn't make you pay the cover charge."

"Sounds like a plan." Giorgio had been the club's bouncer for as long as I could remember. Maybe longer than Austin and Remy had performed there. I definitely didn't want to get into a dispute with him over the twenty bucks it cost to enter the club on performance nights.

"You could invite your new friend, too, if you want," Remy said.

"I don't know if he's into drag shows." And I could never bring Lochlan to the club, any more than I could bring him into the apartment. Those places were Austin. Lochlan and I were only friends, but bringing him into Austin's spaces just didn't feel right.

"You could ask." She shrugged. "Or not. It's up to you, but I'd like to meet the guy."

"You met him when you brought me to the cat café," I pointed out. Remy meeting Lochlan. I wasn't sure how I felt about that. If Remy was her usual self, she would probably be Lochlan's new best friend within minutes of being introduced. Where would that leave me?

And why the hell did I feel jealous about the possibility of Remy and Lochlan becoming friends? It wasn't as if friendship was an exclusive thing.

"We should get to work on those clothes." Remy stood. "Do you want a takeout break at some point? I'm buying. Unless you get sick of me, I'd really rather stay here until after supper so Georgia has time to get home and get her head out of her ass."

Relieved that she'd dropped the subject of bringing Lochlan to the club, I stood too. "Are Mondays that bad?"

"For Donnie, apparently. He's talking about finding a new job." Her switch from referring to her roommate by drag persona to using his daily name and pronouns barely registered on me. It was typical for a conversation about the other performers. Austin had done it too. "He's generally cranky all week, is fine over the weekend, and then Monday rolls around and reality smacks him in the face again."

"Sounds like he would be better off working somewhere else."

She took a box from the stack she'd left by the front door and headed toward the bedroom. I grabbed a box and followed her. "Marco and I would be better off too," she said. "They almost got into a frigging fistfight last week. Donnie goes to bed early on Mondays, so if I can hang out here until seven or eight...?"

"Fine with me." Nights were when the apartment felt the emptiest. Even though for a while I'd preferred that, today the thought of Remy sticking around for a while boosted my mood. I wouldn't be alone.

We started with Austin's drag closet. The things we'd left during our previous round of cleaning were among his fancier drag, far too elaborate and sparkly for daily wear. Not things we could give to Casilla's Closet, though some of the kids might have enjoyed them. Remy inspected the first dress, a rainbow-patterned confection of tulle, satin, and beads. "He wore this for Pride. Every year, I think. Even the couple of years they didn't have the festival, he wore this to walk around, didn't he?"

"Yeah. He was sorely pissed that they had to cancel the festival those years. Said he wasn't going to let a pandemic keep him from showing his pride." I couldn't help laughing at the memory. "He went to the freaking laundromat wearing it the second year. Got some pretty weird looks." I frowned. "I was embarrassed." I'd been a shit about it, too. All it had taken was one half-heard mutter about "fags" for me to turn my back and leave Austin by himself. I hadn't gone far, only out to the sidewalk, but still.

"He told me about that. He felt bad for upsetting you." She carefully took the dress off its hanger. "He said you asked him not to wear the dress, and he was so determined to prove a point that he didn't stop to think about why you might not be comfortable. Then the guy in the laundromat started in and you couldn't handle it."

"I should have been able to handle it." The familiar lump rose in my throat, along with a pang of fear that made no sense given that we were talking about something that had happened years ago. No one had hurt me then, and despite the rantings of a homophobic asshat, no one had hurt Austin either.

But I'd seen too much hatred in my life, starting with my own family, and remembering the day I'd been too afraid to stand by Austin was more than I could handle.

"I was a horrible partner." Leaning against the door frame, I sank to the floor. "That wasn't the only time I didn't stand up for him when I should have."

"Del, he didn't expect you to be a knight in sparkly armor." She draped the dress over the box and knelt beside me. "I'm sorry. I thought this dress would bring happy memories. You didn't do anything wrong by not being Austin, you know. He understood that you couldn't be out there the way he was. He didn't blame you for it. He just wished you had the option to be a little less hidden."

She was trying to comfort me, but it only made me feel worse. Austin should have been angry with me for not defending him. He should have expected me to have his back around homophobes and assholes. That was what partners did. They had each other's backs, the way Austin had had mine when the mother of a boy who'd just come out as trans tried to have me fired for "grooming" her son. Austin hadn't even considered leaving me on my own to deal with that. He'd even gone with me to the meeting the administration had called to try to mediate between the parent and me, though he wasn't allowed in the room.

"I should have done more for him." My voice was thick, choked by the tears I was unwilling to shed for the thousandth time in front of Remy. "He always stood up for me. I should have stood up for him."

"Del, you're dwelling on something that happened a long time ago." Remy's tone, while still sympathetic, was a little less patient now. "What's the point of kicking your own ass about it now?"

"I don't know." There was no point, but that didn't mean I could shut off the self-loathing. My partner had needed me however many years ago it had been, and I'd been unwilling to be there.

No wonder I was alone so often now. I deserved to be.

"Stop it." Remy sat down next to me and put her arm around me. "It's hard, huh? Not having him around. Not being able to tell him all the things you wish you'd said. I'm right there with you. But we don't do ourselves any favors when we get sucked down like this."

"Yeah." I swallowed hard and pressed the heels of my hands against my eyes. "Shit. Sorry, Rem. I thought I was up to this."

"We can take a break."

"No." I uncovered my eyes. She was looking up toward all the gowns still on their hangers. "We took a break when you got here. These things need new homes, because I'm sure as hell not going to use them. I can't promise to be perfectly serene while we sort everything, but I want to get it done. At least most of it."

"Okay." She touched the rainbow dress. "Would it bother you to have one of the queens at the club wear this? I don't know if any of them would want it, but it would fit a couple of them, and it would be another way to remember Austin. Or maybe I'll hold onto it. We get new queens sometimes, and they don't always have their drag together yet. One of them might be able to use this."

"Austin would like that." When Austin started out in drag, he'd had support and mentorship from older queens. As he'd gotten older and more experienced, he'd chosen to take on that role with the newer performers. More than once, he'd literally given a new queen the dress off his back. "If you think it would fit any of them, offer it."

"I will. Thanks." She got up and somehow managed to compress the dress into the box. Hands on hips, she studied the remaining items. "Some of these others can go to the club too, if you're okay with it. Some...there's an organization that gives away gowns for proms and such to girls who can't afford to buy them. I think some of these would be perfect for that. Prom season isn't too far off."

"It's January. Prom season is still a few months away." But I liked her plan. I'd had girls come to my office in tears because they wanted so badly to go to their proms but couldn't even begin to pay for dresses and tickets and such. Sometimes staff members had taken up collections to pay for tickets for the lower-income students, and we'd steered a few of the girls to the organization Remy mentioned. "Yes, that would be good."

"Okay. So two piles, one for the club and one for the prom dress organization." She took a blue satin evening gown off its hanger. "Help me out here, Del, if you're ready."

I decided I needed to be ready. Austin's clothes weren't doing anyone any good collecting dust on these hangers. They certainly weren't anything I would use, though I did save one. A red dress with hanging strands of sparkling red beads. The dress was so short I'd teased Austin about being able to see how tight his tuck was. He'd worn it the first time he talked me into going to the club to watch him perform. More than any of his other dresses, this one reminded me strongly of him, and I couldn't stomach the thought of anyone else wearing it.

Eventually, we managed to get all of the dresses boxed up. It took longer than I'd anticipated; some of the dresses brought Remy or me on a detour down memory lane, and neither of us wanted to deny ourselves the time to remember Austin. By the time we finished, it was dark outside, and my stomach was growling.

"Supper?" Remy closed the last box and turned to look hopefully at me. "Delivery, I think, unless you're in the mood to be out in public." The twinkle in her eye showed that she already knew the answer to that.

"Chinese sounds like a plan." I left the closet and tried to remember where I'd left my phone. "The place down the street delivers."

"Or pizza." Remy followed me. "I'm kind of in the mood for pizza."

"I'm flexible."

"So Austin mentioned." She snorted. "Sorry. Couldn't resist."

I rolled my eyes. "It's fine. Pizza, then. Where's my phone?"

Remy took out her phone and sent me a text. The chime indicated that my phone was somewhere near the couch. I found it on the floor and picked it up to see that I'd missed a message from Lochlan. It wasn't anything important. Just Hi, how's it going? But it put a smile on my face.

Of course, Remy noticed. "Cat guy?"

"His name's Lochlan, and yes." I debated whether to answer and decided it could wait. One advantage of texts was that they didn't require immediate replies. "Pizza."

"You aren't going to answer him?" Remy sat on the couch.

"No. I'm going to order pizza."

I placed the order then sat down beside Remy to wait for food. Remy leaned back and put her feet up on the coffee table. "It wasn't the easiest afternoon, but it's been nice," she said. "Hanging out and talking with you. Sometimes I get the feeling you think we're only friends because I was Austin's friend, but I actually like you as an entirely separate human."

"Likewise."

The pizza arrived, and Remy and I ate in companionable silence. After we finished, I helped her bring the boxes to her car and gave her a hug. "Thank you for helping."

"Thanks for calling me." She slammed the trunk shut and turned back to me. "Call me when you need me, Del. Please. And I'll see you Friday night, right?"

"Absolutely." I put my hands in my pockets. "And you call me if you need me, okay? Just because I fall apart a lot doesn't mean I can't help someone else hold things together."

She smiled. "I'll keep that in mind. See you Friday."

She got into her car and left. I stood on the sidewalk for a moment, breathing in the cold, sea-scented air. I felt good. So long had passed since I'd felt that way that I barely recognized it. I felt good.

And that feeling lasted right up until I walked into the apartment and found myself alone again, with more empty space than had existed that morning. I spent the rest of the evening curled up on the couch trying to forget that Austin's closet was completely empty now.

CHAPTER SIXTEEN

After a week of texting back and forth with Lochlan, during which neither of us said anything memorable, I was looking forward to seeing him on Thursday. Probably more than I should have been.

Thursday morning, just before I logged onto the telehealth app for my counseling appointment, Lochlan called me. "Hey, am I interrupting anything?"

"I have an appointment in about..." I looked at the clock on my laptop. "Two minutes. I can call you back after."

"No need. I'll see you this afternoon, right?"

He sounded a little out of breath. I wasn't sure if it was nerves or something else. "Were you running?"

"I...Um, no." He made a noise that sounded vaguely like a laugh. "Look, it's not a good time, obviously. No worries. Um, can I give you a ride to the café this afternoon? I don't have to be there until twelve-thirty. I know that's earlier than you usually go."

Something was definitely going on with him, and I had the sense he needed to talk about it. I couldn't shut him down. "That's fine. What time will you need to pick me up?"

"Let's say...If we do eleven-thirty, I can treat you to a quick lunch before we go to the café? Would that be okay?"

"Sure." We'd done coffee. Lunch wasn't much of a step beyond that. And I really didn't have time to debate it with him anyway. "Eleven-thirty. I'll meet you in front of my building."

"Sounds good. Thanks." He hung up.

I logged into the telehealth app and tried to focus on talking with Tammy for the next forty-five minutes. My mind was nowhere near the discussion, though. I answered her questions, but I was distracted by wondering what was going on with Lochlan.

I thought Tammy didn't notice, but at the end of the session, she said, "Del, I'm not sure where you were today. I hope it was somewhere happy."

"Yeah, sorry." I ran my hand through my hair. And immediately wondered if I needed to check my hair before going outside to meet Lochlan, since it was quarter past eleven. "I'm having lunch with a friend. My mind was already there, I guess."

She smiled. "I'm glad you're socializing. I hope it's a good lunch. Next week, same time?"

"Same bat time, same bat channel," I said.

"I'm not sure what that means, but you're in my calendar. Have a good week, Del." She logged off.

She didn't know what "same bat time, same bat channel" meant. Admittedly, the Adam West *Batman* TV show had aired well before my time too, but still, realizing Tammy had never heard the phrase made me feel ancient.

I put down my phone and went into the bathroom to check my hair. It was completely fine. I had no reason to care, of course. Lochlan wouldn't, if he even noticed.

What was going on with him? The week before, when he told me about the first two spirits he'd guided to the light, he was nervous, but nothing like the way he'd sounded on the phone this morning. Something must have happened.

When I went downstairs, his car was already stopped by the curb several yards up the street. I walked over to it and tapped on the passenger window. In the driver's seat, Lochlan jumped, then smiled at me and reached over to unlock the door. "Hey," he said as I got in. "Thanks for letting me pick you up."

"Thanks in advance for lunch." I fastened my seat belt. "Is everything okay? You sounded a little..." I trailed off, unable to come up with the right word.

"Off?" he supplied. "Anxious? Yeah." He drove away from the curb. "Where do you want to have lunch? I'd suggest fast food, but I don't know how you feel about that."

"It sounds fine to me. Healthy eating is overrated." I smiled, but my heart wasn't in it. "What's going on, Lochlan?"

"Let's wait until we're at the restaurant," he said. "That way, if you don't want to talk to me, it'll be easier for you to walk away."

"That doesn't sound good." I shifted a little in my seat. Maybe I shouldn't have agreed to this. But despite Lochlan's words, I didn't think he was as worried about me not wanting to talk to him as he was about whatever had happened "You already told me you send ghosts to the other side. What are you going to say that you think might make me not want to talk to you?"

"Del, please." He tapped his horn as a car whipped out of a side street in front of us. "Do you trust me?"

I didn't need to think about that. "Yes."

"And you believe the things I've told you about myself."

"Yes."

"Then please wait." He glanced at me. "I need to pull myself together enough to tell you."

"All right."

We drove through East Boston into Revere and stopped at a fast-food restaurant in a shopping center off the main route. Inside, we got our food and sat at a table away from the few other customers.

Lochlan unwrapped his burger but didn't pick it up. "How have you been? I should have asked when you got into the car."

"I've been fine. We've been texting, so you know that." I dipped a fry into the little cup of ketchup I'd gotten and ate it. "And I thought you were fine until this morning. Something happened?"

"Yeah." He picked up his burger. "I don't know if I can eat this. It was a kid, Del. A kid came to me this morning. Four, maybe five. A little girl."

"Oh, hell." I wanted to comfort him somehow. Touch him. Hold him. Something. But all I could do was sit across from him at the table. And nothing I could have done would have made this go away anyhow. "I'm sorry. That must have been hard."

"She was..." Shuddering, he put the burger down again. "Someone did it to her. She said someone hurt her and then she was lost. I was at the shore, just taking a walk, and she was standing there by herself. She was crying. She asked if I could take her to her mommy."

The only way he could have done that was if her mother was also dead. I was afraid to ask. "Could you?"

"No." He sighed and sagged a bit. "She was afraid of the light. She thought someone in it would hurt her. I don't know if the person who killed her was in there. I hope to hell not."

"Oh, Lochlan." There had to be something I could say. "What did you do?"

"I brought her to the light." He closed his eyes for a second. "I told her it would be okay. That she would be safe. What if I was wrong, Del? What if she isn't safe there? I don't know who or what's on the other side of it."

My eyes were tearing up, but I couldn't let myself cry right now. This was Lochlan's story. His pain. I was here to listen. I drew on my counselor training and tried to at least appear neutral. "You said with your great-grandmother and the neighbor boy, people met them at the light. Did anyone come to meet this girl?"

"Yeah." He nodded. "Yeah. There was someone. She didn't know him. I did."

Maybe it was the pronoun "him." Or the way Lochlan wouldn't look at me when he spoke. Or maybe it was just that I knew my partner. "It was Austin."

"Yeah." Biting his lip, he glanced up at me then back down. "It was Austin."

"And you recognized him because you..." The realization hit as I spoke. Abruptly, I stood. "You took him there. The night he died, you brought him to the light."

Any doubt I'd had about Lochlan's experiences evaporated. He could have still been lying, of course. A made-up story to prove his point or to hurt me, I didn't know which. But he had no reason to hurt me, and the twisted, crumpled expression on his face, the anguish radiating from him so strongly even I, with zero inclination toward empathic powers, could feel it, wasn't something easily faked.

He was telling the truth. About his great-grandmother and neighbor, about the little girl—and about my Austin.

"Yes," he said quietly, bowing his head further.

"He isn't gone. I've heard him." Once. And that had probably only been my imagination. But I needed to cling to something that would mean Austin hadn't crossed into that fucking light, because as I understood it, once a spirit entered the light, they were gone forever.

"That's possible." Lochlan spoke in a dull monotone, but his voice grew stronger as he spoke. "Entering the light means they go to whatever afterlife exists, but they can visit our world. Like if you move to a new city, you can go back and visit the old one from time to time, conditions permitting. They can also speak to us from the other side even if they aren't present here."

"I don't want a lesson in how the afterlife works." So much for neutrality. I was furious. "Why didn't you tell me? How the fuck can you say you want to be my friend and not tell me something like this?" My voice rose, and a couple of other customers turned to stare at me. With effort, I reined in my temper enough to sit down and speak a little more quietly. "Why didn't you tell me?"

"At first, I didn't realize you were his partner. Then I was worried you'd react this way." Mouth in a grim line, he looked up. "I'm sorry, Del. I really am. It probably feels like I took him away from you. If that's what you're thinking, I get it."

"No." I took a deep breath. Part of me hated him for not telling me sooner. Then again, a week earlier he'd been afraid to tell me about what he was able to do at all. And he'd certainly been right to worry that I'd be angry with him about this.

Lochlan regarded me with a mix of defiance and fear, unshed tears in his eyes. He'd asked me to have lunch with him because he needed someone to talk to about the little girl, and here I was yelling at him. Turning on him. Not because of his ability, but because he'd used it to guide my Austin away from me.

Guide. Not take. Lochlan hadn't caused Austin's death. He'd just made sure Austin ended up where he needed to be.

"You didn't take him away." My voice shook. "That fucking driver did. Shit, Lochlan, I don't know where to go with this."

"I'm sorry." His voice caught, and he looked down again. "I wasn't going to tell you like this. I was going to tell you. I promise. But not like this. I just...that little girl, and then Austin was the one who came to meet her, and..." A sob burst from his throat. "I'm sorry, Del."

I couldn't just let him break down in the middle of a fast-food restaurant. I got up and put my arms around him. He clutched at me, openly crying now, and my heart ached for him. I was still angry, but I couldn't stand seeing him in so much pain.

Others were staring at us again, and I shot death glares at each of them. Most, looking sheepish, went back to their food. One elderly woman glared right back at me.

"Hey, Lochlan?" I said softly. "Let's bring our food out to the car, okay? We can talk more out there."

"Huh?" Sniffling, he pulled back and looked around. "Yeah. Probably a good idea." He raised his voice. "Losing someone hits hard. I wouldn't want my grief to ruin other people's burgers and fries."

This time, even the elderly woman looked away. With a faintly triumphant expression, Lochlan rewrapped his burger and put it back on the tray. I went over to the counter and talked the cashier into giving me a bag, and Lochlan and I gathered up our uneaten food and took it outside.

Once we were settled in his car, I said, "You don't owe me an apology."

"I should have told you." He took a shuddering breath. "As soon as I realized who you were, I should have told you. Austin talked about you before he went into the light. He told me how much he loved you and how he hated leaving you alone. He was worried. The first time you and I met, I didn't realize you were the Del he'd mentioned, but then you told me about how you lost your partner, and I knew. I should have told you then."

"You didn't know if I would believe you." My anger was starting to subside, though it still simmered beneath the surface. "You weren't sure until the day we got coffee whether you could tell me anything."

"Yeah. And I've had a few bad experiences telling people I guided their loved ones. I wasn't keen on having my nose broken again." He sniffled. I handed him a napkin from the bag, and he dabbed his nose with it. "I still could have told you."

"You didn't, and there's no changing that." Though I spoke gently, the words seemed harsh to me. "Wishing you'd told me won't rewind anything, so let's put that aside. You told me now, when you knew I'd believe you."

"You do believe me." Eyes widening, he turned to face me. "You're pissed, but you believe me."

"Yes." There was no way not to. Even though I'd never believed in an afterlife or spirits or any of that, I believed it now. Listening to Lochlan, seeing and feeling his pain, it was impossible not to believe him.

And it was impossible not to feel pain of my own. Austin had died on a city street. Alone, or so I'd thought. I wasn't with him. Remy and his other friends weren't there either. I'd believed he was alone, and that had made losing him even harder.

But he wasn't alone. Lochlan was there. Someone who could see and speak to Austin after the life left his body. He'd brought Austin someplace where Austin would never be alone again.

I was glad Austin hadn't died with no one there to support him. Whether or not I believed in an afterlife, I was glad someone who did was present to show Austin how to get there. Now, though, I was the one who was alone. I hadn't gotten to say goodbye to the man I loved —but a total stranger had.

Except Lochlan wasn't a stranger anymore. He'd entered my life, and now he was here.

Maybe Austin had had something to do with it. There was no way to know.

CHAPTER SEVENTEEN

Lochlan touched the napkin to his nose again. "Shit. We're going to be late getting to the café. And we haven't eaten yet."

"I think there were more important things going on." I took his burger out of the bag and held it out to him. "Can you eat? You said you weren't sure."

"I'm not, but I need to. Dealing with spirits uses energy. I'm supposed to eat afterward." He unwrapped the burger and took a bite.

I started eating my own, and for a few minutes we didn't speak. Which was a relief to me. I had no idea what else to say to him. My emotions were in a tug of war over whether to hate him for being the last human to speak to Austin and not telling me until now, or whether to hold him and comfort him about the little girl. And thank him for taking care of Austin when Austin otherwise would have died alone.

"You still didn't run." Lochlan swallowed and crumpled his burger wrapper. "I was sure this would be more than you would want to deal with."

"I don't know how to feel about it," I admitted. "It's going to take a little time to process. I have so many questions. Right now, though, we need to get to the café, and you're still struggling with helping that little girl. At least you know someone safe met her in the light."

"Yeah." He sighed. "I know Austin wouldn't hurt her. I'm just afraid that the person who did harm her is there and will find her. But I can't do anything about it. I'm not in that world. I'm here. All I can do is bring them to the light and hope that's where they're supposed to be."

"I don't know a whole lot about going into the light or that kind of thing, but I'm pretty sure it's where all of them are supposed to be, isn't it?" I stuffed a couple of fries in my mouth. "Maybe we should talk about this while you drive."

"Yeah." He glanced at his watch. "Shit. Yes, we should."

He started the car and drove out of the parking lot while I finished my fries a little too quickly and wound up coughing. Without taking his eyes off the road, he reached over and thumped my back. "Okay?"

"Yeah. When fries attack." I coughed again and wished I'd thought to bring my soda along with the food. "How are you doing now? I understand why you were so upset when you called earlier."

"I rarely encounter children." With a finger, he brushed something away from his eye. "And the other kids I've helped, I knew how they died. Usually illness. I've had a couple who died in accidents. When I was a kid, helping other kids wasn't as hard as it is now, because now I understand how painful it must be for their parents. I didn't really grasp that when I was a kid, because my own parents didn't much care if I was around or not."

"I'm sorry," I said quietly.

He shrugged. "Thanks. It was what it was. Anyway, it's hard enough when a child who died a relatively peaceful death shows up. This wasn't that. This little girl...Someone did that to her. Someone killed her. Guiding any kid freaks me out a little, but this just pushed me over the edge." He glanced at me. "And right now, you're the only human I can talk to about any of this. I didn't know who else to call."

"I'm glad you called me." I genuinely was. Even though I wished I'd learned about his connection with Austin in a less painful way, knowing Lochlan trusted me to support him felt good. And my anger over the Austin thing had ebbed. The fact that Lochlan hadn't told me sooner still rankled, but I understood his reasons. He'd told me now. That was what mattered. "The other people who know what you can do?"

"Two of them aren't in my life anymore. Their choice." The edge in his tone warned me not to ask why they'd made that choice. "The other passed on last year."

"I'm sorry," I said again.

"Me too. They were a good person. I miss them." He quirked the corners of his mouth. "They intentionally did *not* come to me for help reaching the light. They told me before they passed that they wouldn't. Anyway, I didn't have anyone else to talk to. So thank you."

"You're welcome."

As we continued on the way to the café, I tried to wrap my head around everything he'd told me. It was a lot. I didn't know what was harder to digest: that Lochlan had brought Austin to the light or that he'd helped a murdered child.

Who was the girl? Had anyone reported her murder? Children sometimes went missing for months or years before anyone noticed they were gone. It was incomprehensible to me, but several such reports had aired on local news over the past few years. Usually—and even more incomprehensibly, even though I'd seen how horrible people could be to their own children—the child wasn't reported missing because a parent or parental figure was responsible for the death.

Lochlan hadn't seen the child's mother in the light, which meant she was probably still alive. But he was afraid the girl's murderer might be on the other side. Did he have a reason to believe the murderer might also have died?

If the girl's killer was dead, they hadn't met her at the light either. Austin had.

Why?

It wasn't out of character for Austin to help a child. He loved kids, though he'd always specified that he loved them as long as they belonged to someone else. He had no interest in being a father, which was fine with me. After spending all day five days a week working with kids, some of whom were well on their way to being broken beyond repair, I'd had no illusions about whether I would be able to handle children of my own.

But why had Austin helped this girl?

"Why does a spirit meet another spirit at the light?" I asked.

"It almost always happens," Lochlan said. He didn't seem surprised that I'd asked. "Sort of an afterlife orientation, I guess. I—and others like me, I assume—guide spirits from our world to the light, then, most of the time, a spirit meets them to guide them through the light to wherever they go once they cross. Usually it's either someone the just-passed spirit knew in this lifetime or one of their ancestors. Sometimes, though, there's no one there with a connection. I've seen it happen before, a few times. The new spirit doesn't have anyone on the other side, or they do but that spirit couldn't come to meet them for some reason. Not everyone needs a guide on the other side, though, so sometimes the spirit just goes into the light on their own if no one meets them."

"And sometimes someone random shows up?" The dearly departed welcoming committee. Why not?

"I think sometimes when someone crosses over, they take on a role on the other side." Lochlan glanced at me. "Have you heard of spirit guides?"

"Like psychic 'if you're there, knock three times' stuff?"

He snorted. "Not quite. There's a school of thought that says all humans have guides. Beings who work with us to help us live our lives. Some of those guides are the spirits of those we've known, usually in past lives. It's pretty rare, from what I've read, for someone's spirit guide to have known them as a human in the current lifetime, but some people disagree about that."

"This is all getting really out there," I said.

"You asked." He paused. "Well, I guess you didn't, actually. But anyway. Yes, it stretches belief. Point being, sometimes after someone crosses over, they take on a role until it's time for them to incarnate again, assuming they ever do. Maybe acting as a guide to a living human. Maybe meeting people at the light so they don't have to cross over alone."

"Like you said, the flip side to what you do." It made sense when I put it that way. He helped spirits enter the light. If I believed that, I believed spirits existed. If spirits existed, and humans helped them enter the light, why couldn't other spirits also help?

"Yeah."

"I'm glad the girl had someone to help her." I still didn't completely understand why it had been Austin. Maybe because Austin already knew Lochlan. That was the only explanation I could think of.

And of course my brain was going to stick on that point instead of the fact that Lochlan hadn't told me he was the one to bring Austin to the light. Because right now, that was way more than I could deal with.

"I just wish I knew who she was." He sniffed. "And what happened to her. Whoever did this to her should be held accountable. And whoever lost her should know what happened."

"If they don't already." I didn't mean to say it, but I spoke without thinking.

"Yeah." He blew out a long breath. "Can we drop the subject for now, please? I'm trying to get myself on track for working with the cats. If I'm wound up, they will be."

His agitation was noticeable even to me, so he probably had a point. "Sure."

We didn't say anything more until we arrived at the café. Lochlan parked near the building, and we walked in together. "Thanks for being there for me," he said as we sanitized our hands.

"It's what friends do." I smiled at him. "You were there for me. It was my turn."

"I don't think we need to keep score." He faintly smiled back, and we went inside.

Lochlan greeted Liam and immediately went to the shy cat room. I stood in the middle of the space for a moment, trying to decide where to go and which cat to pet first. To my disappointment, Charlie the Sweater Cat already had a human. An older woman with a laptop sat beside him on the black couch, occasionally reaching over to scratch him between the ears. He didn't seem to mind lying on the couch instead of a lap, but I was a little sad not to be able to sit with him. There was no way to do so without crowding the woman, though.

"Charlie's been popular today." Liam came over to me. "We had a few visitors this morning who gave him attention too."

"That's good." Impulsively, I decided to ask the question I'd had for a couple of weeks. "What's the process for adopting?"

His face lit. "You want to adopt? Charlie, I'm guessing."

"Yeah." I looked over at the Sweater Cat, who had lifted his head and appeared to be looking straight at me, though it was hard to be certain. "I don't know if I'd be the right human for him. I'm on leave from work, but eventually I'll be going back. He'd be on his own for seven or eight hours a day during the week."

"Cats are pretty self-sufficient, but Charlie does need a lot of attention." He folded his arms. "He has some medical concerns, too."

"Lochlan told me. Seizures?"

Liam nodded. "We went to the vet yesterday. There's protein in his urine, so he'll need treatment for that. He's going to have to stay here a while longer so we can get him in better shape. But eventually, if all goes well with the treatment, we'll be looking for a home for him. If you want to fill out an application, I can hold onto it until we have a better idea of what's going on with him. And if it turns out this is his final home, you could decide whether you wanted one of the other cats instead."

"That would be great." It would also give me time to decide whether I actually wanted to adopt a cat or just thought it was a good idea because I was lonely.

"Come with me." Liam led me to his desk and took a couple of stapled sheets of paper out of a folder. He handed them to me. "You can fill it out now if you want. I'm sure one of the cats would love to help you."

As if to prove the point, Ice rubbed against my legs. I bent and petted him. "I'm sure our illustrious mayor will be a huge help."

Liam laughed and handed me a pen. I went over to sit at one of the two small tables in the space. Ice followed and jumped up on one of the other stools.

"I didn't think you would actually help me, Ice." I patted his head and started filling out the application. It was fairly straightforward: my income, a guarantee that my landlord would allow me to have a pet if I was approved, a promise that I would get regular veterinary care for the cat. It only took me a few minutes.

When I finished, Liam was talking to two people who had just come in. Ice had gone to investigate the newcomers. The woman with the laptop was still sitting beside Charlie. I didn't begrudge Charlie the attention, but I'd been looking forward to sitting with him on my lap and forgetting about the rest of the world for a while.

I left the application on Liam's desk and went in search of an unoccupied cat. Remembering that Remy-the-Cat liked to stay in the shy cat room, I decided to check there. Remy-the-Cat was there, lying on the floor beside Lochlan, who was staring blankly at his phone.

I sat beside him and started petting Remy, who immediately moved onto my lap. "Hi, Remy-the-Cat. Lochlan, are you all right?"

He shook his head and held out the phone. "I shouldn't have looked. This is her."

Still petting Remy, I leaned over so I could see Lochlan's phone. The screen was mostly filled with a picture of a little girl. Four or five years old, by my guess. Curly black hair held back from her face by a butterfly-patterned purple headband matching her purple shirt.

"That's her?" I kept my voice down without thinking about it. This was not a conversation Liam or the visitors needed to overhear.

"Yeah." He spoke barely above a whisper. "Anissa Williams. Grandmother reported her missing two days ago after her mother didn't bring her for a scheduled visit. Anissa's father's out of the picture, but his mother—the grandmother—had court-ordered visitation." He thumbed the phone screen. "It says the mother claimed Anissa was sick, but when the grandmother asked to talk to her, the mother hung up and then wouldn't answer the phone. Police are trying to track down Anissa's mother and the mother's boyfriend."

He dropped the phone on the floor. Startled, Remy bolted off my lap into his carrier, where he crouched glaring at Lochlan.

"Sorry." Lochlan blew out a breath. "Sorry, Remy."

"I'm sure Remy will forgive you." I lay down, leaning on one elbow, and reached into the carrier. Remy-the-Cat pushed his head against my hand. I looked up at Lochlan. "Lochlan, are you all right?"

"I need to be." He closed his eyes and breathed slowly for a moment. "The cats need me calm. *I* need me calm." He opened his eyes again. "I shouldn't have checked the news. I knew better. I just wanted to see if there was anything."

"Are you going to..." I didn't finish the question. Of course Lochlan wasn't going to tell the police he'd seen Anissa Williams. At best, they would think he was full of shit. At worst, if he told them Anissa was dead, they might think he had something to do with it. "Never mind."

"I thought about it." He picked up his phone. "Calling the police. But that wouldn't help anyone. I know where her spirit is. That's all. I can confirm she's gone, but I don't have any actual information. And telling them she's gone might not be a good idea."

Remy-the-Cat emerged from the carrier and went to Lochlan, who petted him. "Thanks, Remy. I'm sorry I scared you." In response, Remy took over Lochlan's lap. "I guess you do forgive me."

"I'm sorry you're dealing with this," I said, wishing I could say something that would actually help.

"Me too." He sniffed. "Nothing I can do about it. At least I have a name for her now."

"She's safe now." It was a strange thing to say about a dead child, but on the other side, especially if Austin was looking out for her, Anissa was safe from whoever had done this.

"Yeah." He hesitated. "Yeah, I think she is. Earlier, I was afraid the person who killed her might have crossed over, but—"

He broke off as the visitors, two women with glasses and tightly curled gray hair, appeared in the doorway of the room, talking animatedly about the cats. Hopefully Lochlan and I had been speaking quietly enough that they hadn't overheard us.

"Is it okay to come in?" one of them asked.

"Oh, what a beautiful cat!" The other, not waiting for an answer, came in and bent down to take a closer look at Remy-the-Cat. "I love his little nose smudge."

"This is Remy." Lochlan's tone was smooth and confident. "And yes, of course it's okay to come in. Remy's brother Bailey is around here somewhere too."

"I'll be in the main room." With a questioning look at Lochlan, I got up. He nodded. Relieved, I left the shy cat room. Four humans in there were two too many, and as much as I wanted to support Lochlan, I couldn't tolerate being in such a small space with three other people.

For a little while, I wandered around petting and playing with various cats. Finally, the woman with the laptop left, and I was able to get some quality Charlie time. Maybe because he'd been denied the woman's lap, he made his way into mine the second I sat down.

Petting him didn't quiet my thoughts as effectively as usual. Nothing could completely shut down thoughts of a little girl who had died at another's hands. Or thoughts of the man who sat in the other room and the pain he was in.

I didn't want to leave the café. Resting with a lapful of Charlie was soothing, even if I wasn't able to completely shut off my mind. And I didn't want to leave Lochlan there to deal alone with the aftermath of bringing Anissa Williams to the light.

The two older women left after helping Liam set out the cans of cat food. Liam came over to me. "I have some cleaning to do and a bit of paperwork to finish up before I leave, so feel free to stay a little longer. I don't think Charlie's ready to have you go yet."

"Thanks." I looked down at the curled-up ball of fur. "He does seem pretty content."

"I'd say so." He smiled. "I'll hold onto your adoption application until the rescue decides whether Charlie's available."

"Thanks."

"No problem."

He went out to the entryway. Through the window above his desk, I watched him start cleaning the coffee area. I wanted to go check on Lochlan, but there was no easy way to extricate myself from Charlie. I just hoped Lochlan was doing all right.

After a couple of minutes, Lochlan joined Charlie and me on the couch. He leaned back and closed his eyes. "It's been a long day."

"You've had a lot going on," I said, ignoring the urge to rest my hand on his arm. Instead, I petted Charlie, who squinted at me then returned to his snooze.

"Yeah." He lowered his voice. "Sometimes I hate what I can do. This is one of those times. I'm not doing anyone any good right now. Including myself."

"What do you need?"

He looked at me with widened eyes. "I'm not used to being asked that."

That didn't surprise me. He was the one who gave others what they needed. Like cups of coffee in a tiny shop. "Do you have an answer?"

"I need to go home." He sighed. "I can't. I'm supposed to be here until eight tonight working with the shy cats."

Liam came back in carrying the coffee urns. He stopped to study Lochlan. "Lochlan, you don't look well. Is something going on?"

"No, I'm fine." Lochlan gave him a forced-looking smile. "Tired, that's all."

"If you need to take off, don't worry about it," Liam said. "I can give Gloria a call to see if she'll come sit with the cats for a little while this evening. You could come tomorrow if you're feeling better."

I thought Lochlan would take him up on it, but he shook his head. "Thanks, but I want to be here. I'm not sick, I promise. I'll just take it easy tonight. Hang out with the couch dwellers."

Liam laughed. "Okay. I'll be here a little while longer, so just let me know if you change your mind." He continued into the back room.

"Are you sure you shouldn't go home?" I asked Lochlan, again lowering my voice.

"I can't." He scratched Charlie's head. Charlie looked up at him. Apparently deciding Lochlan and I needed privacy—or maybe realizing it was food time—he plopped himself off my lap onto the floor and headed into the back room. "I didn't mean to chase him away."

"He's hungry, probably. And he's been just lying on this couch since we got here." This time, I gave in to impulse and rested my hand on his shoulder. He leaned slightly into the touch. "Lochlan, you need to take care of yourself."

"I know." He paused. "Being here is taking care of myself. The cats help. Keeping my word helps." He looked at me, and the depth of those hazel eyes nearly pulled me under. "Not being alone helps. I live alone. If I go home, all I have are thoughts and memories. Unless another spirit shows up, which I hope doesn't happen for a few days. I need time to process this one."

"I understand. Being alone makes it tougher."

"Yeah." He studied me. "Yeah, you do get it. You live alone too."

"Since December." Reluctantly, I pulled my hand back. "Do you want me to bring you food or something?"

He shook his head. "I'll be fine. Lunch was pretty filling, and I have some snacks stashed here for the later nights. Thanks for offering, though." He leaned forward and clicked his tongue. Piper, who I hadn't noticed entering the room, ran over and jumped up on his lap. He started petting her, and she settled down, eyes closed, purring so loudly I could hear it. "Good girl, Piper."

"I guess you'll have someone looking after you." I wanted to pet Piper too but didn't want to disrupt Lochlan. I stood. "Call if you need. Or text. I'm just going home." To the empty spaces, which felt emptier now after the time with Lochlan.

"I will." He gave me a quick smile. "Take care, Del."

"You too."

I went outside to summon and wait for my rideshare. Fortunately, the wait was only a few minutes and I had a quiet driver. During the entire ride home, my thoughts were with Lochlan.

CHAPTER EIGHTEEN

For the rest of the day and most of the next, I haunted the news channels and websites for updates on Anissa Williams. I wound up wishing I hadn't. As I read the grandmother's claims against Anissa's mother and the mother's boyfriend, my imagination filled in the blanks about what the child might have gone through. It didn't help that over the years, I'd worked with a number of kids who had told me in horrific detail about similar experiences.

The police insisted it was a missing person investigation. They had no evidence indicating Anissa wouldn't be found alive, and they preferred to hold out hope that she would be. A valid hope if it hadn't been for Lochlan's encounter with the little girl—which of course the police didn't and couldn't know about.

Through the first day or so of trying to support Lochlan and seeking more information about Anissa, I lost sight of one very important piece of it all. Austin. Lochlan had seen Austin.

Lochlan had brought Austin to the light the night Austin died. The night I'd told the doctors to turn off the machines and then walked away because I couldn't bear to watch the man I loved leave me.

That realization hit me Friday afternoon as I set down my laptop to make some lunch. I was actually hungry, which wasn't a bad thing but surprised me after what I'd spent the morning reading. Then I thought about Austin, and my appetite vanished.

"I'm sorry, Austin." I spoke out loud without thinking. "I should have stayed. You shouldn't have been alone."

I wasn't expecting an answer, and none came. Not even an echo of his voice in my mind. That made it worse.

Being alone made almost everything tougher. But the night he died, did Austin even know he was alone? The doctor had said he was too far gone to be aware of anything. During the hours I sat in the waiting room, hoping for positive news even though part of me had already known how the vigil would end, Austin had, according to the doctors and nurses, shown no sign of consciousness. He'd suffered a severe head injury that had affected his brain. He might have already been gone long before anyone switched off the machines that gave his body the appearance of life.

I went to the kitchen, barely aware of taking the steps. My traitor mind had seized on the question of whether Austin was mentally present when the machines stopped and whether he had—or ever would—forgive me for not sitting with him until he took his last breath. Those questions were the only things I could focus on. I moved mechanically, bread out of the breadbasket, meat and mayo out of the fridge, a knife out of the drawer. I'd made enough sandwiches in my life that I didn't need to think about what I was doing.

I could ask Lochlan about Austin. That thought was clear. Austin might have told Lochlan about me walking away—and whether he forgave me for doing so. And while I wasn't entirely clear on how much awareness Lochlan had of what was going on in the real world while he did his 'guide to the light' gig, he might have noticed what time he'd guided Austin. That would tell me whether Austin had actually crossed over while his body was still attached to the machines.

The idea appealed. Lochlan would have the information I needed.

But asking him wouldn't be right. Not after what he'd been through the day before. I'd texted him a couple of times the previous evening to make sure he was okay. Both times, he'd simply replied with I'm fine and hadn't seemed inclined to continue a conversation. I hadn't heard from him yet today and didn't know how he was doing. I didn't want to drop my angst in his lap when he was quite likely still trying to handle his own.

I sat on the couch with my sandwich and managed to resist the urge to open my laptop and check the news sites again. I didn't need to know what was going on with Anissa Williams's case. I needed to know what was going on with Lochlan.

Just as I picked up my phone, he texted. I'm doing a little better. Want to go for a walk?

I hadn't anticipated an invitation, and I needed a few seconds to decide how to respond. I liked the idea of seeing him again so soon, but at the same time, was it okay to like that idea? And then there was my determination to ask him questions about Austin, questions I had no business asking.

I hadn't left the apartment yet today, though. I would be going to the club later, as I'd promised Remy, but that wasn't the same. Going for a walk with Lochlan would get me outside. Sure. Did you have somewhere in mind?

I like walks on the shore. Revere Beach? I can pick you up.

Even in January, Revere Beach was likely to be crowded. Walking along any beach was likely to remind me of Austin and all the times he'd tried to talk me into doing exactly that. While I'd acquiesced a handful of times as part of our excursions, I'd said no far more often than yes.

Which was all the more reason I should say yes to Lochlan. I have to be somewhere around eight tonight but any time before that is good.

Now? I'm around the corner.

I did a doubletake. I didn't know what he did for work, so maybe he had a reason to be in my neighborhood other than seeing me, but I couldn't help wondering if I was his only reason for being here. Something I could ask when he picked me up, though I wasn't entirely sure I wanted to know.

I knew I wanted to go, though. It would be better than staying here getting sucked into a mental spiral. Give me five minutes to get ready and I'll meet you out front.

I'll be there.

I hadn't touched my sandwich. I should have asked for more time. Five minutes wasn't enough to eat the whole thing. I took a couple of bites as I walked from the couch back to the kitchen, where I shoved what was left into a baggie which I stuck in the fridge. It could be tomorrow's lunch.

I put on my jacket and sneakers and headed downstairs, exiting the building just as Lochlan pulled up beside the nearest parked vehicle. I hurried over and got into his car, and he drove away as an oil truck came up behind us.

"Thanks for going with me." He glanced at me as he turned the next corner. "I need fresh air, but I didn't want to go alone."

He'd encountered Anissa while he was walking on the shore. I'd forgotten that until now. "That's understandable."

"Thanks."

He didn't seem inclined to talk, and I was fine with that. I liked silence. Neither of us said anything else until we were on Route 1A heading toward Revere.

"What I told you yesterday." Lochlan pressed his lips together. "About Austin."

"What about him?" I did not want this topic. It would only lead to me asking the questions that had come up while I made lunch. The questions I'd decided wouldn't be appropriate to ask.

"I'm sorry I didn't tell you sooner."

He couldn't have been dwelling on that all night. Could he? "I told you yesterday, you don't owe me any apology."

"You told me that because I was having a freaking breakdown about the little girl." He shuddered. "Anissa. She was a real child. She deserves to have people say her name."

"I told you that because you don't owe me an apology," I said. "You had a good reason for keeping it from me. You told me when you felt safe telling me."

"Yeah." He sighed. "You deserved to know, but it isn't something I can just blurt out to people."

We were silent again for a little while until my curiosity got the better of me. "Can I ask you something?"

I regretted it as soon as I asked and hoped Lochlan would say no. But he said, "Of course. Ask me anything."

There was no way out of it now. "You said Austin told you about me. The night he...When you helped him." I hesitated and took a long breath. "What did he say?"

Lochlan gave me an odd look. "That he loved you. He didn't want to leave you. He was worried about how you would handle it."

"Did he say..." I trailed off again, trying to figure out how to ask. Or whether to. Maybe I was better off not knowing. Except I would always wonder. "Was he angry with me?"

"Why would he be angry?" Lochlan asked. "He wasn't, Del. Not at you. I think he was angry that he had to leave you, but mostly he was sad."

"I didn't stay with him." I looked down at my hands. "They asked if I wanted to keep him on the machines. I had to decide whether to keep him alive or let him go. But they said he wouldn't really have much of a life. He was too badly injured."

"They were right." Lochlan glanced at me again. "He was on the machines while he and I were talking, Del. His body, I mean. He told me how bad the injuries were. He said he wished he had some way to let you know that it was okay to turn everything off, because he didn't want to be there like that."

"Are you telling me the truth?" He had to be. He couldn't be cruel enough to lie to me about something like this. But it sounded too good to be true. Too much like what I wanted to hear.

"I promise I am not lying to you." For just a second, Lochlan's voice seemed to echo. "I won't ever lie to you, Del. The machines were keeping his body alive, but Austin wasn't there anymore. He couldn't enter the light until they turned everything off, but he was ready to go."

"He still looked alive." I wanted to believe him, but I couldn't. I'd been in the room with Austin while he was still breathing and the heart monitor still showed a heartbeat. His eyelids had been closed, so I didn't know if I would have seen any life in those gorgeous blue eyes of his, but other things had indicated life.

"That was the machines, Del," Lochlan said gently. "The machines made it look like he was alive. That's why he couldn't enter the light."

I held up a hand, hoping he would take the hint and stop talking. I needed to process what he was saying. Austin's doctors had said they'd done everything they could but that he needed the machines to keep him alive. Maybe he would have woken up eventually, but they hadn't seemed too hopeful about that. Even if he had awakened, he would never have been who he was before the accident. He wouldn't have been able to perform. He might not have been able to walk or take care of himself.

He would have hated that. Austin loved performing. He loved being out in the world. And he was far too independent to tolerate needing someone else to take care of him. For him, living that way wouldn't have been living at all.

I'd done the right thing by telling the doctors to let him go. Walking away while Austin's life faded, though...I wasn't sure about that.

But Lochlan said Austin had come to him while the machines were still on. I'd walked away from Austin's shell, not from *him*. I couldn't stop thinking of myself as a coward for doing it, but I hadn't left him alone while he died. He was already gone. The only signs of life, if I believed Lochlan, were the signs the mechanical devices imposed.

Lochlan pulled over to the curb in front of a random triple-decker apartment building. Without a word, he rested his hand on my shoulder. That broke the dam. All these weeks, on top of losing Austin, I'd blamed myself for not staying in the room with him. More than that, I'd blamed myself for telling the doctors to turn everything off. But I hadn't done anything unforgiveable.

I cried for Austin, stuck between our world and the light until I made the choice that had to be made. And I cried with the relief of knowing I'd chosen correctly. Sobs tore painfully from my throat, and I felt like a fool sitting there bawling on the side of a Revere street, but I couldn't stop.

With gentle hands, Lochlan unfastened my seat belt and pulled me to him. A tiny traitor corner of my mind marveled at how right his arms felt around me and how wrong it was to feel so right. The rest of me neither noticed nor cared. I was crying too hard for that.

"It's all right," Lochlan murmured. "Let it out, Del. I'm here."

Words Austin would have said. *Had* said. I didn't cry often, but the few times I'd done so over the years, Austin had always been there to hold me as Lochlan was doing now. Just as I'd been there to hold Austin when he cried. It was part of caring about someone. Holding each other when the pain grew too strong to hold in alone.

Hearing those words from Lochlan only brought a stronger wave of tears. And I did as Lochlan said. Let it out. There was nothing else I could do.

CHAPTER NINETEEN

We didn't get to the beach that day. By the time my crying jag wound down, I was too exhausted to take a walk. I didn't need to tell Lochlan that. He didn't even ask if I still wanted to go. Once I quieted, he simply said, "Put your seat belt back on. I'll bring you home."

"You wanted to go to the beach." I fastened my seat belt and sat back, pushing back against the guilt that blossomed as I realized I'd spoiled Lochlan's plans. This was what I got for asking a question I never should have asked.

"I did, but I don't think you're up for it. It's okay." With a glance over his shoulder, he drove away from the curb. "It's too cold anyway."

"I'm sorry." My nose was running. Not the most attractive look.

"There are some napkins in the glove compartment." He turned a corner.

I opened the glove compartment and grabbed a napkin, which I used to wipe my eyes and nose. "I'm a mess."

"You're fine." He glanced at me. "Did you find out what you wanted to know?"

Something hard in his tone stopped me from answering. He was angry. I couldn't blame him. I'd asked a question out of the blue that I knew I shouldn't have asked. He probably felt like I'd used him. Bad enough at any time. Worse today, when he was still wading through the aftermath of helping Anissa Williams enter the light.

"I'm sorry," I said again.

"Don't be." He sighed. "I knew you would ask sooner or later. It's fine, Del."

He still spoke in that hardened voice. It wasn't fine. But I didn't apologize again. He wouldn't want to hear it, and apologizing wouldn't change the fact that I'd asked about Austin. Or that I'd broken down at the answer.

We drove back to East Boston on side roads instead of Route 1A. Traffic was beginning to pick up with the end of the school day and beginning of the afternoon rush hour. Neither of us spoke. The silence this time wasn't pleasant. Lochlan had offered friendship and needed my support, and I'd screwed it all to hell.

"I'm not mad at you," Lochlan said as we approached my street. "A little disappointed, maybe. But like I said, I knew you would ask sooner or later."

"This wasn't the time for it." I inhaled deeply and let out the breath slowly. "I'm sorry, Lochlan. That question was on my mind all day, but it wasn't the time."

He shrugged. "Yesterday wasn't really the time to tell you I brought Austin to the light, but here we are."

Despite his claim that he wasn't angry, his phrasing felt like he'd slammed the door on any further conversation. My fault, of course. I'd suspected asking about Austin would be a bad move and I'd done it anyway. And now, as Lochlan said, here we were.

At the same time, a bubble of frustration rose in me. I'd asked a simple question. Lochlan could have declined to answer. He could have said he didn't want to talk about Austin, and I would have respected it. Instead, he'd told me what I wanted to know, and now I was paying for having asked.

I took a long breath. My irritation wasn't fair to Lochlan. I was the first person he'd trusted in a while with the truth about what he could do, and I'd used the knowledge to gain information about the partner I'd lost. Of course he was unhappy with me. He'd reached out to me today because he needed someone to lean on, and instead, I'd flipped everything around to be about me.

He stopped in front of my building, blocking two parked cars and most of the street. There wasn't time for me to say much. I needed to get out of the car so he could move. But I didn't want to leave things like this between us. "Do you want to find a place to park and come inside for a little while?"

"No." He put the car in park and turned to face me. "Not this time, Del. I have a lot going through my head right now, and I can't deal with this." He motioned between us. "I'm not mad. I said I wouldn't lie to you, right? I'm not mad, but I just can't deal with you anymore today. I understand why you asked about Austin. I probably would have done the same thing. And yes, I could have refused to answer you, but that would have upset you. You put me in a no-win position. I did what seemed best for you, but it wasn't best for me. I need some space."

This time, he didn't sound upset. Only sad. I'd let him down, and there was no way to fix it.

"I'm sorry," I said again. "Thank you for telling me about Austin. And for being there for me. I'm sorry I wasn't here for you the way you needed."

"I forgive you." Again, a faint echo underlay his words. "Just please get out of the car, Del. I will talk to you soon, I promise, but I can't anymore right now."

I hesitated. I needed to say something to make this right. But he didn't want me to say anything, and putting my needs ahead of his had brought us to this point in the first place. "Whenever you're ready," I said instead and got out of the car.

I didn't watch him drive away. I couldn't cope with that. I went up to my apartment and started trying to figure out what to wear to the club.

Not that I was in the mood for an evening of drag performances now. Especially since I'd planned to invite Lochlan to go with me. But I'd promised Remy, and I wouldn't break my word to her. She deserved to have me follow through, and I didn't want to let down another friend today.

The moment I walked into the club, I was surrounded by the performers—the ones who weren't backstage painting their mugs and putting on their clothes—and a few regulars who had been friendly with Austin and me. Greeting everyone and answering their questions occupied my mind, which was a welcome distraction. The performance itself was entertaining enough, and I left the club shortly after midnight with a decent buzz both from being in public and from the free drinks the bartender had insisted on providing me all night.

Saturday, I woke up with a headache and a stomach that felt like it was doing cartwheels. The bathroom became my best friend for a few hours. I should have known better than to booze it up when I hadn't touched a drop of alcohol in months. The traitor part of my brain considered the hangover penance for hurting Lochlan, and the rest of me didn't entirely disagree. I didn't even take my walk around the block that day. I was afraid to be away from the bathroom that long.

Sunday, I felt better. Fortified with coffee and toast, I sat down with my laptop to check emails and the local news stations' websites. The emails were a bust. More junk. The websites were worth reading. Anissa Williams's body had been found the day before. Early this morning, police had tracked down Anissa's mother and the mother's boyfriend, who were now in jail awaiting arraignment for Anissa's murder.

The people responsible for Anissa's death would pay. People were already coming forward offering to pay for Anissa's funeral. And she— her spirit, at least—was safe. It wasn't a happy ending by any stretch, but it was the best anyone could hope for.

I wondered whether Lochlan had heard. I picked up my phone to text him but immediately put it down again. He'd asked for space. I'd told him to get in touch when he was ready. Since I hadn't heard from him yet, clearly he wasn't ready. I didn't want to push.

I looked around the room. Once again, its emptiness overwhelmed me. Finding out what Austin had said to Lochlan had only emphasized his absence, and his wasn't the only absence I felt now. Even though I'd only known Lochlan a few weeks, I'd come to think of him as part of my life. It was stupid, and it was probably wrong given how short a time had passed since Austin's death, but Lochlan fit into an empty space I hadn't realized existed. He wasn't a replacement for Austin, nor was he a partner or lover. He was just someone who belonged in my life, and I hadn't known it until he was there.

No. That wasn't right. I hadn't known he belonged in my life until he *wasn't* there anymore.

I didn't reach out to him on Sunday. Or Monday or Tuesday. On Wednesday, Remy came over for lunch and reminiscing, and I tried to stay present with her even though my mind was stuck on blond-streaked black hair above a pair of hazel eyes.

She noticed, of course. "Where are you today? Is this too much?" She motioned at the photo album she'd brought, which was open on her lap. The pictures were a twenty-year timeline of Austin's drag career.

"It isn't too much," I said. "It's perfect. Thank you for bringing it."

"You're welcome." She closed the album, with her finger in the page we'd been looking at, and looked at me. "So what's wrong? I've seen you grieving. This isn't the same."

"No. It isn't." I was still grieving, of course, but she was right. This wasn't that.

"Tell me." She moved the album to the coffee table and crossed her legs, slightly turned to face me. "Cat guy?"

I should have known she would guess my mood had something to do with Lochlan. Still, I was reluctant to admit it. Feeling the way I felt about him seemed disloyal to Austin. I was afraid Remy would see it that way too.

I wouldn't lie to her, though. Not to Austin's best friend/sister, who had become my best friend. I wouldn't have gotten through the past several weeks without her. At the very minimum, I owed her honesty.

"Yes, cat guy. His name is Lochlan."

She smirked. "I know. I just like calling him cat guy. What's going on with him?"

"We had a...dispute, I guess you could say. I haven't heard from him in a few days." I really hoped she didn't ask what the dispute was about. Honesty or not, I couldn't give away Lochlan's secret.

Fortunately, she didn't ask. "Have you tried getting in touch with him? Or are you just sitting around waiting for your phone to ping?"

"He said he needed space. I told him to reach out when he was ready." I leaned back and pulled my phone out of my pocket. Naturally the only texts were from Remy. "Apparently he isn't ready yet. I said something really stupid to him, Rem, and I don't blame him for being pissed. I apologized, but apologies don't make everything go away."

"They sure as hell don't." A fleeting hardness crossed her expression. She'd heard too many half-assed apologies from people who had hurt her and those she cared about. Mostly parents of people who, unlike Remy's family, had thrown away their children like trash for not being straight cisgender humans.

She took a deep breath. "Sorry. Hot button topic, as you know. I'm assuming you didn't say anything completely heinous to Lochlan."

"I asked him something I had no business asking." I paused, weighing my words to make sure I wouldn't give away too much about Lochlan. "He answered, and it set me off. Not because of what he said, but it reminded me of Austin. He was kind while I was trying to pull myself together, but once I calmed down, he said he was disappointed that I'd asked the question, and he wanted some space from me."

"Oof." She patted my knee. "That sounds like it was tough for both of you. And now you don't know where you stand with him because you haven't heard from him."

"Exactly."

"And you aren't sure why it matters."

I stared at her. "Yeah."

She chuckled. "It was the look on your face, Del. Plus I've been in that position. Someone I cared about who I didn't think I *should* care about, so when they stopped talking to me, part of me wanted to be glad. At least I didn't have to worry about whether I was doing something wrong by being interested in them. You aren't doing anything wrong."

"I'm not interested in him," I said quickly.

That only made her laugh again. "Methinks thou dost protesteth too much, or however that line goes."

"I'm not." I gritted my teeth. "How the hell could I be, Rem? Austin hasn't even been gone two months yet."

"Hearts can't tell time." She sobered. "Interest doesn't mean you're about to propose. Or jump into bed. It just means he's someone you care about and want in your life. It isn't betraying Austin. If it's a betrayal of anyone, it's of yourself, judging from how opposed you are to feeling that way. When my Aunt Jana passed, Uncle Lloyd remarried two months later." She caught her tongue between her teeth. "Then again, they were in their seventies. And Uncle Lloyd was dating the woman before Jana passed. Not cheating. She told him to go ahead and be happy once she got too sick to do much besides sleep."

"Whatever works, I guess. Completely not the same thing, Remy."

"The point is, grief and love are not mutually exclusive," she said impatiently. "You can grieve Austin and still be in love with him, while loving—or being interested in, or caring about, or however you want to put it—someone else. Feelings happen. Isn't that one of those counselor-y things you're always saying?"

I snorted. "Yeah. I'm all about the counselor-y things." She was right, though. I'd learned, and had always taught my students, that emotions were things that happened whether we wanted them to or not. How we handled those emotions might be within our control, but the emotions themselves were simply there.

"How do you feel about Lochlan?" She leaned toward me. "Be honest."

"I don't want to, Rem." Despite my resolve, I couldn't be honest with her about this. Not when I was so unable to be honest with myself that I didn't even know the true answer. "He's a nice guy. We've hung out a couple-few times, and I like spending time with him. I don't know if that will happen again. I'm in a holding pattern until I hear from him."

"You'll see him tomorrow, won't you? At the cat café?"

"Yeah." I'd been trying not to think about that. If Lochlan was still unwilling to talk to me, being at the café with him would be awkward. I'd considered not going, but that wouldn't have been fair to Liam or the cats, and I was looking forward to seeing Charlie again.

"Maybe that will give you and him a chance to sort things out," Remy said.

"Maybe."

"I hope it works out. You need more people in your life, Del. Friends or otherwise."

"Friends," I said firmly. "That's all I'm looking to have in my life right now."

"Then don't let yourself lose this one," she retorted. "Talk to him."

I didn't respond. She made it sound so easy, but I had told Lochlan to get in touch when he was ready. If I contacted him, I wouldn't be respecting his need for space.

If I didn't at least try to talk to him at the café, the afternoon would be far less pleasant than an afternoon with cats should be.

CHAPTER TWENTY

Thursday afternoon, I took a rideshare to the cat café after debating all morning about whether to cancel. Fair or not, I wasn't sure I could handle being at the café with Lochlan if he still wasn't speaking to me.

As it turned out, I had no reason to be concerned. Lochlan wasn't at the café that day. According to Liam, Lochlan had come down with something and didn't want to expose any humans or cats to it. I had to wonder whether that was true. Lochlan didn't strike me as someone who would make false excuses, but if he was invested in avoiding me, maybe he would.

That was placing myself pretty damn high in importance, though, and I had no justification for it. Lochlan was an honest person. He wouldn't suddenly decide to be dishonest simply to avoid me. It was winter, after all. Plenty of illnesses going around.

Being in the café without Lochlan felt odd. Not exactly empty. That sense was reserved for my apartment in Austin's absence. Here at the café, I wasn't alone. Liam bustled about talking to the visitors, and we had several visitors. But something was definitely missing. I sat on the couch with Charlie the Sweater Cat on my lap, but my sweater-clad little friend didn't bring me the peace he usually did.

About halfway through the afternoon, Liam came over and sat next to Charlie and me. "We're going to be keeping Charlie a while longer. He needs a special diet and some medical treatment. We're hoping he'll be ready to go home with someone in a month or so."

"I'm glad he's getting the treatment he needs." I stroked Charlie's head. He lifted his head and blinked at me a few times, then settled down again. "He's a good cat."

"He is. We're not happy about why he has to stay, but we do like having him around." Liam reached over and scratched between Charlie's ears. "I just wanted to let you know since you applied to adopt him. If you want to bring someone home sooner, we can talk about one of the other cats."

"I think I'd like to wait for Charlie." I liked the other cats. But Charlie was the one I'd bonded with the most. He was the one who felt like he would belong with me.

Liam nodded. "I thought you might say that. I think Charlie feels the same way. He comes right to you every time you're here."

"Unless someone else is already giving him attention."

Liam grinned. "Well, sure. He does love attention. But he definitely likes you. I'll let the rescue know you're still interested when he's ready to leave."

"Thank you."

Across the room, one of the visitors jumped as Piper loudly hissed at Ice. Liam hurried over to break up whatever spat was going on between the two cats.

I petted Charlie again. "Get better soon, buddy. Then you can come hang out on my couch."

He blinked lazily at me, this time without raising his head, and purred. Apparently he was in favor of that plan.

I left the café that afternoon in a slightly better mood than the one in which I'd arrived. Something was still missing, though. In the back seat of the rideshare on the way home, I fidgeted with my phone, debating whether to text Lochlan. Just to find out if he was all right, of course. I could tell him Liam had said he was sick. That would be a reasonable excuse for contacting him.

Something held me back, though. If he wanted to talk to me, he would. It wasn't up to him to fill my need for contact. My empty spaces weren't his problem. He wanted space, and I needed to respect that even if it was unpleasant for me. This wasn't about me. It might have been *because* of me, because I'd asked him about Austin, but it wasn't *about* me.

It was about how people had treated Lochlan most of his life when they found out what he could do. It was about him trusting me with his secrets, and me using that knowledge for my own benefit. It was about his need for support and comfort after bringing a four-year-old child to the light, and the fact that instead of helping him hold himself together, I'd fallen apart.

He would reach out if he wanted to talk to me. Unless he did, the least I could do was leave him alone.

Days passed. I took my walks outside, even on a few days when the wind chill made being outside unpleasant at best. I visited the club again and was invited backstage to hang out with Remy and the others, those who had become Austin's family and were willing to be mine if I let them. I'd decided I wanted to let them. I liked having time alone, but I couldn't keep completely shutting out the world. I needed to exist again.

Remy came over a couple of times to help with the last of Austin's belongings that I didn't want to keep. We cleaned out some of my things as well, clothes I hadn't worn in months or years, items I'd forgotten I even owned. I'd mostly let go of the idea of moving, even though keeping an apartment in East Boston would stretch my finances to the breaking point. Leaving the place would mean leaving Austin, and despite the emptiness left by Austin's absence, I wasn't willing to let go of our life together. The apartment was that life.

When I went to the cat café the second time after the issue with Lochlan, Liam informed me that Lochlan had changed his schedule. Liam gave me no reason or details, and I didn't ask. I just kept reminding myself that if and when Lochlan wanted to speak to me, if and when he decided his life was any of my business, he would reach out.

As more time went by, though, I convinced myself he never would reach out. He'd promised he would talk to me "soon," whatever that meant, and he didn't strike me as the type to break a promise. Even so,

I no longer anticipated his keeping this one. I didn't think what I'd done was heinous enough to warrant a complete cutting of ties, but that wasn't my call. I'd hurt him, and how he felt and what he chose to do about it were valid. I wished I could apologize, sort things out, at least gain some closure, but that would only happen if and when Lochlan decided he was ready.

February moved toward March with fluctuating temperatures that kept me indoors with a headache while I tried to stay warm. I spent the time curled up with a book and an often-refilled cup of herbal tea. I didn't mind not leaving the apartment. The only thing I didn't enjoy was missing out on that week's visit to the cat café.

At the end of the month, Charlie the Sweater Cat was cleared for adoption. I brought him home two days after the rescue approved me as his new human. Adjusting to having another living being in the place took some doing, especially as Charlie, in his determination to explore his new surroundings, developed the habit of walking directly where I intended to put my feet as I walked. After a few near misses and one unfortunate encounter between his head and my shin, we got the hang of navigating around each other.

Even during those first few days, though, having Charlie around was nice. His presence didn't replace anything, but it filled a few empty spaces, and taking care of him and making sure he got his medications and food gave me a sense of purpose I sorely needed.

Around the same time, in response to a nudge from my principal, I applied to extend my leave of absence through the summer. The counselor they'd brought in to cover for me had formed a connection with the students who most needed it, and it didn't seem fair to cause more upheaval for them during the current school year. And I wanted more time. Time to continue adjusting to Charlie and monitoring his health. Time to figure out who I was when I wasn't half of Del-and-Austin.

Time to take the trip Austin had planned. At first, going to Prince Edward Island alone had seemed like a bad idea. The trip would have been Austin's gift to me, and going without him would only remind me that he was no longer around. But as the days and weeks moved me further from the moment of losing him, I stopped seeing the trip as emphasizing his absence. Rather, it became a symbol of his presence.

Something he'd wanted to do because he loved me. Because even if he didn't understand *why* a forty-something-year-old man gave a damn about Anne of Green Gables, he understood that I did, and he had wanted to share it with me. I booked the trip for the middle of May.

Taking advantage of the free time I'd granted myself by extending my leave, I added a second volunteer gig to my roster. The teens who frequented Casilla's Closet needed adults who supported them, and the people who ran the organization were happy to have a volunteer with a background and degree in counseling.

After the first couple of days working with the kids there, I started contemplating a career change. Not away from counseling, but away from the constraints of public schools. Organizations like the Closet took volunteers, but they also sometimes had paid positions. And seeing these kids, what they went through just to be themselves, reminded me of the teenage Del Nethercott trying to find his way in a world that had made its disapproval far too clear. I wanted to help kids like the one I'd been.

That was a decision I chose to table for a while, though. It was barely March. I could wait a few more months to decide for sure whether I would return to the high school in September.

By this point, I'd stopped constantly thinking about Lochlan. Periodically, he crossed my mind, but not on a daily basis anymore. I accepted that he'd chosen to end our friendship, even though I wished I could have said something to change that choice, and it didn't make sense to keep thinking about him.

With Anissa's death all over the news again, maybe I shouldn't have been surprised on the afternoon of the third Friday of March, shortly after lunchtime, when Lochlan texted. Del, it's Lochlan. I'd like to talk.

Sitting on the couch, my lap occupied as usual by Charlie the Sweater Cat—in a cute new pastel-striped sweater the volunteer who knitted had given me for him the day before—I stared at the phone. I wanted to demand to know what Lochlan thought we had to talk about after a month and a half of silence. I wanted to lie and say he had the wrong number.

I wanted to see him. Talk to him. Make things right.

That last impulse won. Okay. Long time no hear.

Yeah. I'm sorry. Can we please meet?

Reading his apology, I felt my anger ebbing. I'm sorry too. Coffee shop one hour?

I'll be there.

I set down the phone and petted Charlie. "I have to go out, buddy. I'm seeing your old friend Lochlan. Any message I should give him from you?" Charlie purred. "Duly noted."

I waited a little while before extricating myself from Charlie. I wasn't entirely certain meeting up with Lochlan was wise. I missed him, but sometimes missing someone was for the best.

He'd reached out, though. Whatever his reason might have been, he had decided it was time to reconnect. I could at least give him some of my time. And the apology I'd been sitting on for the past two months. Maybe it would end up with a permanent cutting of ties, but at least I would know for sure.

CHAPTER TWENTY-ONE

I walked out of my apartment into the crisp March air. The chill cut through my jacket more than was typical for this time of year, but a hint of spring hung in the air nonetheless. As I headed down the street, I texted Remy. You'll never guess who I heard from.

Cat guy? she replied almost immediately.

What are you, psychic?

Nah. Just been hoping. What did he say?

I dodged around a dog walker and the five canines whose leashes he was desperately trying to keep untangled. He wants to talk. We're meeting up in a few minutes.

Let me know how it goes. Bring him tonight if it works out.

I will.

I put the phone back in my jacket pocket and kept my hands in my pockets. It was a little too chilly for bare hands, but I'd forgotten my gloves after a few days of not needing them. I nodded to a few neighbors I recognized along the way, and reached the coffee shop in time to see Lochlan walking toward me from the opposite direction. He looked thinner. Haggard was the word that came to mind. Stubble marked his chin and upper lip, and his hair was only black now, no blond streaks. He looked older. Still attractive. Still Lochlan. But something had changed in him.

He walked up to me, a tentative smile playing around his lips. "Hi."

"Hi." I smiled back. "It's good to see you. How have you been?"

"Can we not with the small talk, please?" He pressed his lips together. "I'm sorry, Del. It's been a long week. I just... I haven't talked to you in weeks, and I don't want to waste time on how are you, nice weather we're having."

"I'm fine with that. I never liked small talk." I held out my hand. Looking surprised, he shook it. "I'm glad you texted. Let's go inside. It's too cold to talk out here."

He nodded and followed me into the coffee shop. We ordered our drinks and sat at the one unoccupied table, where Lochlan sat looking toward the counter. Without saying anything. And we stayed like that until our drinks were ready.

I went to the counter and got the cups. When I returned to the table, I said, "You wanted to talk. I'd like to hear whatever you want to say." I put his cup in front of him and sat down. "But I can't just be here watching you not say anything."

"Yeah." He picked up his cup and held it in both hands as he blew out a breath. "I missed you. God, that sounds weak. But I did."

"I've been here." I took a sip of my coffee. As impatient as I felt, I wouldn't push him. I needed to let him say what he wanted to say, even if it took him longer than I would have liked.

"I wanted to reach out sooner. I kept talking myself out of it." He put down his cup and leaned on his elbows. "The last time I saw you was hard for me. I knew you would ask about Austin sooner or later, but I hoped you wouldn't. I didn't realize how much it would hurt when you did. It was..." He held up a hand. "I know this wasn't what you were thinking, but when you asked about Austin, I felt like you were only using me to stay connected to him."

"I'm sorry," I said. "I shouldn't have asked you about him. You told me you helped him, and I wanted to know. But I didn't *need* to know."

"You did need to know, though." He tapped the rim of his cup. "That's one of the things I wanted to talk about. I've helped people to the light since I was five years old. I thought about them and what they needed. I never really thought about the people they left behind. You did need to hear what Austin said before he entered the light, and I was the only one who could tell you."

"We were friends." I gestured at him. "You and I, I mean. I wasn't thinking of it as taking advantage, but it was. I took advantage of the fact that I was talking to the last person Austin said anything to. I knew how it might seem when I asked, but I asked anyway. I'm sorry for hurting you."

He looked surprised. "Thank you."

"You're welcome."

We each picked up our coffee and sipped at the same time. I couldn't help laughing at that. Lochlan grinned as he returned his cup to the table. "I guess we're on the same wavelength. Anyway, yes, it did hurt. I got over it pretty quickly, but then, like I said, I kept talking myself out of contacting you. I knew you hadn't intended it as using me, but what if I was wrong? So I kept not reaching out."

"What changed today?" I asked.

He bit his lip. "The trial is bringing up a lot. You know the one I mean."

"Yeah." The trial of Anissa Williams's mother and her boyfriend had started a few days earlier. Coverage of it was all over the news.

"You were there for me the day I brought her to the light." He folded his hands on the table. "You supported me. Hearing about the trial all over the place brought back how I felt when I guided her, but also how I felt when you were there. You were still stuck in your own grief, and you were kind of pissed at me for a minute or two when I told you I'd guided Austin, but you still wanted to help me. That's the kind of person you are. Kind." He made a face. "I'm not doing so well with the word thing. You're compassionate, and even though you were struggling the times we were together, you were also someone I wanted to be around. I reached out today because I realized I'd still like to be around you. And I'm sorry it took me so long."

"I'm glad. I missed you too." It was true. Even when a few days at a time had passed with no thoughts of him, he always came back to my mind. And I always wished he would come back to my life, even when I'd given up hope that he actually would.

"Friends?" He extended his hand across the table.

I clasped it. "Friends." I paused. I had to be out of my mind to think what I was thinking. The club was Austin. Drag was Austin. There was no way I could bring Lochlan to a show. But I wanted him there. "Hey, what do you think about drag queens?"

Looking confused, he shrugged. "They look amazing, and I can't even comprehend how they manage all that makeup. Not to mention the shoes."

"Come with me to the show tonight. The club Austin used to perform at."

His eyes widened. "You'd be okay with that? And his friends?"

"Remy—the human, obviously—tried to get me to bring you a couple of months ago." I paused again. "The day I screwed things up with you, I was supposed to ask if you wanted to go with me to the club that night."

"Maybe it's better you didn't. It gave you time to be okay with bringing me there." He grimaced. "I sound like a therapist."

I laughed. "One of us has to, I guess. Anyway, show's at eight. You can meet me there." I looked at my watch. It was only two o'clock. Sitting in the coffee shop for a few hours wouldn't be possible, but I didn't want to let Lochlan leave. Two months had passed. We had things to catch up on and to settle. "Or you can come to my place until it's time to go and save me a rideshare."

I hoped he would laugh at that. Instead he looked a little too serious. "Your place?"

"Yes. My place. The place where I live." Though he didn't say it, I had a pretty good idea of what he was thinking. "I'm okay with you being there, Lochlan. And there's someone else there who might be happy to see you."

"Charlie." His face lit up, and his expression relaxed. "Liam said you adopted him. I'd love to see Charlie if you're sure. I've missed hanging out with him at the café."

"I'm sure." To my surprise, I was. The apartment was where Austin and I had built our life. It was and always would be the place that reminded me most of him. But time had passed, and the apartment no longer seemed the sacred shrine I'd tried to create during the first couple of months after Austin's death. It was the place where he and I had built a life together. Now it could be a place I built my own life.

Even so, a little while later as I unlocked the apartment door, a pang of guilt stabbed my heart. This was the first time someone with no connection to Austin had visited the apartment. I wasn't sure Austin would like that.

Except Lochlan did have a connection with him. Austin had gone to Lochlan for help in entering the light. Lochlan was the last living human Austin had spoken to. I didn't fully understand how Austin had found Lochlan that night, why he'd chosen to ask Lochlan for guidance, but there was a connection there.

We went inside. From his spot on a folded fleece blanket on the couch, Charlie the Sweater Cat looked up and meowed.

Lochlan let out sound partway between chuckle and gasp. "I've never heard him meow before."

"Neither have I. Maybe he recognizes you." I gently nudged him inside. "Go say hi."

He sat down and started petting Charlie. I closed the door and went to the kitchen. "Do you want anything to drink? Or some food?"

"Water, please."

I brought him a bottle of water and sat on the other side of Charlie. Charlie appeared quite content to see his friend again, and Lochlan had relaxed. He belonged here. Weeks had passed since the last time I'd seen him, but it no longer felt like any time had gone by at all. And although this was the first time he'd been in my apartment, having him here felt right.

"He looks good," Lochlan said. "You're obviously taking good care of him. I mean, of course you are."

His discomfort bothered me. I wanted him to feel the way I did, that he was meant to be here. "He's easy to take care of. I'm a little worried about what happens when I go back to work, but that won't be for several months yet. I decided to stay on leave until next school year."

"That's good for Charlie." Still stroking Charlie's head, he leaned back with a contented smile. "What are you going to do with your time besides being a cat servant?"

"Mostly just get used to living my life again." I crossed one leg over the other. "You might have noticed I wasn't exactly doing that before."

"You'd only been without Austin for a few weeks when I met you."

"Yeah, and I'd never stopped to think there might be a time when I wouldn't have him." I considered that. "Well, okay, I'd thought about it, but I figured I would be in my eighties and have dementia or something so I wouldn't know he was gone. You never really think about losing someone to anything other than old age. Or at least I never did."

"I always have, but that's because I'm the one who takes them to the light." He frowned. "The neighbor boy. Anissa Williams. There have been others over the years. None like Anissa, thankfully, but other kids. And of course there have been plenty of adults who were young. It's hard not to be aware that someone could die at any moment when you see it happening all the time."

He spoke in a near-monotone, but pain permeated the words. He'd seen too much loss in his life, even though most of the spirits he'd guided were complete strangers.

"I wasn't thinking," I said quietly. "About how difficult it is for you."

"I wouldn't expect you to. It isn't something most people can understand." He gave me a quick smile. "I'm not upset, Del. Honestly, it's nice to be able to talk to you about this. As long as it isn't too much for you."

"Nothing you say is too much." I probably shouldn't have claimed that. I had no way of knowing what he might choose to say. But I wanted to be a safe person for him to talk to, and that required me not to place limits on what he told me.

"You might regret that." He scoffed. "Your name came up again."

"Huh?" I turned to face him. "What do you mean?"

"Last week I brought a teenage girl to the light." He bit his lower lip. "She said her name was Admire."

"Oh, no." My heart sank. Admire was a beautiful Latinx trans girl who'd come to the Closet a couple of times when I first started volunteering there. She'd been ejected from her home by an extremely Catholic grandmother who considered being transgender to be an "abomination." Something too many kids heard from the family members who were supposed to love them.

Admire had been on the streets for a couple of months by the time she first visited the Closet, and she'd refused to talk about the things she did to keep herself fed and warm during that time. We gave her clothing and vouchers for food, along with the phone number of a shelter for LGBTQ+ teens.

She'd told me she wanted to die. That she couldn't live with knowing her *abuela* hated her or with the things she'd done after leaving home. I listened, tried to help her. Gave her contact information for a couple of therapists I knew, including one who specialized in working with LGBTQ+ teens who didn't have stable homes or families. She promised to make the calls, but I didn't know if she had. That was the last time she showed up.

Obviously she hadn't gotten what she needed.

"I'm sorry," Lochlan said softly. "She took her own life. She said she wished she hadn't, but when she did it, she didn't know what else to do. She said people at Casilla's Closet tried to help her, but that she couldn't accept the help because she didn't feel like she deserved it." His voice lowered, and sympathy filled his eyes. "She said you were the one who helped her the most. I told her I knew you, and she asked me to say thank you and that she's sorry she couldn't try harder."

I swallowed hard and closed my eyes to push back tears. Admire had deserved better than the life she'd had or the ending she'd given herself.

"Did anyone meet her?" I asked, my voice thick.

"She said her *abuelo* was there. And that he was calling her '*mi niña.*' She seemed very happy about that."

"Good." At least one member of Admire's family had accepted her as her true self. I just hated that it had taken her death for that to happen.

"Are you all right?" He reached over Charlie and rested his hand on my arm.

"Yeah." I swallowed again. "I didn't know her very well. I met her a couple of times a month or so ago. But I was hoping she would make it."

"You made an impression on her," he said. "She wanted to make sure you knew that you did help, even though she ended up making this choice."

Realization struck me, and I pulled my arm away from him. "Is that the real reason you texted this morning? Because Admire asked you to?"

"No." He sighed. "And yes. It's a reason. But not *the* reason. It was the motivation to finally get over myself and contact you after all this time, but I didn't do it because she wanted me to. It was because *I* wanted to. I wasn't lying when I said I missed you."

"You said you would never lie to me." I was reminding myself. "I believe you. But are you saying you would have gone on not reaching out if you hadn't encountered Admire?"

He quirked his lips. "I'd like to think eventually I would have gotten some sense in my head, but I can't deal in what ifs, Del."

"Fair enough." I took a long breath. "Thank you for telling me. I wish things had worked out differently for Admire, but at least at the end, she had someone kind to help her."

"And her grandfather accepted her," he said. "I think that was pretty big for her. She lit up when she told me."

"Being accepted is huge." *For anyone.*

The look Lochlan gave me said he heard the words I didn't speak. "Yes, it is."

We sat without speaking for a moment. For me, it was partly to honor Admire. In death, she more than deserved the recognition she hadn't received in life. I had a feeling Lochlan intended the silence to honor her as well.

But my not speaking was also because I needed to process what Lochlan had told me. Admire's death and her mentioning me as the one who had helped her the most. I'd only done what I did for any kid who came to me for support. For Admire, it wasn't enough. If it had been, she would have chosen to continue to live. It had, however, made an impression on her.

"How are you doing?" Lochlan asked.

"I'm okay." I took a breath. "Thank you for telling me. Did she..." I hated the next question. "Do you know if someone took care of the, um, remains?"

"Her grandmother." He scowled. "She made the arrangements under Admire's deadname, of course."

"Of course." Anger rose in me but faded quickly. It was horrible that Admire would be remembered by her deadname, but there was nothing I could do about it.

Nothing except memorializing her under the name that was truly hers. "We should do something for her at the Closet. I'll talk to them about it when I'm there on Monday."

"I think she'd like that." Lochlan touched my hand. "This is what I meant. You care about others. It's something I don't see enough of. I like it."

My face grew warm, and I looked away. I wasn't sure if I was reacting to the compliment or his touch. Both were affecting me in a way I hadn't experienced since Austin. I was far from prepared to have that kind of reaction to Lochlan. "It's hard not to care about kids like Admire. They don't deserve the shit they've gotten in their lives."

"They don't, but too many people think otherwise." Lochlan took his hand away. "Del, did I mess something up?"

"No." I shook my head, but I still couldn't quite bring myself to look at him. "It's only been a few months since I lost Austin. I can't... Fuck, I can't even figure out what I'm trying to say. I like having you here. If things were different, if I'd had more time to grieve...Too many ifs."

"I think I get it." He moved toward the end of the couch, still close enough to Charlie to pet him, but far enough not to touch me. "If more time had passed since losing Austin, there might be something between us."

"Yes." My emotions wavered between relief that Lochlan had filled in what I couldn't say and irritation with myself for not saying it. "There *is* something between us. Friendship, the same as before. I can't handle more than that. Not yet."

"I get it," he said again. "Friendship is all I'm asking for, Del. Nothing more than you're able to offer. Grief doesn't just let go of you because you want it to, and neither does love. You're still grieving Austin and you're still in love with him. I would never ask anyone to ignore those feelings. Or to rush through them."

"Thank you." I looked at him. In his eyes, I saw only compassion and understanding. "Tell me what's been going on with you. It looks like you've been having a hard time." I paused. "This isn't small talk. I actually want to know."

He gave me a thin smile. "I know you do. Long story short, I've had to bring more people than usual to the light. Illnesses, accidents." He closed his eyes for a moment. "Murders. It's been a long winter." He turned his gaze back to me. "And I was foolish enough to cut off the one person I could have turned to for support."

My heart ached for him. All the times I'd considered reaching out and chosen not to because he was the one who'd asked for space flashed through my mind. He'd needed me, and I hadn't been there. But I was here now, and maybe it was better that I hadn't been previously. I'd had time to process and work through enough of my grief and pain to be actually available to help someone else. "I'm always here for you."

"I know." He clenched his fists and released them with a long exhale. "I'll tell you about some of them, but not now. Right now, I'd really like to pet Charlie and just kind of *be*, if that makes sense."

"It makes perfect sense." I motioned to his bottle of water. "Hydrate. Let me know if you want food. I'm actually keeping up with my grocery shopping now."

He let out a small laugh and picked up his water. "Congratulations. I don't need anything else right now. I just want to be here."

I nodded. "Then I'll be here with you."

CHAPTER TWENTY-TWO

Monday morning, I emailed the director of Casilla's Closet to inform her of Admire's death. She filled in the staff and other volunteers, and that afternoon, she and I sat down with some of the kids to break the news to them. Unsurprisingly, most of them had already heard through whatever networks existed in their world.

We discussed ways in which we might honor Admire's memory and decided as a group to paint a mural in the corner of the "shop" where we kept the donated shoes and boots. Admire had been, as one of the other girls put it, a "shoe whore," and the group agreed that having the shoe area become "Admire's Corner" would have pleased her.

I also listened to four of the kids privately tell me that they'd considered the same action Admire had taken. Two of them admitted to actively planning their suicides. I was able to persuade all four of them to speak to therapists from my resource list, and one of them, at his own request, was admitted to the hospital that afternoon. I couldn't change the prejudice and rejection they dealt with in their lives, but at least for now, for those four, I'd been able to ensure they kept living.

I told Lochlan about it, to the extent I was able without violating confidentiality, when we met for coffee Tuesday afternoon. "You're doing your work so I don't have to do mine," he said. "I guide them to the light when they pass. You guide them to find light while they're still living."

It was, as Anne of Green Gables might have said, a "poetical" way to phrase it, but as I pondered his words, I realized he was right. We were both guides of a sort. And while I'd done similar work as a high school counselor, after hearing about Admire and working with the kids at the Closet in the wake of her death, more and more I realized that was the kind of work I needed to do. Not sitting in a former closet at a rundown urban high school listening to some kids whose lives were fifty shades of hell followed by other kids who hated their parents for buying them the wrong iPhone, but being at an agency or organization that existed specifically for LGBTQ+ kids. I needed to be with the kids who actually needed me.

Over the next few days, I started putting things in motion. I sent my resume to a few agencies in the area whose caseloads either included or consisted solely of LGBTQIA teenagers. I agonized over how to phrase my letter of resignation to the high school, since only a couple of weeks had passed since I assured my principal I would return in September. I felt ungrateful for resigning after the school had bent over backward to accommodate my need to grieve, but it was the right thing for me to do.

With Austin, I'd seen how suddenly a life could end. I needed to start doing what was right for me, within reason of course, while I still had a life to live.

That included spending more time with Remy and the others from the club, especially Solara and Mitch. Mitch was growing on me, though as Remy put it, sometimes that growth was more like a tumor. He'd lived through things that might have killed someone weaker. When I genuinely talked with him, I recognized in him many of the qualities I saw in the kids at the Closet. Although he was doing well at the club, Mitch, with his substance use issues and severe trauma, had become what some of the kids might be without the support and help they deserved.

Yet despite not having had the help he needed, Mitch was the star of the show in his Starry Daye persona. He had friends. Family; he and Solara both considered her his mother, in the real sense as well as the drag sense. And during the dark days of February, while I'd been rebuilding myself in Lochlan's absence, Mitch had found someone to love, a guitarist named Hunter who had joined the show at the club. Around the time Lochlan and I reconnected, Mitch was released from a month in rehab, and he was happier and healthier than I'd ever seen him.

Doing what was right for me also included spending time with Lochlan. He resumed volunteering on Thursdays at the cat café, partly because his schedule worked best for him that way and partly, as he told me privately, so he could see me without either of us feeling any pressure. Being around the cats was good for both of us, and the furry little beasts gave us something to focus on and talk about.

We had times alone together as well, though. Tuesdays and Fridays became our standing coffee dates, though naturally neither of us referred to them as dates. Sometimes we simply sat at the coffee shop until we finished our drinks, then parted ways. Other times, Lochlan came back to the apartment with me, ostensibly to hang out with Charlie. During those visits, while he sat on the couch beside the Sweater Cat, we began to build something. We called it friendship, with a heaping helping of sharing our life stories. But I felt the potential for more. And I began to see the possibility that someday, "more" might be exactly what I wanted.

April launched with weather that would have been more expected in June. Lochlan and I started taking longer walks after our coffee meetups. I couldn't quite bring myself to take him to Piers Park, but we wandered around Jeffries Point and the Maverick Square area. The walks gave us time to talk without feeling awkward about being alone together.

That lasted until Mother Nature played an early April joke on us by throwing a blizzard at the area. It hit on a Tuesday when Lochlan was visiting Charlie and me. He'd intended to leave before the storm got bad, but as it turned out, there was no "before." The storm arrived full force, with such heavy snowfall I could barely see the building across the street and wind wailing between the houses.

"Shit." Lochlan stood, much to Charlie's dismay. "I need to go."

"You aren't going anywhere." I motioned for him to join me at the window. "You might get there okay, but I wouldn't count on it." My voice caught. "And I'd rather not have you risk it."

"I'll stay," he said quickly. "What about my car?"

"We aren't on a major street. You might get plowed in, but you won't get towed." Though depending on how much snow we got, leaving his car on the street might not be the best idea. "I can check with one of the neighbors to find out if there's a lot where we can put your car if you'd rather. Other people are parked out here, though, so you should be fine."

He leaned closer to the window. "Yeah, I think staying put might be the better idea." He turned to me. "Are you sure? We'll be stuck together at least overnight. Maybe longer depending on how bad this storm gets."

He spoke in a lilting tone. I decided to play along. "That would be terrible. You might get sick of petting Charlie. Or of my cooking."

"You might get tired of having me here. Have I mentioned I snore?" He sobered. "I'll sleep on the couch."

"In that case, I probably won't hear you snoring." I paused. The couch wasn't comfortable for sleeping unless one was a cat. It didn't seem quite fair to Lochlan to make him sleep there. But the only other place he could sleep was the bed. The one I'd shared with Austin. I'd gotten used to Lochlan coming to the apartment, but I wasn't even close to ready to let him sleep in the bed.

"Del." He rested his hand on my shoulder. "I'll sleep on the couch. It's fine. Charlie will keep me company."

"Yeah." Charlie usually sacked out on Austin's pillow when I went to bed, but maybe he would stay with Lochlan.

"I can still probably get home if I leave now." Lochlan looked out the window again. "Or find a hotel or something. We're near the airport. There must be hotels. I grew up around here, Del. I do know how to drive in this kind of weather."

"You aren't going out in this." My chest tightened. The snow appeared to be falling even harder. I was not letting Lochlan drive in this. Maybe he would be fine, but his ability to drive in a storm didn't account for whether other drivers could handle it. If he got into an accident...

I couldn't let myself think about that.

"Okay," he said gently. "Then I'll sleep on the couch. And you do what you need to do."

"I need to be glad you're staying." I turned to the window again. Having someone—anyone—spend the night here would be strange. I braced myself for guilt that didn't come. Then again, it wasn't as if I was actually spending the night *with* Lochlan. Only in the same apartment, and only so he would be safe. I was pretty sure Austin would have done the same. "Being snowed in alone would suck. Hot chocolate?"

He raised his eyebrows. "Do you have any?"

"I went to the grocery store yesterday. Had to stock up for the French toast emergency."

He snorted. "The what?"

"French toast emergency. Milk, eggs, and bread. Staples for the storm." I grinned, and my tension ebbed. "And hot chocolate, even though that isn't exactly a French toast thing. But it is something I always had during snowstorms when I was a kid." That was one of the few positive childhood memories I'd held onto after cutting ties with my parents. "Should I get the milk boiling?"

"Wow. Hot chocolate made with milk. Fancy." He smiled, lighting his eyes.

I quickly headed for the kitchen. This was not the time to notice how attractive Lochlan was.

We spent the afternoon and evening drinking hot chocolate and watching a random selection of movies from the 1980s and 90s. I'd seen some of them as a kid. They were far cheesier now, but cheesy movies seemed to go well with a blizzard. The wind howled outside, but fortunately, the electricity stayed on and so did the heat.

At around nine, I decided to go to bed. It was much earlier than usual, but we'd run out of movies and I was running out of resolve. I couldn't let Lochlan share the bed with me. The implications were something for which I was definitely not prepared. Platonic friends shared beds sometimes. Austin and Remy had slept in the same bed plenty of times, and other than one brief "experiment," as they both called it, in high school, they'd always been platonic.

But my traitor brain didn't want my connection with Lochlan to remain platonic. And my entire brain agreed that bringing him into the bed Austin and I had shared our entire life together, with a few mattress changes over the years, might lead to something I would regret. Not to mention feeling even more like a betrayal of Austin than simply bringing Lochlan to the apartment had.

To save myself, I chose to end the evening. "I'm pretty tired. I'm going to call it a night." I looked at Charlie, snoozing on his spot beside Lochlan. "As soon as I bring you some bedding and something to sleep in."

"I can sleep in my clothes," Lochlan said. "I've done it before."

"We don't know how long you'll be here," I pointed out. "If this storm is as bad as it sounds, it'll take the city longer than tomorrow to dig out enough for you to get home. Having something else to wear might be a good idea."

He glanced toward the window. The sound of howling wind filled the pause. "You may have a point."

"I'll be right back."

I went into the bedroom and took a sweatshirt and pair of sweat-pants out of my bureau. After a moment of hesitation, I added a pair of Austin's boxer-briefs that had escaped the final round of clean-out. A corner of my mind yelled a protest at giving away something of Austin's to Lochlan, but I ignored it. Underwear wasn't exactly sacred, and it wasn't as if Austin had any use for them anymore. Lochlan couldn't spend two or three days in the same pair of underwear. These would fit him. I'd given away the rest of Austin's clothes; this was no different.

If I insisted on that long enough, I would believe it.

I added a couple of blankets and a spare pillow from the closet to my pile and returned to the living room. Lochlan, legs curled up behind him, still sat on the couch beside Charlie. He'd switched the TV from the streaming service to one of the local channels my digital antenna picked up. "They're saying it's a full-on blizzard and the governor has asked everyone to stay off the roads." In a fluid movement, he rose and took the armful of stuff from me. "Thank you. For this and for letting me stay."

"I'm glad you're here." My arms twitched as a strong impulse to embrace him ran through me. I ignored that too. "Just let me know if you need anything else. You know where the bathroom is. There might be a spare toothbrush in the drawer under the sink."

"If not, I'll brush my teeth with my finger. I've done that before." He smiled and put the pile down on the couch. "Oh. Um, flashlights? Or candles and a lighter, or something? In case the power goes out." He motioned at the TV, where a map labeled "Power Outages" showed that what appeared to be half of Massachusetts was in the dark.

My little corner of East Boston rarely lost power, but then again, we rarely had storms like this. I tried to remember where Austin and I had stashed the flashlights and batteries we seldom used. The junk cupboard in the kitchen, above the built-in microwave, seemed like the logical place, and fortunately in this case, Austin and I had been logical. We had two flashlights. I tested both of them and brought one to Lochlan. "I don't know if I have a charger cord that will fit your phone, but there's a brick in the outlet over there." I gestured toward the wall under the window.

He looked at his phone. "Yeah, I probably should zap this up a bit. My charger cord's in my car, though. I have a portable charger I carry around. Which, of course, I didn't think to bring in here. I was ill-prepared to weather a storm here."

I couldn't help a little chuckle at his phrasing. "Hang on."

My charger cord, along with a couple of spares, were in the bedroom. I brought them all out to Lochlan. Fortunately, one of them did fit his phone, which he plugged in. I took my time saying good night to Charlie but finally reached the point where standing there felt awkward. "Let me know if you need anything," I told Lochlan again. "I'll be out of the bathroom in a minute."

"Okay." With a tolerant smile, he sat down and used the remote to turn off the TV. "Good night, Del."

"Night."

I rushed through getting ready for bed and settled in for the night. I didn't sleep right away. There was no way I could with my mind racing. I'd done the right thing by asking Lochlan to stay. He wouldn't have been safe on the roads between my place and his. Not with how rapidly the storm had escalated. Here, I knew he was safe.

But I knew he was here, and that kept me from sleep longer than I would have liked.

At a loud thud, I jolted awake and sat up. The room was darker than when I'd gone to bed, and the silence seemed almost as loud as the noise that had awakened me. The clock on my nightstand was dark. We'd lost power.

I fumbled for the flashlight and my watch, which I'd set beside the clock. Two a.m. Four hours, give or take, until sunrise. Maybe the power would be restored quickly, but it was possible we wouldn't have it back until well into the daylight hours. It must have just gone out. The room was still warm, and the furnace didn't work without electricity.

The silence wasn't absolute. Outside, wind still roared. The storm clearly wasn't over. From the living room, I heard a faint voice. Lochlan was probably talking to Charlie. I could stay here, alone in my bedroom, or go join them. I chose to go. Something about the storm and the absence of electricity felt eerie, and for a change, I didn't want to be alone.

I made my way out to the living room. As I approached the couch, Charlie growled.

I stopped short. I couldn't remember if I'd ever heard Charlie growl before. A hiss here and there, but not a growl.

"It's safe," Lochlan said softly. "Someone will meet you there, I'm sure." I shone the flashlight on him. He was lying down, Charlie pressed against his side. His eyes were closed. "I know you don't want to leave, but it's time. Otherwise you wouldn't have come to me."

At another growl from Charlie, I realized what was happening. Someone had died. Lochlan was guiding them to the light. Of course his body remained on my couch. The way he'd described the process, he didn't physically leave whatever location he was in. His soul, his spirit, whatever term one chose to use, did the guiding.

This wasn't something for me to interrupt. Nor was it something I should watch. I was intruding on Lochlan's work. As reluctant as I was to be alone in the overly-dark apartment, I returned to the bedroom. Over the sound of the wind, as I settled back under the covers, I continued hearing Lochlan's voice, though I could no longer make out the words.

CHAPTER TWENTY-THREE

Sometime later, I awakened again. I hadn't been aware of falling asleep, and any dreams I might have had evaporated the second I opened my eyes. The room was chilled, the clock still dark. But a faint tinge of daylight permeated the curtains. I checked my watch and discovered it was nearly six-thirty.

Lochlan spoke in the other room. "Charlie, I don't know where Del keeps your food. Patience is a virtue."

I pushed back the covers and immediately wished I hadn't. I couldn't guess how much the temperature had dropped since I'd gone back to bed, but it was definitely below comfortable room temperature. The wind still blew loudly outside, but it sounded weaker than earlier. Maybe that was wishful thinking on my part, but it seemed as if the storm might be winding down.

"Charlie." Lochlan laughed. "*I'm* not food. Del will serve you shortly, I'm certain."

Obviously my cat would not look favorably on me if I chose to stay in bed. Wrapping the comforter around myself, I got up and left the bedroom.

Lochlan was sitting on the couch, wrapped in the blankets with one arm free to pet Charlie. Charlie was also sitting up, blinking balefully at me. It was time for his morning meal, and lack of electricity didn't mean anything to a cat's schedule.

I went into the kitchen and opened the fridge just enough to retrieve Charlie's food can, which I placed on the floor. At the cat café, all the cats ate directly out of the can, and I'd seen no reason to change that for Charlie even though he rarely finished all the food at one go. I changed the water in his drinking bowl and left him to fortify himself while I joined Lochlan on the couch.

"Did you sleep all right?" he asked with a yawn. "Sorry. I'm guessing coffee won't happen."

"I have some instant, and I think the hot water tap will still run hot enough." I shrugged. "It's worth a try. I slept pretty well, but we both need caffeine and something that resembles a warm drink."

"Yeah." He yawned again. "I thought I slept pretty well. Now I'm not sure."

I hesitated. Had he forgotten his wee-hours visitor? I didn't know whether to bring up what I'd witnessed. "Are you sure you slept?"

Head tilted, he studied me. "I was. Now I'm not. Why?"

Still uncertain, I took a deep breath. "I woke up when the power went out. You were talking out here. I thought to Charlie, but when I came out, you were saying something...I think you were bringing someone to the light."

"Ah." He pressed his lips together. "I wasn't sure if I dreamed that. Sometimes it's hard to tell, especially when they wake me up. So you saw me?"

"Yeah."

A thoughtful expression crossed his face. "What was it like? Obviously I've never seen myself from the outside when I'm guiding someone. I've always wondered."

At least he didn't seem upset that I'd witnessed it. "You were lying there like you were asleep. Charlie was guarding you. He full-on growled at me when I came out of the bedroom. You weren't moving, just talking. It sounded like the person was reluctant to enter the light, and you were trying to talk them into it."

He nodded. "Yeah. She was young. Early twenties, maybe. Car accident. She went out to get food and milk for her kids because she hadn't had a chance to earlier." He wet his lips with his tongue. "That was why she didn't want to go. She left her kids alone. She said she knew it was wrong, but she didn't want to bring them out in this, and she thought she would only be gone a half hour or so."

I sat up straighter, shifting into counselor mode. If this young woman had died, her kids might still be alone. "Did she say how old the kids are?"

"Six and four. She said she told them to keep the door locked until she got back." He inhaled sharply. "Shit. She didn't tell anyone she was leaving them there. And they probably don't have power either. Those kids must be terrified."

"Did she enter the light?"

"Yes." He paused. "I told her whoever she was leaving here would be happy to know she'd gotten where she was meant to be. That was pretty frigging stupid of me. Of course her kids won't be happy."

"Kids understand heaven." I moved a little closer to him. "They won't be happy to lose their mom, but they'll be happy to know she's in a good place."

"If they know anything." Anguish twisted his features. "What if no one finds them, Del? They're barely more than babies. They can't take care of themselves, and if their power is out and they don't have heat..." He shuddered, and a tear ran down his cheek. "They might be the next ones I guide."

The last word broke on a sob, and he flung himself against me. Without thinking, I extricated my arms from the comforter and pulled him closer, my heart echoing his pain. He'd only wanted to help this young woman, just as he only wanted to help any of the spirits who came to him. And now two children were motherless and alone. I knew what being alone felt like, but from an adult's view. My only understanding of losing a parent came from the students I'd worked with who'd had that experience, and all of my students were teens.

Those children would struggle. Hopefully someone who cared would help them.

But first, we had to make sure they made it through the storm so they could be helped.

Lochlan was still crying, and I wasn't sure he would hear me, but I had to ask. "Lochlan, do you know where her accident happened? Where she lived?"

"Huh?" He pulled away, sniffling. "Sorry. Tissues?"

"I'll get some." I went into the bathroom, stumbling a bit over the comforter since I didn't want to unwrap myself, and returned with a box of tissues, which I set on Lochlan's lap as I sat beside him again. "Do you know where the woman's accident happened? What town, at least?"

Staring into space, he wiped his nose. "Her light was at the Topsfield Fairgrounds," he said slowly. "The gate into the grounds. She said she grew up around the corner from there and went to the fair every year. She kept wanting to bring her kids, but they were so little and she was afraid they would get lost or hurt. But they could hear the fair from their apartment."

"Topsfield, then. Maybe she was going to one of the convenience stores on Route One."

Brow furrowed, he opened and closed his mouth a couple of times, then nodded. "I think so. She didn't say, but the fairgrounds are on Route One, right? So she had to live on that road or close to it if they could hear the fair at home."

I'd left my phone in the bedroom. I stood again. "I'm going to call Topsfield police. If I can't get them, I'll call the state police. They have a barracks near there. Someone will know about the accident, and we can get them to send an officer to find her kids."

"And what are you going to tell them, Del?" Eyes narrowed, he wiped his nose again. "Your friend has a side gig escorting spirits to the afterlife, and this woman's ghost said she left her kids alone?"

"Probably not," I said calmly. "I'll think of something."

I had no clue what I could say that would make the police believe me, but I had to try. I went into the bedroom and did a quick search on my phone for the Topsfield Police Department number, then placed the call.

A gruff, impatient male voice answered. "Topsfield Police dispatch. This line is recorded. Is this about the power being out?"

"No, sir." I never called anyone "sir," but something in his tone made it feel like the right decision in this case. "This is going to sound odd, but please bear with me."

"Everything sounds odd today," he grumbled. "Go ahead."

"There was a fatal accident there." I tried to remember what time I'd awakened to Lochlan's voice in the living room. "Sometime between one and two this morning, maybe. A young woman, twenties-ish."

"Go on." The grumble was gone. He sounded guarded but alert.

"She had two kids," I said.

"No kids with her in the car." He paused. "A couple of pictures in her wallet, though."

"That's my point." I took a breath. This was where he was going to question me, and I had no answers. I just had to hope he would listen. "She left the kids at home. Two little ones, maybe four and six. They're alone there."

"How do you know this?" he demanded.

Nothing I could say would sound at all realistic, and I didn't want to lie to law enforcement. "I can't answer that. Please, just send someone to her apartment to get those kids. The power's out there, right? Their mom didn't come home, and they're probably terrified and freezing."

I was certain he would accuse me of lying, if not outright hang up. He did neither. "Are you connected to the family?"

"No. Just a concerned citizen." I didn't know where that phrase came from, but it sounded suitably neutral.

"We haven't been able to get hold of any next of kin." He paused again. "I shouldn't be telling you this. We'll send someone out to her place. Got a name and number so I can follow up with you? Or is that something you can't answer either?"

I would probably regret this, but maybe giving him my name and number would help me seem more credible. "Del Nethercott." I recited my phone number. "That's my cell."

"Got it." He exhaled loudly. "Okay, Mister Nethercott. We'll send someone out and call you back if we need more information."

"Thanks. Stay safe in this storm."

"Yeah." He sounded a little surprised. "You too."

He hung up. I brought the phone into the living room and set it on the coffee table. Charlie had returned to the couch and was curled up on Lochlan's lap. Lochlan was absently stroking Charlie's head, staring toward the window. He jumped a little when I walked over to him. "You actually called."

"I don't know if it'll do any good, but yes." I sat down and reached toward Charlie, who raised his head and glared at me. I decided not to pet him in case he took offense. "They said they'll send someone to her apartment."

"Do you think they actually will?" Lochlan asked.

"I think so. He sounded like he meant it." Of course I had no way to know for sure, but that wasn't what Lochlan had asked. He'd asked what I thought, and I'd given an honest answer for that.

"Thank you." He held out his hand.

I took it. I hadn't held hands with anyone other than Austin in longer than I could remember, but this wasn't exactly holding hands. It was a gesture of comfort.

A few minutes passed. Lochlan continued petting Charlie with his free hand, and I listened to Charlie's purring mingled with the sound of the decreasing wind. Lochlan's hand in mine occupied most of my attention. I didn't want to let go.

"This is nice," Lochlan said finally. "But you mentioned coffee?"

With a reluctant chuckle, I released his hand and stood. "Yeah. It won't be great, but the hot water heater's gas, so I should be able to get the water hot enough to make drinkable coffee. Do you want anything to eat while I'm up?" I paused. "The stove is gas too, but I don't think the burners ignite without electricity."

"The burners on my stove don't. I've had a few power outages." A smile slowly spread across his face. "This might sound weird, but do you have peanut butter and jelly?"

"Not something I tend to keep on hand, I'm afraid." Not something I'd eaten since I was a kid. Lochlan's disappointed expression made me wish I had some, though. "I have butter. Maybe preserves of some kind." Austin had liked raspberry preserves. He probably hadn't finished the jar he'd had, but I wasn't sure if they would still be good after four months.

"Don't open the fridge just to indulge me," Lochlan said. "Right now, coffee is the most important thing. We can figure out something to eat after we've had some caffeine. Maybe by then, a miracle will happen and we'll have the power back."

"Anything's possible," I said as I walked over to the kitchen. Possible, but it seemed unlikely.

I hated instant coffee, but it was better than no coffee. I mixed two cups with hot water from the faucet and powdered creamer I found in the cupboard with the mugs. It must have been something Austin had bought, because it wasn't anything I would have used, but I was glad to have it. It saved me from opening the fridge again. Back in the living room, I handed Lochlan his mug and sat beside him again.

He took a sip. "Not horrible."

"That's high praise, I suppose."

"It is." He grinned. "Thank you, Del. Not only for the coffee."

"You're welcome." An impulse to reach for his hand again rushed through me, and I shoved it away with the excuse that his hands were full. One held the coffee mug, one was petting Charlie, who, judging from the purring and the way he pushed his head into Lochlan's touch, wouldn't respond favorably if Lochlan stopped.

"We'll have to find some way to occupy ourselves today," Lochlan said after a few minutes. "No TV. Oh. Can you check the weather on your phone and find out when this storm will wind down? I'm not in a hurry to leave, but I should go home eventually."

"You're welcome to stay as long as you need to." I smiled. "Or as long as you can stand the couch, whichever comes first."

"Duly noted." He yawned. "The couch is tolerable. I just feel like I should go home at some point. Like I said, I'm not in a hurry. Just wondering."

"Sure." I picked up my phone and opened the weather app. According to that, the snow had already stopped falling. A glance out the window proved the app wrong, though it wasn't snowing anywhere near as hard as the day before. I clicked on the hourly forecast. "This says it's mostly over. Scattered snow showers for the rest of the day."

"How much snow did we get?"

I switched to one of the local news channel's apps, which was filled with stories of accidents and power outages. One story caught my eye. A fatal crash on Route 97 in Topsfield near the intersection of Route 1. Single car, single occupant, dead on scene. The name of the female driver was being withheld pending notification of the next of kin.

"What is it?" Lochlan leaned toward me.

Letting him see that story didn't seem like a good idea, but before I could pull the phone away, he gasped. "That's her, isn't it?"

"I think so." I put the phone face down beside me, away from Lochlan. "Are you okay?"

"I mean, I'm never really okay after I guide someone." He leaned back. Charlie made a "mrrup" sound, and Lochlan started petting him again. "Sorry, buddy. I got distracted. No, Del, I'm not really okay. It helps knowing—well, believing, anyway—that the spirits go someplace safe. Where they're happy. Maybe they reconnect with lost loved ones. I don't know for certain that's what happens, but it's how things appear. But even believing that, it isn't easy watching people leave their lives, you know? And some of them tell me in a little too much detail how they died. Usually the ones who had violent deaths, because they're still trying to process, and I'm the only one who can listen to them."

"I can't even imagine how hard that is for you." Sensing his need for human touch, I rested my hand on his lower thigh. He made a small sound and relaxed slightly. "You do something amazing for them, but you pay for it every time."

"Yeah." A distant look in his eyes, he sipped his coffee. "I don't look at it like that, though. It's hard to watch, and I'm usually exhausted afterward." With his mug, he sketched a circle around his face. "All this yawning and stuff isn't only because my sleep was interrupted. It takes energy to do what I do. I'm usually kind of out of it for a little while afterward."

"Good thing I managed to give you some coffee, then."

He gave me a faint smile. "Yes. That and Charlie will keep me awake and sort of functional. Did you notice the snow totals?"

He must have known I hadn't. I took the question as a change of subject and picked up my phone again, quickly scrolling past the story about the accident. "Looks like about eighteen inches at Logan," I said. "Planes are grounded, roads are closed, and the governor and Boston's mayor are still asking people to stay off the roads. Schools and businesses are shut down too."

"Okay." He held out his mug. "Would you put this on the coffee table for me? I don't think Charlie would appreciate me bending over."

"Sure." I took the mug and set it down along with my phone. The cup was still almost half full. "Do you want more? I can add more hot water if it's getting too cold."

He shook his head. "Not right now. Thanks. I think I just need to sit here for a few minutes and process."

I started to ask what he was processing. I didn't let myself speak. For one thing, his statement was a clear request for quiet. For another, the answer was pretty obvious. "I can go back into the bedroom if you want," I said instead.

Again he shook his head. "Please stay. It helps having you with me. I just don't want to talk."

"Got it."

I leaned back and looked out the window. The trees and other buildings were visible now, though snow still fell. The branches I could see still moved wildly in the wind, but the storm did appear to be slowing. It would, of course, take time for the city to clear side streets like mine, and I had no idea what Lochlan and I would face when it came to clearing his car. He would definitely be here for most of the day, if not another night.

I was fine with that. Even more than before, Lochlan belonged here. Eventually, of course, he would go home, but for as long as he wanted and needed to stay, I was glad to have him.

After a little while, my ringtone shattered the silence. Startled, I fumbled for the phone. My eyes widened at the words "Topsfield MA Police" on the screen.

"Is it...?" Lochlan asked in a hushed voice.

Nodding, I yanked up the phone and thumbed the screen. "Del Nethercott speaking."

"Mister Nethercott, this is Officer Reynolds from Topsfield PD." The voice was the same one as earlier, though somewhat less gruff. "I wanted to follow up with you about your call earlier."

"Yes, Officer." Tensing, I sat back. This might be good news. On the other hand, it might be an interrogation.

"Just wanted to let you know, two of my guys went out to Serena Lawrence's apartment." He paused. "Two kids there, like you said. They're here at the station now getting warmed up and fed. You said you aren't a relative, right? We have a call in to DCFS about finding a place for these kids to go, but if there's family who can take them, that would be better."

"I'm not a relative." I turned to Lochlan, who was staring intently at me, and gave him a thumbs-up. "I'm sorry I can't help with that part."

"No worries. DCFS says they'll send someone as soon as the storm lets up enough. Meanwhile, the kids seem okay here." He cleared his throat. "Care to tell me how you knew they were there?"

"As I said earlier, I'm afraid I can't answer that." I kept my tone carefully neutral. "I appreciate you taking me seriously even without that information."

"I'm glad I did." He paused again. "All right, then. Thanks for calling us. Stay safe."

"You too."

I waited for him to hang up, then dropped the phone onto the cushion beside me. "They have the kids," I told Lochlan. "They're safe. Children and Families is going to take care of them if the police don't find any family members."

Lochlan closed his eyes for a moment. "They found the kids."

"They did."

"Thank goodness." He opened his eyes again and let out a long breath. "Thank you, Del. For believing me and for doing something about it. I wouldn't have thought to call the police. I would have just... I don't know, kept angsting or something."

"It's all good." I smiled. "We make a good team."

"Yeah." His expression relaxed. "Yeah, we do."

Afterward, I couldn't remember which of us moved first. But we both moved, disrupting Charlie from Lochlan's lap. Hands on shoulders, which became an embrace as our lips met.

A kiss. One both tender and needful. One which excited me as much as it terrified me. For two decades, I'd kissed no one other than Austin. I didn't remember how to kiss anyone else, not that I seemed to be doing too badly.

I didn't remember wanting to kiss anyone other than Austin during those two decades, but I wanted this. The closeness with Lochlan. The passion building between us. I wanted it even as a black wave of guilt pushed me toward panic. This was wrong.

This was right.

I did know which of us broke it. That was me. I couldn't take the physical intimacy, and the emotions behind it were beyond tolerance. Breathing heavily, without taking my gaze from Lochlan, I slid away from him on the couch.

"I'm sorry," he said quickly.

"No." Pressing my lips together—the faint taste of Lochlan had to have been my imagination—I pulled myself together. "Don't be sorry. It was good. I just..." Uncertain how to finish the thought, I trailed off.

"You're just still grieving," he said softly. "It's only been a few months."

"Yes." And no. I wasn't thinking about Austin right now. Only about Lochlan. The safety and comfort of his arms around me. The softness of his lips against mine. The unexpected hunger within me for more, maybe even without clothes in the way.

Something I was far from ready for. Sex in and of itself wouldn't have been a bad thing, but right now, I would have done it for the wrong reason. Because I wanted *someone* to be close to. A substitute for the closeness I'd lacked since Austin's death. Not because I wanted *Lochlan*. I wouldn't do that to Lochlan. It wouldn't be fair.

"You aren't ready." He rested his hand on mine. "We're friends. And until you can honestly tell me you're ready for more, we'll stay friends."

"And when I am ready?" When. Not if. For the first time, it seemed possible that I might reach a point of being able to handle having a partner again.

"I'll be here."

Three simple words, spoken in a low, quiet voice. But I heard the promise behind them. The meaning within the tone.

We made a good team. A platonic one for now, while I continued getting my shit together and grieving Austin. But I wouldn't be alone. What we had begun to build would continue to grow, and someday, hopefully soon, there would be more.

When I was ready, Lochlan would help me continue to fill the empty spaces in my life. And I would help him fill his.

CHAPTER TWENTY-FOUR

Lochlan stayed with me again that night. With the power still out, meaning no traffic lights in some places, I worried that the roads wouldn't be safe and didn't want to send Lochlan out to drive on them. And although Lochlan seemed a bit calmer after learning that the accident victim's children were safe, he was still visibly agitated. I wasn't sure if being around me helped at all, but Charlie seemed to recognize Lochlan's need and spent most of the afternoon and evening on his lap.

We didn't talk about the kiss. What was there to say? I cared about Lochlan, more deeply than friendship might explain, but I was far from ready to accept any stronger emotion. The physical affection between us certainly awakened something in me that I'd thought had died with Austin, but I was absolutely not willing to act on it. Not until the tiny voice in the back of my mind stopped insisting that sex with Lochlan—even kissing him—would constitute cheating on Austin.

By the following morning, the power was back on, and a bright sun shone in a blue sky above the city. As I prepared the coffee maker for real coffee, as opposed to instant, the sound of people clearing cars and sidewalks filtered up from the street.

"I should definitely go home today." Yawning, Lochlan leaned against the counter beside me. "It looks like it will be possible."

"Seems so." I waved toward the window. "We can go out in a little while and check on your car. I'll help you clear it off."

"You don't have to." He bit his lip. "But I'd appreciate the help and the company."

"And the coffee." I turned on the machine and stepped back. "Did you sleep all right?"

As he so often did, Lochlan heard the question I didn't ask. "No one visited. As far as I know, I slept straight through, other than a couple of times when Charlie thought I was a scratching post. I'm good, Del." A slow smile spread over his face. "Except for the desperate need for caffeine."

"My coffee won't be as good as the shop up the street's." I took our mugs from the day before off the dish drainer where I'd left them. "And I can't make a foam cat face. But it will definitely be caffeine."

He chuckled. "I don't need a foam cat face."

While the coffee maker did its thing, I opened the fridge, then realized most, if not all, of its contents would have to be thrown away. The power had been out for a full day. "I don't know what to feed you. I'm going to have to do some major shopping later." I closed the door. "Except everyone else will be shopping too, and the stores might be out of things. Shit."

"I'm fine with toast and butter." He opened the cupboard closest to him. "Uh oh, spaghetti-o's. I'm good with those too. Reliving my childhood and all that." With a snort, he closed the cupboard. "Actually, I'd really rather not relive it. Second childhood, maybe."

"At least I have the ability to heat things up." I wasn't keen on spaghetti rings for breakfast, though. Cereal was possible. Except the milk was almost definitely spoiled, and I didn't want to check to find out for sure. "Dry cereal? I wish I'd been able to tell the future. Then I would have bought more nonperishable stuff when I went to the store before the storm, instead of the milk and eggs we can't eat now anyway."

"It's fine, Del." He hesitated. "I can contribute to your food replacement fund if you want. After all, I did eat some of your food the past couple of days."

"I'll think about it." For a normal round of grocery shopping, I would have turned him down. I probably still would. But replacing an entire fridge and freezer full of food would cost more than I'd budgeted for the next two or three weeks of grocery shopping, so I might not have much choice.

The coffee finished percolating, and I toasted a few pieces of bread for our breakfast. Not the most ideal meal, but it was food.

While we sat on the couch eating, with Charlie making occasional attempts at scamming bites of toast from us, Lochlan's phone rang. He snatched it up off the coffee table, almost dropping his toast in the process, and answered. "Liam?" He paused. "Ah, yeah, that makes sense. I can let Del know so you don't have to call him. Tomorrow?" He waited a few seconds. "All right, just let me know in the morning. Thanks. Stay safe."

He dropped the phone onto the cushion beside him. "That was Liam, obviously. The café's closed today. He's trying to get hold of the owner of the plaza to clear the parking lot enough that he can go in and check on the cats, but he doesn't want anyone else trying to drive up there."

"Oh. It's Thursday." I'd lost track of the week. "I'll miss seeing all the cats, but I'm sure Charlie will keep us entertained."

Grinning, Lochlan scratched Charlie between the ears. "I'm sure he will. I'd like to try to get out of here around noon. By then, the roads should be clear enough."

"Probably." My heart sank a little. On Tuesday, I hadn't been sure I wanted Lochlan to stay. Now I was pretty certain I didn't want him to leave. But of course he couldn't remain in my apartment indefinitely. "Just let me know when you're ready and I'll go with you to get your car out."

"Yeah." It might have been my imagination, but he sounded disappointed

We took our time drinking the coffee while Charlie occupied Lochlan's lap. Lochlan clearly wasn't in any hurry to leave, and I wasn't eager to have him go. Having him in the kitchen trying to wake up while I made coffee had felt more right than I wanted to admit. He belonged here. Which I sure as hell wasn't about to say to him.

"This was good." He took a sip of his coffee. "I don't mean the coffee. I mean, that is good, but...Damn. Maybe I should have gotten more sleep so I could be coherent." He snorted. "Staying here was good. Thank you for letting me."

"I'm glad you were here." That sounded sappier than I wanted. "Being alone during the blizzard would have sucked." I reached over and rubbed Charlie between his ears. "I wouldn't have been completely alone, but you know what I mean."

"Yeah." He frowned. "And I *would* have been completely alone. I'm glad I wasn't."

The pain in his tone almost broke me. For a change, the tears that welled up in my eyes weren't for me or for Austin. They were for Lochlan and his loneliness. I was alone because I'd lost the man I loved, but at least I had loved someone and been loved in return. Lochlan hadn't had that.

"I'm glad too," I said quietly.

"I've lived alone my entire adult life. Not even a pet fish. No one's ever made coffee for me first thing in the morning. Or toast. Or spaghetti rings." He pressed his lips together. "No one's ever sat with me after I guided a spirit and listened to me tell them about the person and the crossing. And I've definitely never had anyone who cared enough to take action on what I told them the spirit said." Looking hesitant, he cleared his throat. "Not that I've become a fan of blizzards or anything, but I'm not sorry this one happened. Or that I was with you for the past two days."

"I'm not sorry either." Impulsively, I rested my hand on his shoulder. "Having you around was nice." That wasn't what I wanted to say. "Nice" was a pale word for what I meant. But I couldn't find any other words, at least none I was willing to speak aloud.

"Can we just be here?" Looking rueful, he shook his head. "I don't know what I mean."

Maybe he didn't, but I understood perfectly. "You want to just sit here and not talk. I'm down for that. Pet Charlie and drink your coffee, and I'll be here."

He flashed me a grateful smile. "We both will be."

So we were. Silently, other than the sounds of us sipping our coffee and Charlie purring, we sat there together. I was relieved Lochlan had suggested it. I'd run out of non-cliché things to say, and simply existing beside Lochlan was exactly what I hadn't realized I needed.

Shortly before noon, after a lunch of microwaved spaghetti rings, we left a disgruntled Charlie and went to dig out Lochlan's car. In the sunshine, the air felt unexpectedly warm, and my weather app informed me that the temperature had risen to nearly fifty degrees. Whether because of the wind direction during the storm or the rising temperature, or maybe a kind neighbor, Lochlan's car was already partially cleared of snow. Someone nearby who was digging out their own car helped us shovel enough for Lochlan to be able to leave the parking spot. And then it was time for him to leave.

He got into his car and rolled down the window. "Thanks for letting me stay, Del. For being supportive. For everything." He gestured at the sweatpants he wore. The clothes in which he'd arrived on Tuesday afternoon were in a bag on the seat beside him. "Including the clean clothes. I'll wash them and bring them back next time we have coffee."

"No rush." I could live without the sweatpants, and the other clothes weren't mine. Better that Lochlan have them than that they go back to collecting dust in Austin's bureau. "Do me a favor and text when you get home, okay? I want to know you made it all right."

His face lit, and he nodded. "I will. I should get going. I'm sure my clients are waiting to hear from me. And I probably have a fridge full of stuff I'll have to throw out and go replace. Let me know if you need a ride to the grocery store at some point." He looked thoughtful. "We could go now, actually."

"The stores might be out of a lot because of the storm," I reminded him.

"Yeah." His expression crumpled. "Okay. Well, like I said, let me know. I don't mind driving you to the store whenever it makes sense to go."

"Thanks."

He opened and closed his mouth, then shook his head. If he had anything else to say, apparently he'd decided not to say it. He closed the window, and I stepped back as he maneuvered out of the spot. I stayed where I was until he turned the next corner, then reluctantly headed back to the apartment to start the process of cleaning out the fridge and freezer.

Charlie kept me company while I worked, though I suspected he hung around mostly because he knew the fridge was where I kept his partially-eaten cans of food. Which I also threw away, unsure whether the food in the open can would be safe for him to eat. At least I had several unopened cans of Charlie food stacked in the cupboard.

The clean-out distracted me for a little while, but once it was complete, I had no way to occupy myself other than watching TV. Which might have been fine if I could have decided what to watch— or if Lochlan had still been there with me.

"Nope." Sitting on the couch, I continued scrolling through one of the streaming services while Charlie purred on my lap. "Not going there." I was definitely not going to think about the kiss Lochlan and I had shared. About how right it had felt.

Damn it. I seriously hoped Lochlan wasn't tapping into my thoughts just now. The last thing I needed was for him to realize what I was thinking about him.

We were friends. Close friends, maybe closer than was wise, but still only friends. That was all we could be until I healed enough from my grief to be open to anything more.

But reality and logistics didn't have much impact on how I felt. I cared about Lochlan. That wasn't news. After two days with him in my apartment, just the two of us plus Charlie, I knew "care about" was far too shallow a description for my true emotions.

I loved Lochlan.

I shouldn't love anyone other than Austin, not romantically, but I loved Lochlan.

This might be a problem.

And it was a problem I didn't want to think about right then. I didn't have the bandwidth. I stood at the edge of a yawing pit of grief, and trying to sort out my feelings for Lochlan would only push me into the pit.

Someday, I would be ready. Not so long ago, I'd doubted I would ever be able to love anyone else, let alone that I would want to. Now it was something I did want. Thanks to therapy, Charlie, and my friends, I'd progressed enough in healing from Austin's loss that I believed loving again was possible and that wanting to have another partner wasn't wrong. It wasn't a betrayal of Austin.

It simply wasn't something I could handle right now. Despite spending two days and nights with Lochlan, despite the kiss, I was not able to deal with anything beyond friendship.

Something Lochlan and I had both acknowledged after the kiss, so I didn't know why my brain was so tangled up in trying to decide what to do. I'd already decided. Lochlan had already validated my decision. We'd agreed that we were friends.

We'd agreed that when I was ready, we would be more.

I wanted to be ready. I wasn't yet.

"Oh, for crying out loud." Using the remote, I clicked on a TV series I vaguely remembered liking as a kid and turned up the volume as the first episode started. I didn't need to sit there and angst about Lochlan. I didn't need to think about anything. I could just watch a no-brainer show, pet my cat, and let my mind go blank.

Fortunately, Remy's ringtone blaring from my newly-charged phone broke me out of the thought spiral. I fumbled for the phone, which I'd set on the coffee table, and managed not to drop it as I answered. "Hi, Remy."

"Hi." She sounded a little out of breath. "Just making sure you survived the snowpocalypse."

"Yeah, I'm good. We lost power for a while, but it's back now." I reached out to scratch Charlie's head. "Were you shoveling?"

"Snowball fight." She snorted. "Donnie thought it would be a nice way to release the whole cabin fever tension thing. I don't think he liked the result. You said we."

"Yeah." I didn't even realize I'd said it, but of course Remy caught it. "Lochlan was over on Tuesday when the storm started. I was worried about him driving home because the snow picked up so fast, so he crashed on my couch until this morning."

"Oh?" She extended the word to multiple syllables.

"He slept *on the couch*," I repeated.

"Okay, okay." She paused. "Del, you don't have to defend yourself with me. You know that, right?"

"I know." I took a deep breath and slowly released it. "Sorry, Rem. I just..." Having no idea what I wanted to say, I stopped. I was feeling defensive, and there was absolutely no reason for it. Especially not with Remy.

"You just aren't sure letting him stay with you was the right thing?" she suggested.

"Yeah." That wasn't quite what I was thinking, but it was close enough. "It was the right thing. When the storm started, it started *hard*. He might have gotten home all right, but he might not have. I couldn't..." My throat tightened, and I took another breath. "I couldn't take the risk. Or let him take it."

"Exactly." Remy spoke with her usual compassion. "You were making sure a friend was safe. There's nothing wrong with that. For the record, though, even if he'd shared your bed, there wouldn't have been anything wrong with it."

"We kissed." I didn't even realize I intended to say it until I blurted the words. And I immediately wished I hadn't. Not because I was worried about Remy judging me, but because that kiss was between Lochlan and me, and I wanted to keep it that way.

For a moment, Remy was so silent I was afraid she'd hung up. Finally, she burst out with, "What? You did *what?*"

I sighed. This was not how I'd envisioned telling Remy about the kiss. Then again, I hadn't envisioned telling her at all. "Lochlan and I kissed. It just kind of happened, and that was where we left it." A statement which wasn't entirely true. "We agreed that I'm not in a place right now to deal with a relationship or sex or any of that. We're friends, and for now, we're staying friends."

"Wow. This is unexpected." She didn't sound upset, which was a relief, though I couldn't quite label how she did sound. "There's definitely something between you and him, Del. Everyone who's seen you together sees it, except maybe you and him."

"I see it. I just reject it as a reality." I hesitated. "I like him. Care about him. But he isn't Austin, and I'm not over Austin yet."

"Sweetie, you're never going to be over Austin," Remy said gently. "That isn't how grief works. You don't get over it or past it. You get through it. You *are* getting through it. Comparing you now with how you were even a month or two ago, it's night and day, but you're clearly still hurting. And that's valid, but if you're waiting to be over him before you let someone else into your life, you might never stop waiting."

I bristled at the lecture. I wasn't trying to stop thinking about Austin or even stop grieving him. But Remy was responding to the words I'd used, not the thoughts and emotions behind them. She wasn't trying to tell me what to do.

I took a slow breath and released it as I mentally pulled together the words to say what I meant. "I'm not trying to get over or past him. I'm not saying things very well right now. I just mean that right now, the pain and grief are still too much for me to bring someone else into." My voice choked, and I forced myself to keep talking. "I didn't mean I'm waiting to get over Austin. Only that I'm waiting until enough time has passed that I feel like I can handle being with someone else without feeling like I'm cheating on Austin or...or negating our relationship."

Tears ran down my cheeks. *Damn it.* I did not need to cry on Remy's shoulder again. "Does that make sense?" I managed to say, though my voice sounded thick. "I'm not trying to get over him like you get over a bad breakup. I'm trying to get far enough through healing that I can start a new relationship without the grief overriding it."

My voice broke into a sob, and I gave up trying not to cry. I wanted to be with Lochlan. I wanted to wait until I was better. I wanted to have a life that didn't include breaking down during phone calls with friends.

I wanted Austin back. I wanted him to tell me it was okay, whatever "it" might be.

Minutes passed with only the sound of my sobbing and faint but audible breathing on Remy's end of the call. She was giving me time to pull myself together, which I appreciated even though I didn't know whether I could.

But gradually, the tears stopped falling. I reached over Charlie to take a tissue from the box so I could wipe my eyes and nose. "Sorry," I mumbled, unsure whether I was addressing Remy or Charlie, who was glaring at me for having the audacity to lean over him.

"You never need to apologize at a time like this," Remy said. "Are you all right? I can come over if you need me." She paused. "Or not. I still need to dig out my damn car. Shoveling got put aside for Donnie's frigging snowball fight."

I couldn't help laughing, though to my own ears it sounded a little hysterical. "Thanks, but I don't need you to come over. Talking with you is good even over the phone."

"All right. I can stay on for a bit longer."

She wouldn't tell me she had other things to do, but something in her tone conveyed it anyway. "No, it's good. You can get back to shoveling or fighting snowballs or whatever. Is there a show tonight?"

"Club's closed. There's some damage to the roof from the storm, so we might be off for the weekend." She didn't sound too upset about it, though she hated missing shows. "I can let you know if you want."

"Yeah, keep me posted." I hadn't planned on going to the club this weekend, but if they wound up opening, maybe I would change my mind. It would be a welcome diversion after being stuck in the apartment for a few days.

"Will do," she said. "Take care, Del. Give me a call if you need anything, and I'll talk to you in a couple-few days anyway."

I chuckled at her use of my usual time-range phrase. "Okay. Take care."

She hung up, and I let my phone drop onto the cushion beside me. The TV was still on. Charlie still purred beside me. But the apartment felt emptier than before Remy's call. I didn't want to think about why.

CHAPTER TWENTY-FIVE

The good thing about early spring snowstorms was that the snow didn't last long. The temperature remained in the fifties, and the sun shone brightly every day. Within a week, the only signs that we'd even had a storm were the snowbanks that hadn't fully melted. Streets, sidewalks, and even grass were all completely bare, and leaf buds began to unfurl on the trees.

Spring had arrived. A time for new beginnings, for those willing to begin.

Less than five months earlier, I hadn't anticipated ever being willing to start anything new. Living without Austin was enough change. A painful change. One I hadn't been certain I would survive.

Now, as April moved toward May, I realized I already had survived. My life wasn't the same without Austin, of course. How could it be? But it was life. I'd formed deeper connections with Remy and the other performers. I'd made decisions about my career and was applying to agencies where I could do the work to which I felt most drawn.

I'd met Lochlan. I'd weathered the weeks of no contact and reconnected with him. I'd begun to love him.

Spring was a time for new beginnings, and I felt like my life was beginning. A life without Austin, still, but one that didn't see me spending every minute of every day submerged in a dark pit of grief. A life in which I sometimes even looked forward to waking up in the morning.

Lochlan and I continued our weekly coffee meetups. We also continued not mentioning the kiss we'd shared or our feelings for one another. I didn't even know for certain if he had feelings for me other than friendship, but it was pretty obvious that he did. Some nights as I fell asleep, I heard the echo of him promising to be there when I was ready for more. A promise he wouldn't have made if he didn't care for me.

I consciously chose not to overanalyze Lochlan's words. Throughout my life, I'd spent far too much time thinking and anguishing and too little time actually doing things. Even receiving my degree and getting the job at the school had taken months of mental wrangling on my part. Lochlan had said he would be here. I needed to take that at face value. There was nothing to analyze. Simply something to believe.

At the beginning of May, I started preparing for my trip to Prince Edward Island. Though I still looked forward to it, I felt a little reluctant to go. When I booked the trip, I was still isolating from the rest of the world. Now, I would be leaving friends behind, albeit only for a week. I would be leaving Lochlan.

I would also be leaving Charlie the Sweater Cat. Obviously I couldn't leave him completely alone for a week. With his medical needs, even a cat sitter who came in once a day might not be enough. The solution was clear, but I hesitated to ask Lochlan if he would be willing to stay at my place while I was gone. It was a huge favor, maybe too huge.

He knew I was taking the trip, though, and he brought up Charlie's care before I had a chance. The first Tuesday in May was the warmest day of the year so far, nearly eighty degrees, and instead of sitting in the coffee shop we decided to take our drinks to go so we could walk along the waterfront. Not into Piers Park. Bringing Lochlan there still felt wrong. But walking along the sidewalk, we glimpsed the harbor between the condos that had risen over the years. We heard the gulls and smelled the salt air. And we soaked in the sunlight.

"You'll be right at the ocean in a couple of weeks, won't you?" Lochlan asked as we walked toward Piers Park.

"Pretty much, yeah." The travel agent had booked me into an LGBTQ+-friendly bed and breakfast about twenty minutes outside of Charlottetown. The place sat on an inlet, not exactly the ocean, but it was close enough. I would be able to smell the air, hear the waves, and hopefully feel at peace.

"I have to admit I'm a little envious," he said. "I have a travel bucket list, but I haven't managed to check anything off it yet." He paused, looking through a gap between buildings. "I'll miss you."

"I'll only be gone about a week." I wouldn't even miss a Tuesday unless I was too tired for our coffee date the day after I came home. Which I didn't anticipate being the case. "I'll send you pictures."

He flashed a smile. "That would be nice."

"I was meaning to ask." I cleared my throat. "When I booked the trip, I didn't have Charlie. I could cancel everything, but this was the last thing Austin wanted to do for me, and canceling doesn't feel right. But Charlie can't be alone more than a few hours at a stretch. So I was wondering..." I trailed off, trying to put together the words to finish the question. "I know you have work to do and such, but I was wondering if you'd be willing to stay at my place while I'm gone. To take care of Charlie, you know?"

I couldn't look at him, which annoyed me. While I wasn't a big fan of asking for favors from people, I certainly wasn't doing anything out of line by asking Lochlan for this. There was no reason to feel so uncomfortable.

"Can I think about it for a day or two?" he asked after a silence which was probably far briefer than what I perceived. "I think it would be fine, and I definitely wouldn't object to a few days of Charlie, but I need to make sure I can shift a couple of things around so I'd be able to work from your place."

"Yeah, yes, of course." He hadn't said no. That was a relief.

"I really like that you felt like you could ask me, Del." His voice was warm. "That's the kind of connection I want us to have. Where we ask each other for things when we need to and help each other out when we can."

"Same." I wasn't sure what else to say. Of course that was what I wanted as well, but at the same time, that didn't sound like friendship to me. It sounded like a relationship.

A relationship I still didn't consider myself ready to have.

I didn't say that to Lochlan. I didn't need to. Since the blizzard, his "overhearing" of my thoughts had ramped up to the point that I barely needed to say anything to him most of the time. We still talked, because he preferred to hear the words in my voice rather than in his own head, but some things simply no longer had to be spoken. He knew I was still hesitant to have anything more than friendship with him, and until I could honestly tell him I did want more, we would maintain the status quo. There was no need to discuss it. We'd already agreed.

Among my plans for the trip to Prince Edward Island was spending some time genuinely and deeply examining where I was in the grieving process and what that meant for me. My friendships, my relationships, my future career...everything in my life was impacted by losing and grieving Austin, and some things had been on hold since the night I got that devastating phone call. I'd begun living again, not simply existing, but various pieces of my life were still in limbo. A nice, quiet bed and breakfast near the ocean, in a town where no one knew me and I could be alone with my thoughts, seemed like the perfect place to make more decisions.

The perfect place to decide whether to move forward with Lochlan, and if so, what that would look like. For Lochlan's sake and my own, I didn't want to keep us in friendship limbo forever. At the very least, I wanted to be completely sure of whether I wanted a relationship with him eventually, even if I couldn't yet determine when "eventually" might be. Keeping him on hold didn't seem fair to either of us.

"Whatever you need from me, you have," he said quietly. "I hope you know that, Del. Whether it's me watching Charlie if I'm able to arrange it or me hanging back until you know what you want. I told you I'd be here. I will be."

I snorted. "Sometimes I think you know what I need better than I do."

Looking sheepish, he shrugged. "I know you need someone who listens to what you don't say as well as what you do. But I also want you to tell me if I overstep. I know it's weird to have someone know what's going on in your mind. I do it because you don't seem to object. If you do object, please say so."

I shook my head. "Honestly, I feel like it should bother me, but it doesn't. In a way, it's comforting to know you pick up on this stuff."

"Good. I'm glad." He wrinkled his forehead. "Comforting, huh?"

"Yeah." Hearing him repeat it, I felt foolish for saying it.

"Del." He looked away. "You don't have to feel weird about anything you say to me."

"I know I don't have to, but that doesn't stop it from happening."

As I'd hoped, he chuckled. "All right. Just making sure you know. So I'll give you an answer about Charlie in the next couple of days. If it turns out I can't stay with him, I'll help you find someone who can, okay?"

"I appreciate that." Charlie would probably be happier with Lochlan, and I would definitely prefer having someone I knew well staying in my apartment rather than a stranger or even an acquaintance, but I didn't say so. The last thing I wanted to do was pressure Lochlan.

We continued walking toward Piers Park. As we neared it, Lochlan stopped. "We can go back if you want."

"Thanks." I hesitated, torn between going back the way we'd come and continuing up the street and wondering why I was torn at all. Going past the park wasn't the same as entering it. My Austin-connected memories were of being at the water's edge inside the park, not walking along the sidewalk in front of the park's gate.

But the park was Austin to me in the same way our apartment and the club were. It contained Austin. I had no memories of Piers Park that didn't include him.

I'd overcome the overwhelming association between Austin and the club. Lochlan had yet to go with me, but I'd invited him, and I went to a couple of shows a month on my own to support Remy and the others. More importantly, I'd been able to allow Lochlan into my apartment. If I could walk into the spaces Austin had called home and bring someone else with me, there was absolutely no reason I couldn't do the same with a public park.

I took a breath. I hadn't been to Piers Park since the day I broke down. Part of my fear of going back was fear that I would fall apart again. But what if I did? Lochlan wouldn't think less of me. He'd seen me at my worst. Other people might see, but the opinion of strangers wasn't a reason to continue avoiding a place where Austin and I had been happy.

"We can keep going," I said.

Lochlan smiled. "I hoped you'd say that. Are you sure?"

"Yeah." My smile felt forced, but it was genuine nonetheless. "It's a nice park, and I haven't been there in a while. So why not?"

"Why indeed?" Lochlan studied me. "Tell me if it's too much for you."

"I will."

As we approached the park, the sound of children shouting and shrieking reached my ears. No surprise given the heat and sunshine. Parents who stayed home with their young children would want to take advantage of the weather to get them out of the house for a little while.

"It might be crowded," Lochlan said.

It was a bland enough observation, but something in his tone made me stop. "I wasn't necessarily planning to go into the park. We can just walk on up to the shipyard at the end of the street."

"I...Yeah." He shook his head. "Sorry. I think we should go back to your place. Something just feels off. And I'm...Yeah. Can we go back to your place, please?"

"No problem." I wanted to ask what he meant by something feeling a little off, but I suspected he wouldn't want to talk about it in the middle of the street.

"Thank you." He pressed his lips together. "I'm not sure what's going on, Del, but I just need to not go into the park."

"You don't need to explain," I said quickly. I was worried as hell about him, and I wanted to get him off the street and out of the sun. "Come on."

"Thanks." He took a drink of his coffee and made a face. "In this heat, you'd think the coffee would have stayed warm."

I sipped mine, which was still almost too hot to drink. "I..." Something in Lochlan's expression stopped me. "Yeah, their disposable cups aren't great, I guess."

"Yeah." He looked up the street. "Guess I'll have to deal with it. No trash cans."

"You can throw it away at home."

He grimaced at his cup. "Let's go."

I studied him as we resumed our walk, heading up the nearby side street to my street. My apartment was only a couple of blocks away, but I wasn't sure Lochlan could make it. His breathing was heavy and his steps much slower than usual.

Something was happening to him, and as I realized that, I started getting a sense of what it might be. Given how hot my coffee was, his shouldn't have cooled enough for him to react the way he had. Unless it had something to do with why he didn't want to go into the park. The thought made no sense, but I couldn't shake it.

We were almost there. Lochlan was breathing as if he'd scaled a mountain, and his face was the color of the concrete sidewalk, but we only had to go a few more yards. He could make it. I hoped.

Something was affecting Lochlan but not me. Something that led to him wanting to avoid Piers Park and to his coffee being too cold for him to drink.

In TV shows, when a ghost was around, the temperature dropped. Lochlan guided dead spirits.

"Lochlan, is there..." Unsure how to phrase the question, I trailed off.

He glanced at me, eyes wide. "Yeah. Yeah, I think so, but they aren't quite here."

"Do you need to sit down or something?" Given what I'd seen the night of the blizzard, he couldn't exactly do his guiding thing while walking along the sidewalk.

"I don't know." He hitched in a breath as we reached—*finally*—my building. "Help me inside."

"Yeah."

Thank God working as a counselor had given me plenty of practice in hiding my reactions. Though fear and worry roiled through me, I managed to act like nothing was wrong as I put my arm around Lochlan and guided him inside and up the stairs.

He leaned against the wall while I unlocked the apartment door. With the door open, I reached for him just as he suddenly plunged toward the ground.

Screw my coffee. And the fucking floor. I dropped my cup and grabbed Lochlan. I wasn't exactly in the best shape, but I managed to catch him and lower him to the floor inside the door. Somehow I positioned myself so his head could rest on my leg, and I was just able to reach the door to push it closed as Charlie came over to investigate.

Lochlan's eyelids fluttered and his breaths grew shallower. His lips moved as if he were speaking, but his voice was inaudible.

Following an impulse I didn't quite understand, I placed my hand on Lochlan's too-hot forehead.

Which was a mistake. With a dizzying whirl, I was suddenly no longer in my apartment.

CHAPTER TWENTY-SIX

I didn't know where I was. The gray mist surrounding me obscured any features that might have given me a sense of place. I stood on what felt like solid ground, but I couldn't tell whether the ground was natural or manmade.

The one thing I could see clearly was a figure standing nearby. A male figure. One I'd seen countless times over the past two-plus decades.

My mind battled with itself. There was no possible way I was seeing who I thought I was seeing.

Then again, there was no possible way I was in some weird mist-world. Or that a ghost was attacking Lochlan. None of this was possible.

But since the other impossible things were happening, maybe this was real too.

"Austin?" I gasped, my voice barely audible through the rushing in my ears.

"Hey." An uncertain smile playing on his lips, Austin took a step toward me. "You shouldn't be here. I'm not sorry to see you, but you..." He shook his head. "You shouldn't be here," he said again.

"And yet I am." Chest tight, tears welling in my eyes, and such a desperate ache to embrace him that I could barely stand it, there I was. I reached for him but stopped myself. "I can't touch you, can I?"

"Unfortunately, I don't think so." He held out his hand, palm facing me, and I held mine in a similar position with less than an inch between us. The love and longing in his gaze stabbed my heart. "I love you, Del. I wish I'd had a chance to tell you that before...Before."

"I wish you hadn't had to leave me." My voice broke.

For several long seconds, we simply stood there, looking at each other. Words I wished I could speak filled my mind, but I couldn't bring myself to say them aloud. Judging from the expression on Austin's face, though, he knew.

Finally, he lowered his hand. "Lochlan needs you. I can't help him. I tried."

"I don't understand." Despite the urgency I sensed from him and around me, I needed to know what the hell was going on. "Austin, what is happening?"

"You know what Lochlan can do." He hesitated, and his cheek twitched the way it always had when he was trying to figure out what to say. My heart ached at the tiny movement. This was my Austin, right here in front of me but completely beyond my reach.

I didn't know why I was here, but I hated like hell that I was.

"Yes," I said. "I know."

"Someone took their life at the park." Austin grimaced. He loved Piers Park. He must have hated knowing that someone had harmed themselves there. "Some spirits don't want to enter the light. This one... He wasn't a good person alive. To hurt someone else. And he isn't a good person dead. He did what he did out of anger and revenge. Lochlan can't get him into the light alone."

"You can help, can't you?"

Looking grim, he shook his head. "I can't do anything until he actually enters the light. Like I said, I tried. Others are trying. Lochlan needs someone else from the living side of things. He needs you, and you have to hurry. The spirit knows something's happening, and he's going to fight back."

"Shit. Yeah." I had no idea what I could do, but if I was here, there had to be something. "Okay, so this spirit came to Lochlan for help, though, yeah?"

"He came to Lochlan to use him to stay in the living world." Austin blew out a breath. "I shouldn't be telling you any of this. I'm not supposed to interfere. But I love you, Del, and I want you to be happy. Lochlan makes you happy."

"*You* make me happy." My voice shook, and I swallowed hard. "He does, but he isn't you."

"No one's me, and that's probably a good thing." He chuckled but sobered immediately. "Lochlan didn't choose his gift, but he chooses to use it. And he's used it alone all this time. Now he has you. And he needs your help."

I couldn't even being to take all this in. This wasn't my life. I worked at a high school. I mourned my partner. I volunteered at a freaking cat café. Spirits, suicides, entering the light...these were Lochlan's life, not mine.

But Lochlan was part of my life now, and that meant what was in his life was in mine whether I could process it or not.

"What do I do?" I asked.

"Hold him." Austin's voice began to fade. "It's okay to love him, Del. It's okay to keep him with you. Stand with him and help him push that spirit into the light. I and others will take it from there."

His form was fading too. I couldn't let him go. Not yet. "Austin?"

"I'm with you." Now I could barely hear him. "I'm always with you, Del. No matter what. Live your life and know I'm with you. And help Lochlan before the spirit gets him into the light."

"Before..." I couldn't finish the question. Austin was gone. I'd lost him again.

"No!" Lochlan's voice pierced the mist. I whirled around but couldn't see him.

Grief rose within me, threatening to take over as it had so many times before. For just a second, I let the black cloud enshroud me. A tear ran down my cheek.

One tear, and one only. I didn't have time to fall into the grief pit. Not if Lochlan's life was at stake.

Unable to see more than a foot or so in front of me, I started in the direction from which his voice had come. As I walked, the mist began to clear, until ahead of me I saw figures standing before a vibrant white light. One of the figures was a vague outline in the mist. The other, I recognized. "Lochlan."

Though I didn't speak loudly, both of the figures turned toward me as I came closer. Lochlan's face was white and drawn, and he shook his head violently. "No. Del, no. You can't be here. You can't."

"I'm here." I walked over to him, purposely not looking at the other figure.

"He's right." The voice was harsh, the gender unidentifiable, though Austin had referred to the spirit as "he." "You shouldn't be here."

A cold wave of energy washed over me, and I almost lost my balance. Whatever this guy had been in life, in death he was powerful. But I kept my footing and continued ignoring him. "Lochlan, I'm here to help.'

"What?" Eyes wild, Lochlan looked at me, but I wasn't sure he actually saw me.

"I'm going to help you." I put my hand on his shoulder. "Lochlan, I'm right here."

"And you're an idiot," the harsh voice said. The shape loomed closer, his rage tangible. "I'm going back."

"You need to go into the light." Lochlan spoke confidently, but beneath my hand he trembled. He was nearing the end of his strength; I could feel the weakness taking over.

If he grew too weak, the spirit wouldn't be the one entering the light. Heart pounding, I realized that was exactly what the spirit wanted. He would take Lochlan's strength and use it to return to the living world.

I couldn't let it happen. I didn't know what the hell I could do to stop it, but I had to do something.

Hold him, Austin had said. Without stopping to think, I wrapped my arms around Lochlan. Instantly, I felt strength flooding both of us, flowing from me into Lochlan but not taking anything from me. Power. And even though I didn't know what I was doing, I knew what I needed to say.

"It's time to go." I looked toward but not quite at the other figure. "Go into the light. That's where you belong."

"Fuck you," he snarled. Before he finished speaking, he moved toward the light. He braced himself, but something pushed him toward the bright glow.

Something that came from Lochlan and from me. And again, it took nothing from us. I felt stronger even as the sense of strength flowing out of me grew.

The spirit turned, his face twisted. "No. No!"

"Go." Lochlan's voice echoed as it had when he'd made his promise to me months earlier. "It is time for you to leave this plane. Go into the light."

"No!" The voice was a shriek now. I felt Lochlan pushing, not physically but on a level I couldn't name. I had no clue what I was doing, but I pushed too.

"It is time to go," Lochlan said again, and this time his voice held a force I couldn't even comprehend.

The light flared, and the figure disappeared.

A sudden wave of power hit me, and I lost all awareness. No sight. No sound. Not even the sensation of Lochlan in my arms. For a moment, I knew nothing, not even the bounds of my own body.

And then I was back in my apartment, lying on the floor.

"Lochlan?" I looked up. He was lying, unmoving, beside me. I managed to get to my knees, though I felt like I was climbing through sludge, and rested my hand on Lochlan's. "I'm here."

"Del?" His lips barely moved, but the sound came unmistakably from him.

"I'm here," I said softly again. "Right here."

"What..." His eyelids fluttered, then, to my relief, he looked at me. His face was still drawn and pale, but Lochlan was back. "Del? What?" He raised his head slightly and looked around. "Where are we?"

"My apartment." I motioned around. "Do you remember walking back here?"

"Yeah." He touched his forehead and flinched. "Maybe. I felt dizzy. Sunburn, I think. What happened?"

"You don't remember?"

He furrowed his brow, then shook his head. "No idea. We were talking about whether I could take care of Charlie for you while you're away, right? And we had coffee." He glanced around again. "Where's my coffee?"

"You tossed it. You said it was cold." Which was almost certainly because of the spirit that had tried to end Lochlan's life. I shivered despite the heat of the room.

"I don't remember that." He looked up at me, eyes filled with fear. "Del, why can't I remember?"

"It's all right." Maybe it was for the best. I didn't know what he'd dealt with before I showed up. Before Austin told me to help.

Austin. My throat tightened, and I had to turn away from Lochlan for a moment so he wouldn't see the tears in my eyes. I didn't have time to process Austin's presence—or disappearance—right now. I needed to support Lochlan.

"Del?"

I didn't know what to say. I wasn't sure I could speak through the lump in my throat. But the fear in Lochlan's eyes got my voice working again. "Do you think you can sit up? I'd like to give you some water."

"Yeah." Lochlan cleared his throat. "Yeah. Thank you."

"I'll be right back."

I didn't want to leave him lying there, but I didn't know if he could move yet. My mouth was suddenly so dry it hurt; I could only imagine how Lochlan might be feeling. We both needed something to drink. Probably food, too, but one thing at a time.

I took two bottles of water out of the fridge and brought them back to Lochlan. He was sitting up now, propped against the couch. "Hey," he said softly. He touched my arm. "Did I do something? I'm sorry."

"No." I closed my eyes tightly, pushing back the tears that still threatened, then opened them and forced a smile. "No, you didn't do anything. Drink some of this, then I'll try to explain."

Frowning, he nodded and took the bottle. "Okay. Thank you." He opened the bottle, took a sip, and sighed. "Nectar."

"Slowly." I wanted to drain my entire bottle of water in one gulp and suspected Lochlan was even thirstier, but drinking it too fast probably wouldn't have done our stomachs any favors. I opened my bottle and took a small drink.

Lochlan sipped more of his water then put the cap back on the bottle. "I'm starving. What time is it?"

"Um." I checked my watch and did a double take. Although the time in the mist-world had felt like only seconds, half an hour had passed since we'd entered the apartment. "Not quite suppertime, but food would be good." My stomach growled. Apparently pushing combative spirits into the light took more energy than I'd realized.

As if I'd realized anything about any of what Lochlan did until I experienced it for myself.

"Definitely." Lochlan took a deep breath and pulled himself up onto the couch. "Okay, good. I can move. For a little while..." He frowned. "I couldn't move. It felt like I was being held still. Like something was weighing me down. But that couldn't have happened before we got here. I wouldn't have been able to walk."

"You walked here under your own power." I sat beside him, not quite touching his leg with mine, but close enough that I could feel his body heat. The fact that he *had* body heat reassured me. "Then you passed out."

"Tell me what happened."

I was not up to that discussion. Fortunately, my furry sweater-wearing friend saved me with a loud "mrrpp" and a swipe at my arm. At least he didn't use his claws. "Hang on and let me feed Charlie, and then I'll explain."

Lochlan glowered, but nodded. "The fuzzy overlord wins."

Thank goodness for fuzzy overlords. I went into the kitchen, Charlie following so closely I almost tripped over him.

I couldn't avoid telling Lochlan what we'd done. The problem was, I wasn't sure what that was. What had happened. *How* it had happened.

Maybe by the time I finished feeding Charlie, it would make enough sense for me to put it into words.

But I doubted it.

CHAPTER TWENTY-SEVEN

I took care of Charlie's food, then returned to Lochlan. He was leaning back, eyes closed, but he looked at me when I sat down. "So?"

I sighed and took another drink of my water to procrastinate. "It's going to be a long story. Have you remembered anything between walking and waking up here?"

Looking thoughtful, Lochlan took a drink and put the cover back on the bottle. "A bunch of things that don't make sense. There was a spirit, wasn't there?"

"Yeah." I took a couple of slow breaths while I tried to sort out what to tell him and how. "A suicide at Piers Park. That's why your coffee got cold when we got close, I guess. The spirit came to you, but not for help entering the light. For help—or to use you, I guess—to stay out of it."

"Oh, fuck." His eyes widened. "Seriously? Where...I'm here, though. This is real, yeah?"

I ran my fingertip along his forearm. "Feel that?"

"Yeah." He looked slightly relieved. "Okay. I'm here, which means the spirit isn't."

"No. We got him into the light."

"Wait. We?" He stared at me. "You?"

"Yeah. Me." I decided to go with the easy part of the story first. "You said you were feeling light-headed and wanted to come back here. You made it, but just barely, and you passed out as soon as you were inside."

"Which explains why I woke up on your floor." He smiled slightly as Charlie jumped up onto the couch and regally took over Lochlan's lap. Lochlan stroked Charlie's head. "Hello, friend. Del, tell me the rest."

"I don't really understand this part, so don't ask me to explain it." Trying to think, I drummed my fingers on my leg. "I touched your forehead. Then I was in this mist-world kind of place. And..." I cleared my throat, and my eyes watered at the memory. "Austin was there. He said you needed me."

Lochlan stopped petting Charlie and reached over to rest his hand on my arm. "That must have been hard."

"It was good to see him, I guess." My voice cracked, and I cleared my throat again. "Yeah, it was hard. I wanted to hold him and never let go, and I couldn't even touch him."

"I'm sorry."

I shrugged and pushed away the gathering grief cloud. "Thanks. Anyway, he said you needed me. He said the spirit was resisting entering the light, and he and others were waiting to help but they couldn't do anything on our side. He said..." I trailed off, remembering exactly what Austin had said but uncertain whether sharing it with Lochlan would be a good idea.

Lochlan didn't speak, just went back to petting Charlie. After a moment, I decided to start talking again and see what fell out of my mouth. "He said he wasn't supposed to be talking to me but he wanted me to be happy. And he knew you make me happy."

"Oh." Lochlan bit his lip.

He didn't seem inclined to say anything else, so I continued, hoping like hell that I was doing the right thing by telling him any of it. "I found you by the light. The spirit was fighting back. I don't really know what I did, just that I held you. There was...power. That's the only way I can describe it. Just this power that came from us but came to us too." A weird way to put it, but those were the words that came to me. "We pushed the spirit into the light, and the other spirits Austin mentioned took over from there, I guess."

"We crossed the spirit together." Lochlan looked thoughtful. "I wouldn't have been able to do it alone. I remember a little now. He was fighting. He was stronger than any spirit I've dealt with before. I don't know what he was, but there was something there. More than a standard-issue human, you know?"

"Yeah." I'd had that sense too, though I hadn't been able to put words to it.

"I needed you to do it." Lochlan's mouth twitched a few times as if he was trying to speak but had no words. "We worked together. You gave me the strength to fight back against that spirit or whatever he was."

"You had the strength," I said. "I just helped."

"I don't know what this means." He petted Charlie a little too fast. Charlie gave him a half-hearted hiss and stalked off his lap to lie against the arm of the couch. "Sorry, Sir Charles. I've always been alone in this. I know there are other people who can do what I do, but I've never met any of them. And you aren't one of them, as far as I know."

"It's a first for me." I hesitated. "I think Austin had something to do with it. He's shipping us, I think."

Lochlan snorted. "Shipping, huh? Why would..." He tilted his head. "He told me, the night I guided him, that he was worried about you being alone. That he wanted you to be happy."

"Which is what he said to me today." I couldn't believe I was about to say what came to mind, but I went ahead and said it anyway. "You do make me happy, Lochlan. I love you."

I held my breath. He might not answer. He might say he didn't love me. He might get up and walk out.

He did none of those things. "I love you too," he said softly, and turned to me.

My arms were around him before I realized either of us were moving. Our lips met, a tender kiss that rapidly became less tender and far more needful. This wasn't like the kiss we'd shared during the blizzard. This one was both promise and fulfillment.

As if on its own, my hand stroked Lochlan's hair and moved down to trace a line along his cheek and neck. He made a contented sound against my mouth and pressed against me. My cock started to grow hard, and I ached with a need I hadn't felt in months.

For the past several months, I'd barely considered sex. I'd submerged every hint of desire that had arisen, especially with Lochlan. Arousal hadn't even been part of the equation. But now a fire kindled within me, heat dancing over my skin from every point of contact between our bodies. I needed to be touched. Held. Kissed.

I needed Lochlan to do those things.

And for the first time, needing Lochlan, wanting him, didn't feel wrong. As the kiss intensified and my body reacted, I felt nothing except desire and love.

This was right.

His hands moved over my body, and despite my clothing in the way, I felt his touch as if on my bare skin. I needed to be bare for him. Pulling back, without giving myself time to think, I yanked off my shirt.

Lust kindled in his gaze, but beneath it I saw uncertainty. I still held my shirt and wondered if I should put it back on.

"I love you too," he said quietly. "So much. I want this, Del, but are you sure?"

"Yes." I couldn't remember the last time I'd been so sure of anything. I set my shirt on the back of the couch. "Are you?"

"Yes." He scoffed. "I have to be honest, though. I'm not a virgin, but I'm not exactly experienced either. With my life, I haven't had much opportunity for romance. Or sex."

"I haven't been with anyone other than Austin in over two decades." I ran my hands down his arms. He shivered. Pleased, I leaned in to kiss him again, a short, teasing kiss. "We can figure it out together. Or we can stop with this and figure it out another time. I'm not in any hurry." I gestured at my crotch. "I'm hard. I want you. But it doesn't have to happen today."

"What changed?" He leaned forward, pushing me back so I lay against the arm of the couch, though my feet were still on the floor. Charlie let out a disgruntled hiss and plopped down off the couch, and

Lochlan laughed. "Maybe we should continue this conversation some-place that won't offend the overlord."

"Come with me." I was off the couch holding out my hand to Lochlan before the full impact of what I was about to do hit me. I was going to bring Lochlan into my bedroom. My and *Austin's* bedroom. The room where Austin and I had slept, made love, joined our bodies and our souls.

Sappy but true. That room, more than anywhere else, represented my relationship with Austin. Since Austin's death, the only person besides me who had entered that room was Remy, and that was only to help me clean out Austin's belongings. Now I was bringing Lochlan in there.

I waited for the pain to hit me. The grief. The sense of wrongness and betrayal.

None of it happened. Maybe a tiny twinge of guilt, but that was all.

Lochlan took my hand and stood. "I'm not in a hurry either."

"Come lie down with me." My chest tightened, but I pushed away the anxiousness. "I don't want to talk this to death, but right now, I just want..." I lost the words.

"Let's go," he said, giving my hand a gentle squeeze.

We went into the bedroom, and I closed the door so Charlie wouldn't follow. As much as I loved that cat, there were times and places he simply didn't belong. He would be pissed that the door was closed, but he would get over it.

With a questioning look, Lochlan went to the bed. I nodded, and he sat. "What changed?" he asked again.

"What do you mean?" I sat beside him but didn't touch him. The heat that had grown between us in the living room still simmered, but it wasn't as strong, and part of me was still braced for grief and guilt to overwhelm me with the insistence that I was betraying Austin's memory by being in this room, on this bed, with someone else.

"You've been holding back from this. So have I." He took my hand, and the warmth of his touch sparked the fire inside me again. "I've seen you changing, Del. You're more, I guess you could say in the world now. You seem happier. But this..." He sketched a line in the air between us with his finger. "If we do this, I can't just be your friend anymore. I'll want more. Hell, I already do, but I said I would wait."

"I don't want us to only be friends anymore." As I said it, the truth of the words resonated through me. "Am I ready? Honestly, Lochlan, I don't know. Today, yes. I am. I could have lost you, and somehow I helped you come back. And Austin..." My voice cracked on the name. "I will always be in love with Austin. Part of me might always feel a little guilty for moving on. But he was there, Lochlan. He was there at the light, and he said he wants me to be happy."

Lochlan's features relaxed, and something lit in his eyes. "I'm glad you had the chance to speak to him. That's something not many people get. I need to know, Del. Are you really ready to be with me? To be my partner? Or are you just pushing yourself to be ready because you think it's what Austin wants?"

"It's what *I* want." I pulled his hand up and studied it. The thin lines. The barely visible bits of light-colored hair at the knuckles. The way our fingers looked twined together, as if this was how they had always been meant to be. "I can't promise I'm over Austin. In fact, I can pretty much guarantee I'm not."

"I don't want you to be over him." He sounded almost angry. "Getting over someone isn't what grieving is about. Moving on doesn't mean forgetting. It just means not clinging so tightly to one thing that you can't let anything or anyone else in. I'm not asking if you're over him. I'm just asking if you can let me in."

"I think I already have." I brought his hand up further and kissed one knuckle. "I think I started letting you in the day we met." It was true, I realized. Even though back then I hadn't even been ready to let the cats into my heart, let alone another human, I had cracked the door for Lochlan. "I've been letting you in more and more since. While we weren't speaking, I missed you. When you were here during the blizzard, I think I stopped keeping you out at all. You were here and you *belonged* here." I brought our hands to my heart. "Here. I was planning to figure all this out in PEI, but maybe I was just too afraid to admit I'd already figured it out. I love you."

This time, saying it felt comfortable. Familiar. They were the same words I'd said countless times to Austin, of course, but that wasn't where the familiarity came from. Something in me recognized Lochlan as one who belonged in my life. I simply hadn't been able—or willing—to see it until now.

"I love you too. I knew it the day I told you about Anissa." Biting his lip, he looked down at our hands. "So where do we go from here? I know where we were starting to go." He chuckled and surveyed my bare chest. "I'm not turning down sex with you, but is that where we are right now?"

"I don't know," I admitted. My desire still simmered below the surface, but the fire had ebbed. I wasn't hard now. I didn't crave his touch as I had minutes earlier. I *wanted* him to touch me, but I didn't *need* it. "Lie down with me. If we just lie here and hold each other, that's good. If it leads to more, that's good too."

"I like that plan." He yawned. "Sorry. Fighting bad-guy spirits takes it out of me, I guess. If we lie down together, I might fall asleep."

"That's also good." Releasing his hand, I moved to the other side of the bed and lay down, my head on the pillow that had once been Austin's. I held out my arms and held my breath wondering if Lochlan would take the invitation, or if I wanted him to.

To my surprise, he removed his shirt and neatly folded it before setting it on my nightstand. "If you're half-naked, I should be. It's only fair."

"Right." I surveyed his body. His chest, covered with sparse blondish hair, was neither skinny nor muscular. It was, in the immortal fairy-tale words, just right. My mouth watered with the inexplicable desire to lick his skin, and I closed my eyes to push away the urge.

"Okay?" The bed settled as he lay beside me, and after a moment he tentatively lay his hand on my shoulder. "Del?"

"Okay." Opening my eyes and seeing his blue ones so close, so deep, I smiled. "Yes. Okay."

"Good." He moved so our bodies touched, lightly but still together, and rested his head on his hand. "And this?"

"Very okay." Very *right*. I hadn't known how good simply lying with our bodies against each other would feel. I encircled him with my arms and pulled him closer. Heat began to build between us again, but something else subsumed it. Something I couldn't completely name. Belonging, maybe. Connection.

The filling of the empty space in my heart.

"Can we..." Lochlan made a frustrated sound. "I don't know how to ask. Can we just be like this for now? Holding each other? I want you, I do, but right now I just want this. Slow. Just holding each other. Is that all right?"

"Anything is all right." Slow was good. Slow meant I had time to wrap my head around how badly I wanted him, sexually and otherwise. "I like holding you."

"Me too." His voice sounded drowsy. "I'll stay. While you're away, I mean. To take care of Charlie."

"He'll like that." So would I. I didn't let myself say so, though.

"Me too," he said again. "I think I'm falling asleep."

"I don't mind."

The only answer was a deepening of his breathing and the relaxing of his body as he allowed sleep to take over. I lay with Lochlan in my arms, wondering at how I could be here, at how I could let myself love him, and yet knowing that it was right.

I wouldn't stop loving Austin. Not ever. But there was room to love Lochlan too.

Be happy, Austin said, and I didn't know whether it was truly him or my mind's echo of his voice. *Be happy, and be loved.*

And for this moment, as Lochlan's breathing settled into a slow rhythm and mine began to slow too, I was.

ABOUT THE AUTHOR

Karenna Colcroft (she/they) is a nonbinary, neurodivergent survivor whose books try to encourage other survivors to believe they deserve and can find love and healthy relationships if they dare to open their hearts. In her non-writing life, Karenna is a mother, grandmother, and partner, and is preparing to study for a degree in mental health counseling.

She does not compartmentalize love into gender or number, and in her stories, she strives to show that no matter how afraid or reluctant someone might be, and no matter how much work it takes to build a relationship, finding someone to share a life with is worth the effort. Karenna lives in the northeastern United States, where she is hard at work on becoming a forest-dwelling cat person.

You can learn more about Karenna and her books on her website, https://karennacolcroft.com, or Facebook page, https://www.facebook.com/karennacolcroft.

ALSO BY KARENNA COLCROFT

Male/Male romance:

The Real Werewolves Don't Eat Meat series

Salad on the Side

Veggie Burgers to Go

Hummus on Rye

Try the Tofu

Tempeh for Two—Releasing January 11, 2024

Take Some Tahini—Releasing July 11, 2024

"Tofurkey and Yams" (a Real Werewolves Christmas short story, also available as bonus material in Veggie Burgers to Go)

Chance Met (a Real Werewolves universe novel)

Heterosexual romance:

The Real Werewolves True Mates series

Alpha Receptor

Beta Test

NOTE: *Alpha Receptor* takes place concurrently with *Salad on the Side* and shares some plot points; *Beta Test* takes place concurrently and shares plot points with *Veggie Burgers to Go.*

PREVIEW: CHANCE MET

Available in ebook and paperback on Amazon

CHAPTER ONE

Crawford had reasons for not going to the donut shop near his apartment in the mornings. Plenty of reasons. The shop was always far too crowded. Too many cranky people jonesing for their morning caffeine. Too many wound-up kids begging their beleaguered parents for a sugar fix. And too many commuters frantic about missing their train—even though the trains ran every few minutes—and rushing to get to the subway station across the street.

Yeah, he hated crowds and frenzy, and most mornings he avoided the shop at all costs. Today, to his annoyance, he didn't have that option. Thanks to spending the entire weekend working, he hadn't had time to go to the grocery store. Which meant no coffee in the house, not even instant, which meant either no caffeine or dealing with the morning rush hour crowd.

After the weekend he'd had, the shop seemed like the lesser of two evils.

He walked the couple of blocks from his apartment to the shop and joined the line that reached to the door. Fortunately, the people working the counter were used to morning rushes, and the line moved fairly quickly.

As Crawford moved up, others entered behind him and formed a wall of noise and thoughts Crawford could hear even through the mental blocks he'd trained himself to keep in place. The voices and thoughts seeped into his ears and brain like heavy wind through an old single-pane window. The hum in his head was the worst. He didn't care about people's grocery lists or how pissed they were with their kids or whether they were wearing underwear. This was why he disliked crowds. No matter how hard he tried, some of the thoughts leaked through.

I need a frigging vinyl replacement brain block.

"Daddy, I want a frosted donut."

"Mikey, a donut isn't a good breakfast. We talked about this."

Crawford shook his head. The father in line behind him sounded exhausted. The little boy sounded determined. It was pretty obvious who would win this battle. Kids often won. That was why Crawford had never wanted one.

"If you want me to be healthy, you should wake me up to have breakfast at home," the little boy said.

"Let's go outside," the father replied.

He didn't sound even slightly irritated, but his anger was tangible to Crawford. The boy protested but followed his father out to the sidewalk in front of the shop. Crawford turned to look.

The man, tall with messy, slightly too-long black hair, knelt in front of his son in spite of the February cold. At least there was no snow on the ground. It had been an unnaturally mild winter.

The little boy wore a navy-blue hat and blue jacket. Crawford could barely see his face amidst the clothes. He didn't seem worried by his father, and the gentle way the father put his hand on the boy's shoulder showed no anger at all despite what Crawford had sensed.

Realizing he was staring, Crawford turned to face the front of the too-long line.

"Can I have egg and bacon?" The little boy and his father had re-entered the shop.

"Yes. That would be healthy."

"And hot chocolate?"

The father chuckled. "Maybe hot chocolate. We'll see."

The man and boy now weren't even directly behind Crawford, yet his attention was drawn to them. He wasn't completely sure why. He stayed tuned into their conversation, father-son banter now, and wished he could be part of it.

His reaction didn't make sense. Then again, it didn't have to. Crawford had learned early in his life that many things made no sense. He had psychic abilities. He worked for a sorcerer. Compared to those things, nothing was too weird.

He finally reached the counter and placed his order: coffee and a toasted bagel. One of the employees handed him the coffee almost immediately. He moved down to the other end of the counter to wait for his bagel.

A couple of other customers got their beverages, then it was the father and son's turn. Crawford tried not to noticeably watch them, but he was so focused on them he barely realized the bag which suddenly appeared in front of his face contained his bagel.

"Do I get hot chocolate, Daddy?" the boy asked.

"Hang on, Mikey." The man's irritation was beginning to show in his tone. "How much for the sandwiches?"

The woman at the register answered, and the man shook his head. "Sorry, kiddo. We don't have enough for hot chocolate this morning."

Without giving himself a chance to second-guess the impulse, Crawford went over to them. "I'll pay."

The little boy looked up and grinned. A faint glow surrounded him, and Crawford realized why he'd been unable to focus on anyone else. The boy was psychic too. Not only that, but he was something very special.

He could have stood there staring at the boy all morning, except it would have seriously creeped out the boy's father. He looked up at a pair of brown eyes in a face with a very suspicious expression. "Who are you?" the man asked.

"Jeremiah Crawford." His seldom-used first name sounded strange to his own ears. "I'm sorry if I'm intruding. I overheard your conversation."

"Are you ordering anything to drink or not?" the woman at the register asked impatiently.

"Yes," Crawford said.

"No," the father said at the same time. He glared at Crawford, glanced down at his son's hopeful face, and sighed. "Yes. A small hot chocolate, please. No whipped cream."

"And whatever coffee he wants," Crawford added.

The guy shot him another glare and said, "Medium regular."

The cashier rang up the drinks along with the father and son's sandwiches. Crawford waved off the man's attempt to pay for part of the purchase and handed over his credit card again. "Pay me back sometime if you feel like it. My boss has this one."

"I'm sure your boss wouldn't be too impressed about you buying food and drinks for total strangers on his dime." The man took the small cup one of the other counter-people handed over. "Wait a couple minutes, Mikey. It's hot."

"Introduce yourself and we won't be total strangers." Crawford gave him his best charming smile.

The guy didn't seem particularly charmed, but he said, "I'm Trey Damone. This is my son, Mikey. Thank you."

"Thank you," Mikey echoed. He looked up at Crawford with eyes a lighter shade of his father's brown. Those eyes widened. "Oh. Now I get it."

"Get what?" Trey furrowed his brow. "Mikey?"

"I'll tell you on the train." He held up one hand. "I want my hot chocolate, please."

"I said you need to wait." He shook his head. "Kids. They always think they know everything."

"Yeah." Crawford was pretty sure in Mikey's case, he wasn't too far off.

He took his credit card back from the cashier. He should have left. He was already later for work than he liked, though Joel wouldn't have a problem with it and probably wouldn't even find out. Joel rarely started his day before ten. Crawford just preferred to keep things on schedule.

But he didn't want to leave until he found out more about Mikey and Trey. Mikey was like him, no question. And judging from the way the little boy had looked at him, he'd realized it too.

People with psychic abilities weren't uncommon, but there was something about Mikey. Crawford couldn't explain it any better. Something more, and he wanted to find out what.

He wouldn't have minded spending more time around Trey, too. The man was attractive, and Crawford sensed strength in him. The way he managed his son showed a soft side Trey probably didn't often display.

The problem was Crawford had no clue how to express his interest without coming off as a major creep.

Trey and Mikey were called to the other end of the counter. At that point, Crawford decided it would be better to leave. Judging from Trey and Mikey's discussion, they came here fairly often. Crawford usually avoided the place, but he would make an exception if it meant seeing them again.

"Stupid moon-struck moron," he muttered as he shoved the outer door open and stepped out into air cold enough to practically freeze his coffee. He hated winter in Boston. The nearby harbor sometimes helped keep temperatures a bit higher than inland, but wind off the water tended to make things worse instead of better.

He'd lived in the area his entire life, though, and he couldn't think of anywhere else he'd rather be. Not to mention he'd be unlikely to find a job as interesting as the one he had with Joel.

"Thank you," a small voice said behind him.

He turned and smiled at Mikey, whose mittened hands were cupped around his hot chocolate, and extended the smile to Trey, who stood behind his son. "You're welcome."

"Next time, it's on us." Trey put one hand on Mikey's shoulder. "You'll be here again at some point, I assume? This coffee's kind of addictive."

"It's the coffee of champions," Crawford said, joking. "Yeah. I'll be here." *Every morning now that I've met the two of you.*

Mikey frowned and opened his mouth, then quickly shut it again. Crawford had to wonder if the boy had heard his thought. Mindreading was a bit more rare than other psychic abilities, as far as he knew, but it wasn't unheard of.

"We have to get on the train," Trey said. "Mikey, come on. You can't be late to school again after what happened the other day."

"It wasn't Tareth's fault," Mikey said. "She got lost."

"I know, but we need to make sure you're on time from now on." He smiled at Crawford. "See you around."

"Yeah. See you." He wanted to ask who Tareth was but didn't quite dare. Probably Mikey's stepparent. That would be just his luck. The first guy he'd been attracted to lately would absolutely turn out to be straight.

Trey and Mikey crossed the street to the subway station. Crawford stood there, coffee and bagel cooling in the East Boston wind, until he couldn't see them anymore.

Trey and Mikey Damone. He wouldn't forget those names, or their matching brown eyes. He just hoped he would see them again soon.

———

Trey settled Mikey into a seat barely wide enough for the little boy and stood directly in front of him, holding the post beside them to keep himself steady. He hated taking rush hour trains, especially with his son. Too many people around, meaning too much risk. But he had little choice. He'd had to sell his car to move them to Boston, and right now his income barely covered rent and other expenses. A car was far in the future, if he ever managed to buy another one at all.

"Jeremiah was nice," Mikey said, his voice barely audible above the commuter cacophony and the noise of the train itself.

It took Trey a moment to remember the name of the man who'd paid for their food and beverages. "Yeah. You're only saying that because he bought you hot chocolate."

"No. I'm saying it because he was nice." Mikey swung his feet and connected with Trey's shin. Trey yelped, and Mikey immediately stilled. "Sorry."

"It's okay."

Mikey didn't say anything else, which worried Trey more than his declaration had. Mikey knew things. Things he had no logical way to know. Since they'd moved to Boston, the ability had grown stronger, and Trey wasn't sure whether that was a good thing. The boy had nightmares sometimes now, and he refused to even look out the window at the garden beside their apartment building.

Then again, that didn't have as much to do with what Mikey knew as with what had already happened. The garden was where three were-wolves had kidnapped Mikey only a few weeks earlier. And in trying to save his son, Trey had been changed into a werewolf himself.

Yeah, Mikey's fear of the garden was definitely understandable.

The man at the coffee shop was a different matter. Most people wouldn't have offered to buy hot chocolate for a little boy, at least not without a very nasty ulterior motive. Trey hadn't sensed anything off about Jeremiah, though he didn't completely trust his own instincts. He'd gotten better at judging people and situations since his change, but he wasn't always certain of what he detected.

On the other hand, Mikey hadn't had any qualms about the man, and Trey trusted his son's instincts without question.

The train finally reached Government Center, and Trey took Mikey's hand as they were pushed along by the crowd of commuters. They had to change to the Green Line to get to Mikey's school, and fortunately the trolley they needed was waiting when they reached the upper platform. They were even able to find seats next to each other.

As soon as the trolley started, Mikey said, "We'll see him again."

It wasn't a question. It was a prediction. Trey put his finger to his lips. "Remember what I've told you."

"Yeah." Mikey looked discouraged and a bit annoyed.

Trey felt bad. He hated stifling Mikey's abilities or his imagination and curiosity. But they'd learned it wasn't safe for Mikey to share the things he knew in public. If the wrong person heard, it could cause problems.

That was one of the reasons Trey had taken the job offer in Boston. To protect his son from those wrong people.

"Can I tell you at home?" Mikey asked.

"Yes. You can tell me anything you want at home, because it's just you and me there." Trey put his arm around his son, though it was mostly around the boy's backpack. "Time and place, remember?"

"Yeah. Anyway, Jeremiah said he goes there sometimes, so we'll see him again."

Trey hoped Mikey was right. He wanted to learn more about Jeremiah. Something about the man drew him, like something out of a sappy romance novel, minus the romance since Jeremiah had seemed more interested in buying Mikey's hot chocolate than talking to Trey.

He delivered Mikey to school and reminded his son and the office staff that Brianna Wright, Trey's former packmate and one of Mikey's favorite babysitters, would be picking Mikey up at the end of the day. Then he went to his office and pretended to focus on his job. The entire time, he kept thinking about the man at the donut shop.

He arrived home at six-thirty, thankful that his son hadn't been with him. The trains had been even more crowded than usual, and someone on the Green Line had decided the trolley driver insulted him and had tried to stab her. A transit cop had been on board and had brought the attacker under control quickly, but there had still been a few scary moments. Mikey didn't need to be around things like that. It would have been frightening for any child, but Mikey would have experienced it more intensely than most. He would have felt the passenger's fury and the driver's fear right along with them.

Thankfully, the moment he entered the apartment, Trey was able to let go of his day. Home was the safe place, the place where he and Mikey could be together like a normal family. And the smile on Mikey's face when Trey walked through the door made everything worthwhile.

Mikey was sitting on the couch with a clipboard. Brianna was in the kitchen, and the smell of spaghetti sauce filled the apartment. Mikey set his clipboard aside and jumped up to give his father a hug. "You're home! You're late."

"Only a little. There was a problem on the train." He kissed the top of Mikey's head. "I'm sorry if you were worried."

"I wasn't worried. I knew you were all right." Mikey glanced uneasily at the kitchen. "Brianna's in there."

"Brianna can hear you," Brianna said. "It's okay."

"You're allowed to talk in front of pack members," Trey reminded his son. Brianna was a member of the neighboring City Pack, the mate of that pack's Beta, which was why she had left Trey's pack. Mikey didn't interact with most of the City Pack members, but Trey had made sure the boy knew it was safe to be open about himself in front of anyone he recognized as belonging to either of the Boston packs. Compared to being werewolves, having psychic abilities was barely even unusual.

Mikey relaxed. "Yeah. Anyway, I knew you were okay, but you got scared."

"A little. There was a scary man on the train, but the police came and took him to jail." Trey was never sure how much to tell his son. The boy was only six, but he seemed to understand a lot more than Trey would have expected from a child that age.

Brianna came out of the kitchen. "I made spaghetti. I hope it's all right. Mikey said he was hungry, and I couldn't find much else in your kitchen."

"Of course it's okay. I appreciate it." He smiled. "Since you cooked, you're more than welcome to stay."

"Thanks. I might take you up on that." A knock sounded on the door. "Or not. That's Carlos."

Trey opened the door and motioned Carlos inside. "Hi." He was never quite sure how to address Carlos, who wasn't in direct authority over Trey but was definitely higher ranked.

"Evening." Beaming at Brianna, Carlos leaned against the door frame. "Are you ready?"

"I think so," Brianna said.

Mikey jumped up and hugged her. "When are you coming over again?"

"Soon." Face slightly red, Brianna looked at Trey. "When will you need me?"

"Not for a few days. Mikey doesn't have school next week."

"Just give me a call." Brianna released Mikey and took Carlos's hand. "Enjoy the spaghetti."

"Thanks for making it." Trey smiled as Carlos led Brianna out of the apartment. The two of them had found each other only a few weeks earlier, but already they were as close as if they'd known each other forever.

Something Trey hoped to find someday. Love. Companionship. Someone to lean on and who could lean on him. He'd believed he had that with his ex, right up until he and Mikey had to leave. He hadn't trusted Derek enough to tell him the real reason for the move. Nor, when he'd thought about it, had he wanted Derek to go with them. He had cared for Derek, but he hadn't loved him.

He didn't know if he would ever find someone who would accept Mikey along with him. Unless Jeremiah turned out to be that person.

Yeah, right. Nothing like jumping too far ahead.

He closed the door and took off his shoes and jacket. "So we're having spaghetti for supper. Are you hungry now?"

"Kind of." Mikey went to the open doorway between the living room and kitchen. "We're going to see Jeremiah again. He wants to see us."

"You've been holding onto that information all day, haven't you?" Trey went into the kitchen to dish up the spaghetti, and Mikey followed him. "Why does he want to see us?"

"He's like me, and he wants to help us." Mikey paused. "And he likes you."

Trey didn't answer while he put spaghetti on plates. He was tired, and it took longer than usual to sort out what Mikey had said. Even then, it didn't completely make sense. "He's like you? Or he likes you?"

"Both." Mikey sat at the table, his feet swinging above the floor. He was small for his age. It would be a while before he grew into the chairs. "He knows things the way I do, and he likes both of us. But I think he likes you more. Or different, anyway."

"Oh." Trey set a plate in front of Mikey and sat down with his own plate at the other end of the small table.

"He can be your boyfriend. Then you won't be sad."

Trey stopped with his fork halfway to his mouth. Mikey shouldn't have known how Trey felt. Kids weren't supposed to worry about their parents.

"He might not even be interested in men, Mikey," he said finally. It was the only response he could think of. "And if he is, that doesn't mean he'd want to date me."

"If you say so." It was Mikey's usual response when he disagreed but didn't want to argue.

They finished their supper and Trey helped Mikey finish his homework. Then they had a little time to watch TV together before Mikey's bedtime.

Mikey didn't say anything else about Jeremiah, but Trey didn't doubt the man would be brought up sooner or later. He just hoped Mikey was right about seeing Jeremiah again. Even if it wasn't remotely logical, Trey wanted to learn more about him.

Available on Amazon in ebook and paperback!

Made in United States
North Haven, CT
31 October 2023

43445311R00134